A DETECTIVE JARROD O'CONNOR STORY

JACK RONEY

THE SHADOWS WATCH

BOOK THREE IN THE SERIES

Published in Australia in 2023 by Hawkeye Publishing.

Cover Design by Alex Jay MacDonald

A catalogue record of this book is available from the National Library of Australia.

ISBN 9781923105041

Proudly printed in Australia.

www.hawkeyepublishing.com.au
www.hawkeyebooks.com.au

Praise for Jack Roney and *The Shadows Watch*

'Jack Roney has done it again. His latest crime thriller in the detective Jarrod O'Connor series, *The Shadows Watch*, once again projects the reader into a world of the deepest evil. The word 'project' is more than appropriate since Jack mercilessly throws his reader, headlong, into his narrative in his more than captivating prologue: 'The water surface bubbled and frothed. Ringlets expanded like ink on blotting paper. There was no splashing. Tom never surfaced.' As they say in the classics: Read on….'
Gary Crew. Professor Emeritus (Creative Writing) University of the Sunshine Coast. Author of The Watertower and In The Secret Place.

'With plenty of action and realism, this book delves into the psyche of crime victims and those who feel the justice system is lacking, and the importance of protecting vulnerable children. (It also shows the complications of tailing a suspect while having young children in tow, and how difficult it is to keep secrets from your live-in mother-in-law!) Roney draws together a cast of varied and well-rounded characters to show the challenging, dangerous and human side of detective work.'
Eileen O'Hely, Author.

'A nail-biting finish to an epic trilogy, as the stakes rise ever higher, Detective Jarrod O'Connor faces down his most dangerous trial yet. I read this in one go, then had to read it all again, this book delivers on its promises.' *Nita Delgado, Editor.*

'Roney not only brings authenticity to Australian crime procedure in his novels, he writes victims of crime with a nuanced sensitivity that elevates his work above his peers. *The Shadows Watch* is a thrilling conclusion to the Detective Jarrod O'Connor series.'
Cate Sawyer, Author.

PROLOGUE

33 years ago...

EIGHT-YEAR-OLD Tom Baker was lost in his own world, playing on his swing in the shade of a lurching paperbark tree. His mum, ever watchful, hung washing down the side of the house while he played out front. In contrast to the earthy shades of the surrounding fields, the front lawn was a lush green carpet. It was bordered by cottage gardens of pink and violet flowers while a bore ensured a never-ending water supply. *Shhh-tik-tik-tik-tik* sputtered the sprinkler, menacing the butterflies with its spray. The fragrance of wild lavender meandered like a mist of perfume while daffodils and daisies danced in the breeze. Neat garden beds lined the pathway leading to the base of the veranda staircase. A wind chime jingled, playing a rhythmic tune that blended with the chirping of wild finches and the cooing of doves.

'Pssst! Hey, Tommy! Over here!' called Vincent as he rode up to the front fence. He waved, eyeballing Tom to get his attention. Tom hadn't noticed him, cloaked under the branches of a sprawling Jacaranda tree.

Vincent was always like that, sneaking about.

He peered up from behind the rustic milk can mailbox, straddling the shiny red frame of his Dragster bicycle.

'Where's ya dad?' Vincent threw a nod towards the open shed where the ute was normally parked.

Tom shrugged. 'He's gone into town to buy some stuff, I think.'

Vincent, distracted, directed his gaze towards Tom's mother. She hadn't seen him yet. Tom knew what she would say if she did. She would shoo Vincent home and tell Tom to come inside. She would say, "I don't want you playing with that little creep. I don't trust him.

He'll get you into trouble." *The sneaky little creep from down the road*, that's what his mum always called Vincent.

Vincent returned his attention to Tom. 'I've got somethin' to show ya, Tommy. Come on, come with me.' He grinned, like butter wouldn't melt in his mouth. That was another one of Tom's mum's sayings. Weird. *Why would anyone want to eat butter?*

Vincent's hair was slicked back with oil and a comb. Tom had seen Vincent's father preaching at the community church. He wore his hair just like that, all greasy and slicked back. Tom thought Vincent was trying to look like his dad.

Vincent had gotten tall, but he was still skinny. Lanky arms emerged from an ironed polo shirt. He sat on his bike with one foot resting on a pedal and the other anchored to the ground to give him balance.

Vincent waited, leaning his forearms on the elongated handlebars. The longer he waited, the more fidgety he became.

'I'm not allowed to be friends with you. My mum and dad said you'll get me into trouble.' Tom's mousy fringe blew across his forehead from the rush of air as he returned to Earth with each swing.

'Are you a little chicken?' Vincent teased.

'I'm not a chicken,' Tom shot back.

'Don't be a cry baby. Come on, it'll be fun. No one will know.'

'Where ya goin'?' asked Tom, curious.

'To a secret place. It'll be so cool.'

'A secret place? Will I get into trouble?' Tom swung back and forth.

Vincent shook his head. 'You'll be fine. Your parents won't even know you've gone. Come on, it'll be our secret adventure.' Vincent was smiling now, cheeky like.

Tom planted his sandals on the grass to stop the swing and lifted himself from the seat. His baggy denim shorts came to his knees. Clutching the swing chains, he stood rigid, uncertain. He thought for a while and his frown deepened. He peered around the corner of the house to where his mother had her back to him, pegging bed sheets to the Hills Hoist clothesline. She hummed a lullaby, making the most of the morning sunshine.

Tom's eyebrows lifted. He turned and stared wide-eyed back at Vincent who produced a large packet of potato chips and a bottle of Coca-Cola from his knapsack.

'Come on, I'll share these with ya,' said Vincent, enticing. 'But you need to come now, before your mum sees us. Quick, grab ya bike.'

Tom's eyes darted towards his mother and then back at Vincent. Just at that moment, his mother walked back inside with an empty clothes basket.

Vincent beckoned Tom with an urgent wave. 'Quick, now's your chance while your mum's inside.'

Tom surveyed the unattended washing and then looked at Vincent. The temptation of Coke and chips was too great. He released his grip of the chains and tiptoed over to his little BMX leaning against the house. He grabbed the handlebars and wheeled it hurriedly to the front gate where Vincent lingered.

'Come on! Follow me,' insisted Vincent as he scooted off on the Dragster.

Vincent streaked ahead while Tom peddled as fast as he could to keep up. Vincent wobbled on his bike as he glanced back over his shoulder, slowing to allow Tom to catch up. As they followed a bend in the road, Tom looked back towards his home. Trees swallowed his family farmhouse until it disappeared. The sky loomed huge and blue over the ploughed paddocks. They turned down a service track and entered the shadows of the radiata pine plantation. The air became cool. A refreshing piney tang mingled in the air with a hint of eucalyptus. Towering stringybarks grew wild on the fringes of the spiking manmade forest. Endless rows of pines crisscrossed to form a complex matrix, fading to a blur in the distance.

'I'm tired. Please stop,' begged Tom. 'Please take me home. This forest gives me the creeps. I'm scared. I just want to go home.'

Vincent stopped and stared back at Tom who was lagging behind. He looked annoyed now. Vincent sighed and rolled his eyes in frustration as he dropped his Dragster in some long grass. 'Come on then, let's sit here in the shade for a bit,' he said. He retrieved the drink and chips from his knapsack.

'Where did you get those from?' asked Tom. 'Do your parents let you have Coke and chips? I'm only allowed them on special occasions, like my birthday. Mum says they'll rot my teeth.'

Vincent's mouth turned up in the corners and he flashed a set of white, perfect teeth. 'Nah, I knocked them off from the servo down the road. Easy-peasy.'

'You stole them? We'll get into trouble.'

Vincent opened the chip packet and held it under Tommy's nose. The aroma of salty baked potato made Tom's mouth water.

'Suit yourself,' said Vincent. 'More for me.'

Tommy looked around. He figured no one could see them. 'Okay then, I'll have some.'

They munched on the chips and took turns guzzling the Coke until it was all gone. Vincent let out a long, guttural belch from the gassy soda and Tom giggled.

'Come on, it's not far. It's just on the other side of the pine forest. It's so cool.' Vincent sprang to his feet and slung the knapsack over his shoulders.

'What's not far?' Tom asked with renewed excitement.

'If I tell, it'll ruin the surprise. You'll have to wait and see.'

They rode their bikes deeper into the gloomy forest. Shards of sunlight penetrated the canopy, forming a mosaic of dappled light on the forest floor. They rode at a steady pace until they came upon a log fence. Up ahead, a padlocked steel gate blocked the track. They climbed over and dragged their bikes under the gate.

Vincent pointed. 'It's just up ahead.'

They trudged with their bikes along the sandy track until they entered a clearing.

Vincent dropped his bike, walked to the edge of a cliff, and peered over. 'Whoa, this is so cool. Come on over.' He lowered his voice. 'You have to see.'

Tom hesitated. 'I'm not allowed to stand near edges. My mum says it's dangerous.'

'Do you always do what ya mum says?' Vincent teased.

'No,' said Tom with as much bravado as he could muster.

'Well come on, we've come all this way. Don't be a sook now. It's cool, you'll see.' Vincent leaned forward, standing precariously close to the edge.

Tom dropped his bike and shuffled over.

'Come stand beside me. Here, take my hand.' Vincent twisted his body towards Tom with a sinister smile, his hand outstretched. Tom reluctantly took hold of Vincent's hand. Vincent squeezed harder than he needed to and jerked Tom towards the edge.

Tom flinched. 'Ouch, you're hurting my hand. Let go.'

Vincent ignored him and stared out over the shimmering body of water far below. The edge fell away to a sheer vertical cliff of sandstone mottled with pink and white crystals, water lapping against its base. The sun glistened on the surface of the olive-green quarry lake. Fluffy clouds slid across the sky, throwing shifting shadows across the mirror-like water.

Vincent said nothing, the silence stretching on as he gazed at the chasm below. A hush fell over the place.

Vincent looked down at Tom with an icy grin. His eyes narrowed into slits. 'Can you fly, Tom?'

'What? No, let go. I want to go home. I want my mum,' Tom cried.

'Let's see if you can fly,' Vincent leered.

Tom squinted from the sun as he looked up in sheer terror at his tormenter, tears streaming down his face. But Vincent seemed to be enjoying himself.

'No, Vincent. Please don't. This isn't funny. I'm scared. Let me go,' Tom pleaded.

'Okay, Tom. I'll let you go.' Vincent's voice was even. He snorted a short laugh and released his grip of Tom's hand. He took a step away from the edge, shoving Tom's shoulders with both hands. An inquisitive smile formed on Vincent's face as Tom lost his balance and frantically waved his arms to reel himself back.

'Fly, little Tommy,' whispered Vincent before giving him another shove. As he toppled over the edge, Tom's eyes locked onto Vincent's. His eyes were cold and cruel. Gripped by overwhelming terror, Tom made no sound, his lungs defying the instinct to inhale. His arms and legs flapped with futility as gravity yanked hard with all its ferocity. Silently, he hurtled towards the water for what seemed like an eternity.

Vincent watched with curiosity until the little boy's frail body smacked the water hard, the loud splash echoing off the walls of the cliffs. He disappeared beneath the surface, swallowed by the lake. The water surface bubbled and frothed. Ringlets expanded like ink on blotting paper. There was no splashing. Tom never surfaced. The water settled, and all went quiet. Vincent watched and waited. Nothing. He wheeled Tom's BMX to the edge and heaved it over. It too disappeared into the abyss below.

Vincent walked over to his bike and rode away. He didn't look back. And so began the mystery of the disappearance of Tommy Baker. Vincent was home in time for lunch. He never told a soul.

~

As with all his secrets, only Vincent held the key to unlock the truth. He was always in control, savouring the misery he had inflicted on the town.

Years passed and he became lost in his solitude and self-destruction. He emerged from his pitiful existence, a phoenix from the ashes. Reborn, his life had a higher purpose. He journaled his discoveries – his prophecies.

It was all in his book of secrets. *The Book* would be his legacy, long after his corpse had decayed to dust.

ONE

KALEB Carmichael's lungs threatened to burst. His head pounded, every cell in his body craving oxygen. If he gave in, his fate would be sealed. Resisting the urge to suck in air defied all logic, like having a gun to his head and being told not to let his heart beat. Just as his heart would go on, his lungs would eventually inhale, whether it was air or briny water. It wouldn't be long before reflexes took over and his mouth gaped. When that coolness rushed in, he would know he was already dead. Panic and fear set in. Submerged just under the surface, he was swept away by the river's erratic current. He tumbled like he was inside a giant washing machine. His eardrums squeaked and crackled from the pressure on his skull as he sank deeper. Red and black splotches danced behind clenched eyelids, sealed tight against blinding mud and grit. Increased carbon dioxide in his blood fuzzed his brain and awareness dissipated with the onset of asphyxia. To avoid detection, he had stayed submerged for as long as he could, but his limbs gave in to exhaustion.

With no fight left in him, he calmed his mind and let go. He became one with the water, his body limp. His mind cleared, all thoughts and memories erased as he teetered on the brink between life and death. A downward surge pushed him deeper, beneath the frenzied torrent of the choppy surface. He floated in a void of calmness, disorientation taking hold. The river would cast him into eternal darkness; or be his salvation. He lost all sense of up and down, inside and out.

The initial shock from the freezing chill was gone. His body numb, he floated in a blissful state of nothingness. Fate would decide his destiny. Was he already dead, trapped in a watery purgatory? Had his day of judgement arrived? *Bring it on.* He was ready to meet his maker, to wreak havoc amongst the fallen angels.

The toes of his shoes dragged on something, and then a momentary sense of gravity. He searched with his feet, prodding and stabbing until they sunk into mud. He bent his knees and launched himself towards the surface, arms reaching for the heavens. Kicking, he rode a final surge of adrenaline. Every muscle burned and strained. He breached the surface and tilted his head back, gasping for air. The precious first breath flowed down his throat and into his lungs. With barely a splash he was under again, fatigue yanking him like an anchor chained to his ankles. He sank fast and his heart hammered inside his ribs. His feet met riverbed sludge and he pushed again, dragging the water with his hands until he broke the surface once more. He paddled to stay afloat. His wet clothes clung to him, heavy and restricting his movement. He found his rhythm and swam with the current, at its mercy.

A solid object slammed against him like a torpedo. He cried out, pain jolting his shoulder, still raw from the gunshot wound. Grappling with the spinning log as it bobbed on the surface, he slung his good arm over, giving him enough buoyancy to drift while he caught his breath. He kicked with renewed purpose. As the river hooked around the bend, he floated towards the far bank. Soon the police would scour the river. He'd be a sitting duck.

He hadn't thought things through; events had escalated in seconds. First, there was the old man with the rifle, then the gunshot and the screams. He saw his tiny window of opportunity and took it. He cherished his newfound freedom and would rather die than be caught again. It was a sign. The universe wasn't done with him. He'd been given a second chance to finish what he'd started, and be damned if he'd let anything, or anyone, stand in his way. There was a greater power at play.

His shoes found the bottom of the riverbed as he drifted closer to the bank. He let go of the log and paddled until he was crawling, mud oozing between his fingers. He clambered out and flopped onto his stomach, exhausted. Looking back across the river, he spotted the apex of the courthouse's gabled roof peeking over the tree line. He found his bearings and knew he had to make it to the cover of the sugarcane crop just metres away. Staying on the riverbank left him exposed. The echo of voices from the other side of the river bounced off the water. He resisted the urge to lie there in the mud to rest, his body weak and limbs shaking. He pushed himself up and crawled through the mud until he came to dry sand. Pulling himself to his feet, he stumbled towards a seemingly impenetrable wall of sugarcane. He prised the stems apart and entered, enveloped in their embrace.

He flopped to the ground, softened by layers of compost from earlier harvests. A sliver of light penetrated the curtain of green and through the gap, he spied movement on the other side of the river. Clueless cops scampered, pointing and yelling in confusion. Kaleb chuckled to himself. *Idiots.* He'd escaped again, but this time he would take control of his own destiny. His path to redemption lay ahead.

He rolled onto his back, sucking air into his lungs until his heart rate steadied. Sunlight filtered through the bamboo-like sugarcane and warmed his body. Water dripped from his sodden prison browns. Crickets chirped and rats scurried in the undergrowth, oblivious to his presence. He hoped he wouldn't come across any snakes. Swallowing his fear of serpents, he kicked into survival mode. He had to keep going, to get away before they crossed the river and found his tracks, before their helicopter arrived with its thermal imaging. He sat up and crawled deeper into the cane field until he was far enough to get to his feet and hurry away on foot. He laboured through the never-ending maze, scratches on his arms and face stinging from the relentless whips of cane stems. He looked up at the blue sky and followed the sun until he emerged onto a cleared vehicle track dissecting two cane fields. Indecisive, he looked left and right, not knowing which way to go. Closing his eyes, he waited for inspiration. It was a technique he'd been taught by his mentor and friend, Vincent Miles.

'When you lose your way, just close your eyes. Breathe in and focus. The angels will guide you,' Vincent had reassured him. Those words resonated with Kaleb and had served him well.

His thoughts drifted back to his friendship with Vincent, the man who had pulled him from the brink of self-destruction and steered him towards a path of discovery. Vincent had taught him to turn his fears into courage, anger into wrath. It was Vincent who had shown Kaleb how to discover his inner self, to find the real man hidden behind those ghastly scars.

'Revenge heals the soul. Salvation is a road discovered by the chosen few,' Vincent had said. He promised Kaleb that one day they would walk together as equals in paradise. Vincent had his own demons to deal with. He made a promise to Clare and paid the ultimate sacrifice to fulfill her quest to be reunited with her children. But he'd been duped by those copper bastards. That mongrel O'Connor would get his when the time was right. He rubbed his shoulder and grimaced, the clunk of torn gristle grinding on bone audible with each arm movement. A muscle in his thigh twitched and ached, the bullet hole still healing. He embraced the pain, a constant reminder of the payback coming for that detective. *O'Connor.* For now, the cop would have to wait. He had bigger fish to fry.

Kaleb knew Vincent and Clare were looking down on him, steering him towards his own destiny. He opened his eyes and followed the track towards the sun, walking with purpose. He would find his way to the city, where he would inflict punishment on the man who was next on his kill list. The man he blamed most of all for his pain and suffering.

He was destined to follow the path of his master, to finish what Vincent had started. To seek out the truth. Revenge would be followed by redemption. Vincent's secrets and wisdom were yet to be fully discovered, but Kaleb knew the answers were out there.

Vincent had taken his secrets to his grave, yet he had left a written record that Kaleb was determined to find. *The Book* would teach him about the past and reveal the key to unlocking his future.

There was much to be done; his true journey was just beginning.

TWO

A month had passed since Kaleb Carmichael escaped police custody during the mayhem outside the Lockyer Courthouse. He prowled the city streets, hiding in plain sight. His disfigured face made him easily recognisable, so he only ventured out at night, a nocturnal hunter keeping to the shadows. His image still featured in media stories all over the country. *'Scarface serial killer still on the loose,'* read the headlines. His reign of terror in the town of Lockyer had made national and international news. But he was no serial killer. That label made his blood boil. What an insult. There was nothing random about his actions. His killings were driven by revenge, retribution for past sins. Some were killed out of plain necessity, in the wrong place at the wrong time, in the way of achieving his objective. He was working towards a higher plan, every move calculated.

He had resorted to petty crime to survive the gloomy streets of inner-city Sydney. During the day, he hid in whatever refuge he could find. At night, he roamed and stole what he needed to survive. The homeless man he took clothes from had no use for them anymore. He skulked the streets in a hoodie and black trench coat, the collar pulled high to conceal his face. He was a ghost. The heavy stomping of his buckled boots echoed in the dimly lit laneways. He'd tracked down the man he'd been searching for all his life.

He had never known his father. His birth certificate read *'father-unknown'*. Carmichael was Kaleb's mother's surname. She never spoke about his father and refused to answer Kaleb's questions. All she ever said was that he had abandoned her when they found out she was pregnant, leaving her to cope alone. She hadn't seen him since. It wasn't until she lay on her deathbed years later that she finally revealed her secret. Wheezing with each breath, she had motioned for Kaleb to lean closer until his scarred ear nearly touched her lips. She whispered the man's name and drew her last breath. Kaleb was fourteen years old when his mother died.

The man he now stalked had the word SECURITY printed in bold white letters across the back of his shirt, the shoulder patches a cheap police rip-off. Crumpled and untucked over a potbelly, the shirt swam on his hunched frame. He had a habit of licking his pencil-thin moustache, twirling the edges at the corners of his mouth with his nicotine-stained fingers. He removed his cap and ran a hand over his hair, greasy and slicked back. Kaleb had been watching him for over a week, studying his daily routine. The man's address had been easy enough to find. He lived in a dingey one-bedroom apartment in the old part of Kings Cross and caught the subway each night into the city, working the graveyard shift as a mall cop. He was a sleazebag whose ego was inflated by his uniform, swaggering like John Wayne, thumbs tucked behind a utility belt holding an array of unnecessary holsters. It was all part of the façade of being someone with authority, someone important. At the end of each shift, he returned home on the subway and hid inside his apartment all day, like a vampire. That was the sad life of his father, the man who abandoned him all those years ago.

Kaleb had waited so long for this moment, saving the best to last. It would be his sweetest act of revenge. This coward had left Kaleb and his mother to fend for themselves until his drunken stepfather came into his life – the man responsible for his horrific burn scars. That man had already paid with his life. He had screamed in agony as his flesh was devoured in flames. It was now time for his biological father to pay for a lifetime of abandonment.

After going unnoticed just two seats behind, Kaleb followed him off the train carriage and out the station gate. The man lit up a cigarette, snorted phlegm and spat on the footpath. It was 4:00am and the pre-dawn air was brisk. The streets were dark and empty. The man crossed the street and flicked the cigarette butt into the gutter as he entered a 24-hour liquor barn. He came out five minutes later, tucking a new packet of Marlboro Reds into his shirt pocket with one hand, a bottle of bourbon in the other. The same routine, a creature of habit. He continued until he reached the front entrance of his apartment building just around the corner, unaware he was being followed.

He fumbled with his keys to unlock the foyer glass door, and sensing something, looked over his shoulder. For the first time, his eyes met Kaleb's. Under the glow of a fluorescent light, the man's face was pasty, sickly looking.

He squinted his beady eyes. 'You right mate?'

'Kevin De Vries?' said Kaleb, his voice husky.

'Yeah. Who wants to know?'

Kaleb ignored the question. 'Does the name Caroline Carmichael mean anything to you?'

De Vries let go of the keys, leaving them hanging in the door. He turned to face Kaleb who stepped closer to him, pulling the hood away to reveal his face. The man reared back with a look of repulsion.

'Answer me!' Kaleb snapped. 'Caroline Carmichael. Do you know her?'

'I… I haven't heard that name in years.' De Vries stared into Kaleb's eyes, searching. His mind seemed to work overtime, retrieving long-forgotten memories. 'Caroline Carmichael. Now that's a name I haven't said out loud in a long time.'

'So, you knew her?'

'Yes, I knew her. Over twenty years ago.'

Kaleb clenched his jaw. 'You abandoned her.' He kept his voice even. 'She was pregnant and alone.'

'Wait. Who the hell are you? What's it got to do with you anyway?'

Kaleb stepped forward and grabbed De Vries around the throat, slamming him against the glass door. He pressed his face against the frightened man's cheek. 'It's got everything to do with me, *Dad.*'

'What… what did you say?'

'You heard me. Don't you recognise your own flesh and blood? Take a good look at this face. Do I make you proud, *Dad*? The apple don't fall far from the tree, hey? Karma's a bitch, old man. It's time for retribution.'

Kaleb pressed the edge of a hunting knife against the man's throat until blood trickled. He leaned in and studied the man's eyes, wide with fear. Kaleb smiled. Kevin's eyes told him what he needed to know. He knew his past had caught up with him.

He knew this was his end.

THREE

JARROD started the Forerunner and reversed out of the parking space in front of Lucio's Italian Diner, Lockyer's classiest restaurant. He'd been lucky to secure a table for two, even though he booked a week in advance. It was his and Jayne's twelve-year wedding anniversary and the first time they'd been out for dinner without the kids for as long as he could remember. Katie and Matty were being babysat at home by Jayne's mother, Pat.

'God, that chicken and rosemary ragu was divine,' said Jayne as she reclined her seat. 'I'm a bit woozy. I think I've had too much red wine.'

'You're allowed to, sweetheart,' said Jarrod. 'How long's it been since you let your hair down?'

'Too long. We need to do this more often. We need to make more time for us. Especially after everything that's happened this last year.'

'Yeah, I know. I've just been so caught up in the Carmichael case that I've—'

'I know, Jarrod,' Jayne interrupted. 'There's no need to explain. I know that case has worn you down. I can see how it's affected you. But you know I'm here for you, don't you?' Jayne reached over and rested her hand on Jarrod's.

'Yeah, I know,' he said with a smile. 'Where would I be without you?'

She grinned. 'You'd be buggered, that's what.'

'How do you reckon your mum has coped looking after the kids? I hope they haven't talked her into spoiling them too much. Matty has her wrapped around his little finger.'

'Oh, that reminds me. I better call Mum to let her know we're on our way home.' Jayne rummaged through her handbag and pulled out her phone. 'I'll put her on speaker.'

'Hello, darling. How was dinner, you two lovebirds?' said Pat when she answered.

'Hey Mum. Yeah, food was beautiful, and the service was great.'

'Hey, Pat,' Jarrod said over the road noise. 'How are the rug rats?'

'Oh, they've been angels. We've had so much fun. Matty crashed on the couch after dinner. I didn't have the heart to wake him. Katie is just getting ready for bed now.'

'Sounds good. We'll be home in ten minutes. See you soon, love you,' said Jayne.

'Okay love, see you soon. Love you too.'

Jarrod continued along Kent Road with the lights of the town centre disappearing in his rearview mirror. The engine hummed and they drove in silence, enjoying the last of their date night. Jayne reached over and ran her fingers through Jarrod's hair, caressing the back of his neck. His skin tingled with goosebumps.

To his left, bright lights appeared. He snapped his head and squinted out the passenger window past Jayne, blinded by the headlights of another vehicle. *SLAM!* Jarrod's eardrums nearly burst from the explosion of mangled metal and shattering glass. Jayne's window imploded into a million glass fragments and the door caved in on her. Jarrod's body jolted violently against the seatbelt as the Forerunner skidded and groaned, the steering wheel spinning from his grip. He lost all sense of direction as the truck spun out of control. He instinctively planted his foot on the brake, but they hurtled into oblivion. Time stood still. Jayne's muffled cries, the screeching of tyres and the crunch of metal as they collided into a light pole, the bonnet crumpling upwards. Jarrod's head slammed against the side pillar and his brain rattled inside his skull. The truck rocked on its suspension before coming to a complete stop. Then there was silence. A grey pall fell over the world making everything dimmer. Time slipped; moments lost in an inverted sense of reality.

Dazed, Jarrod turned his head towards Jayne, his vision blurred by something warm trickling into his eyes. He reached over and found her limp hand. She was so still.

'Jayne,' he murmured.

There was only the ticking of the engine and steam hissing from the radiator.

He wiped his eyes and blinked, his own blood smeared on his fingers. Jayne's head slumped forward with blood running from her ears and nose. The buckled door pressed against her body. She stared at her feet, the life in her eyes dying embers.

Jarrod looked out through the cracked windscreen. 'Help.' The sound was a pathetic whisper. He filled his lungs. 'Someone help, please!' His voice was louder this time, but the words caught in his throat. He couldn't move. His knees were pinned against the twisted dashboard.

Footfalls grew louder and a man's face pressed against Jarrod's window. Their eyes met and the man's horrified gaze shifted to Jayne's limp body. His eyes darted back to Jarrod, his expression forlorn. He tugged at the handle and the door came open. 'I… I didn't mean for this to happen. I'm sorry.'

His breath reeked of liquor.

'Help us,' Jarrod said, his words slurred.

The man stumbled backwards. He just stood there, shaking his head.

'I'm sorry, I… I can't.' He scurried away and then a car door slammed. An electric whine was followed by the *click-click-click* of an ignition trying to kick over. Another whine and the engine came to life, revving as the vehicle dropped into gear and drove away into the night.

Jarrod and Jayne were alone, the silence ringing in his ears. He reached across and reverently positioned her head back against the headrest. Her hair was matted with blood. He stroked her cheek with the back of his fingers. She wasn't breathing and her face was grey and clammy. He cried, slamming his palms against the steering wheel.

House lights came on, dogs barked, screen doors slammed, shocked voices grew louder. After what seemed like an eternity, Jarrod heard the distant wail of sirens.

He felt light-headed. His head slumped and he drifted into unconsciousness.

FOUR

JARROD'S head lolled and he blinked through blurred vision, his mind foggy. Though his eyes were open, his mind was empty. Images materialised and scattered thoughts made connections. A halo of blue and red lights flashed in his peripheral. Awareness slowly returned. He was lying on his back, his chest rising and falling. He was alive, that much he knew.

Bandaging, wrapped tight around his head, restricted the movement of his eyebrows. Something pressed against his face. He squinted against a bright light in one eye, and then the other.

'Obs are good. Breathe in, mate.' A woman's voice, her words an echo as if she were speaking to him from the top of a well. 'It's oxygen, just breathe. You're in good hands.'

Jarrod's brain replayed the last scene before he had blacked out, and his eyes snapped open. His brain buzzed with sensory overload, then panic set in. 'Jayne. Where's Jayne?' The words fell from his lips as a drawl, muffled by the mask. A sensation of being lifted. Then he was moving. His body jiggled, a strap fastened across his chest, his arms by his sides. He was on a gurney, being hoisted into the rear of an ambulance.

'Where's my wife?' he pleaded.

The female paramedic shot her partner a sideways glance. He shook his head in return, his expression glum.

Jarrod slid his arm from the strap and gripped her wrist. 'Please, tell me.'

Her eyes locked onto his, her lips spread thin on a solemn face. She stared at Jarrod and sighed. 'What's your name?'

'Jarrod. Please, my wife Jayne. She was in the car with me. Where is she now?'

'Jarrod, she took the brunt of the collision. Firies are still trying to cut her free. I'm sorry. There was nothing we could do. She's gone.'

He'd willed himself to believe it couldn't be true, that his mind was playing tricks. The cold reality cut deep, and his heart ached. A groan of anguish erupted from the pit of his stomach, deep and guttural. A wave of hopelessness washed over him.

'I need to stay with her. She's all alone,' said Jarrod between sobs.

'There's nothing you can do for her now, mate,' said the female paramedic. 'Our guys will take good care of her, I promise. We need to get you to hospital.' She placed her gloved hand on his shoulder, gentle and reassuring. 'Do you have kids?' she asked.

Jarrod nodded.

'Best you focus on staying alive for them. They'll need you.'

Was this woman a mind reader? All he'd wanted was to die, to take Jayne's place. But before that thought consolidated, it was replaced by another. *The kids.* The paramedic was right. He had to be there for Katie and Matty, to stay strong for their sakes. He closed his eyes, numb with despair.

~

Every quiet moment was spent watching Jayne die again, playing the *what if* game in his head. In that suspended moment, he was the eye in his own storm until he surrendered himself to grief. Time itself had become irrelevant; the seconds could have been hours, or hours mere seconds. The heartbreak of losing Jayne so suddenly was unimaginable. Jarrod had never known such loss and pain. Her absence ripped a gaping hole in his heart. She was his world, his rock, the mother of his two beautiful children. He could still feel her fingertips caressing the back of his neck, smell her fragrance, and taste her kiss on his lips.

Breaking the news to Katie and Matty was the hardest thing he ever had to do. When Pat brought them into the hospital, Matty ran to him and climbed onto the bed, wrapping his little arms around

Jarrod's neck. 'Where's Mummy?'

Jarrod didn't know what to say and just held onto his little boy. Tears spilled down Jarrod's face, salty on his trembling lips. He could tell Matty sensed something was wrong.

Katie's eyes bulged, unblinking. She stared at the bandaging on his head and the bruising under his eyes. She looked horrified and gripped her grandmother's hand. Jarrod gestured to her to come closer, and she looked up at Pat for reassurance.

Pat smiled through a brave veneer. 'It's okay, Sweetie. Go to your dad. He needs to see you.'

Katie came to Jarrod's side and hugged him tight.

He grappled to find the right words. He wasn't equipped for this. They stared into his eyes, and he placed his hands on their cheeks. 'I'm so sorry. Mummy has gone to heaven. She's gone to visit your poppy.'

'Why?' asked Matty, one eyebrow raised. 'Why did she go without saying goodbye?'

'She didn't want to leave. She died in the car crash. She's with the angels now.' Jarrod thought he might choke on those bitter words.

'No, no, no! Why did this happen?' cried Katie. 'It's not fair!'

They huddled in a tearful embrace and Jarrod held out a hand to Pat. She took his hand and together the four held on tight, engulfed by a profound sadness. Jarrod wondered how they might ever overcome such despair.

They cried until there were no more tears to shed. Red-eyed and puffy faced, they clung together on that hospital bed. Jayne's absence was palpable. Matty cupped Jarrod's cheeks in his hands and examined his face. He patted the bandages and said, 'What's under here, Daddy? Does it hurt?'

'Yeah, buddy. It hurts. I banged my head in the crash and have a big cut. They put stitches in my skin to help it heal.'

Matty frowned. 'What are stitches?'

'The doctors stitched Daddy up with a needle and thread,' said Katie. 'Like when Mummy mends holes in our socks…' Her voice trailed away with a renewed sadness.

Pat put her arms around the kids. 'Come on now. How about we leave Daddy here to rest and we swing by Maccas on the way home?'

'Can we have a chocolate sundae?' asked Matty.

'You can have anything you like,' said Pat.

Katie gave Jarrod another hug and kissed him on the cheek. Pat led them away, holding hands. In the doorway, they turned and waved. Katie blew a kiss and Jarrod raised a hand to catch it. He was left alone to dwell on his thoughts once more.

~

The dappled light of morning brought with it a fresh wave of anguish. It was a painful reminder that Jarrod's first day without Jayne was upon him, that the world outside would go on regardless. All night, shock had kept sleep at bay. He had never noticed how time was so much like water; how it could pass a drop at a time, or even freeze, or rush by in a blink. The hours had passed like thousands of camera frames being shown one at a time. His insides felt as if there was nothing there, nothing to need feeding, nothing to have any need of anything at all. Outside, a tree branch swayed in the breeze, its fingers tapping and scraping against the windowpane, its rhythm hypnotic. His brain stuttered as his eyes took in the intensifying glow of sunlight.

There was a knock on the door and Jarrod rolled his head in his pillow to see a face peering into the room, the man's mouth an uncharacteristically grim line amid his stubble. There was a sadness in his eyes and when he spoke his voice trailed, like his words were unwilling to take flight. 'Hey mate. It's just me.' He waved and a warm smile emerged. 'You up for a visitor?'

The appearance in the doorway of his partner and best friend, Brad Harding, lifted Jarrod's spirits, but in the same breath a lump formed in his throat as an outpouring of emotion threatened to burst. He felt his eyes moisten. 'Sure mate, come in.' Jarrod groaned from the stabbing pain in his ribs as he shuffled to sit up in the bed.

Brad came in, awkward, his limbs moving as if some

inexperienced person was controlling them remotely. Hospitals made Brad nervous at the best of times, but in such dire circumstances he seemed utterly lost for words. He extended his hand and patted Jarrod on the shoulder. Dragging a chair over he sat, leaning his elbows on the bed railing. He cleared his throat. 'I'm so sorry about Jayne, mate,' he said. 'I just can't believe it.'

Jarrod nodded, muted by grief.

'How are you feeling?'

Jarrod shrugged. 'I don't know what to feel.'

'Stupid question. Sorry.'

'It's okay mate. Thanks for coming.'

'I came as soon as I heard.' Brad glanced at Jarrod's bandaged head. 'How's the melon?'

'Pounding, but at least I'm alive.'

Brad nodded, breaking eye contact to scan the room.

Neither spoke. It was a comfortable silence, a pause of mutual thought between best mates, at ease in each other's presence. Nothing either of them could say would make a god-damned difference. Brad just being there was enough for Jarrod.

Brad leaned back and folded his arms, his eyes drawn towards the dancing branch outside. Jarrod followed his gaze.

After a while, Jarrod was the first to speak, still staring out the window. 'I can't believe she's gone. It doesn't seem real. I keep telling myself that I'll wake up and all this will be some shitty dream. I know it'll get worse, but I just don't know if I have the strength to support the kids. They need their mother. I wish I could take her place.'

Brad looked at him. 'Hey, don't say that. It's not your fault. You're not alone, mate. We're all here for you and the kids. Whatever you need, just name it.'

Jarrod's eyes found Brad's. He swallowed. 'Has the other driver been found yet?' A surge of anger rose inside him.

Brad lowered his eyes. 'We're putting every available resource into this investigation, but still no news on the other driver. We'll catch him, Jarrod. It's just a matter of time.'

'Who's leading the investigation?'

'Jacko from the Forensic Crash Unit.'

Jarrod gave an understanding nod. Sergeant Steve Jackson was a full-time crash investigator, the best in the region. He knew his stuff, and this gave Jarrod some reassurance.

'It's really odd,' Brad continued. 'We've put out public appeals through the media and we've canvassed the neighbourhood. Some residents heard the crash, but no one came out in time to get a good look at the other car before it left the scene. Judging by the damage to your car, it's a miracle it could still be driven. One resident said she saw the taillights disappear around the corner, but she can't describe the car. It went straight through a stop sign. You didn't stand a chance, Jarrod. Please don't blame yourself.'

'Did they find anything at the scene?' Jarrod grimaced as a sharp pain in his ribs took another bite.

'Yeah, there were skid marks and fragments of the other car's front indicator lights, but we won't know what make and model they belong to until they're analysed. No one's come forward yet with any information about seeing a damaged car.'

Jarrod reached out and grabbed a handful of Brad's shirt and pulled him close. 'Promise me you'll find the bastard. He has to pay for what he's done. He was full of piss. I could smell it on him.'

'How do you mean? How did you get that close to him?'

Jarrod let go of Brad's shirt and ironed the crinkles with his hand. 'He ran over after the crash. He opened my door, looked at Jayne and then ran off. I'll never forget that man's face.' Jarrod stared at the far wall, playing back the scene in his mind like an old newsreel. Everything else was a blur, but the memory of that face was so vivid.

'Are you up to giving me a quick statement now?' said Brad.

'Yeah, sure. I'll tell you what I can remember.'

Brad pulled out his notebook and pen. 'Have you seen this guy before? Do you know him?'

Jarrod shook his head. 'No, never seen him before.'

'Describe him for me.'

Jarrod closed his eyes. 'He was middle-aged. I'd say around mid to late fifties. Short brown hair, slicked over to the side with hair oil. Or maybe it was wet, I don't know. He was short and stocky with a chubby face. He was right there, looking inside our car. I got a good look at him.'

'Did he say anything?' Brad pressed.

Jarrod thought for a moment and then snorted a cynical laugh. 'He said he was sorry. Can you believe that? He then took off, scared shitless. I pleaded for help, but he just left us there.'

'Did you see the car he was driving? Can you describe it?'

'No, I never saw it. I was blinded by the headlights when he T-boned us. When we came to a stop, we were facing the other way. The sound of the engine when it drove away made me think it was a four-wheel-drive, not a sedan.'

'Makes sense. Your truck's a mess. The passenger side took the brunt of the collision. Jacko seemed to think the other car had a bull bar because of the scrape marks and lack of paint transfer. It would also explain why he was able to drive away.'

Jarrod held Brad's gaze. 'Promise me you'll find him.'

'We will, Jarrod. Get your rest and be there for your kids. Leave this to us.'

'Promise me!'

'I promise, Jarrod. We won't stop until he's caught.'

Grief turned to anger, bubbling inside him, steam building in a pressure cooker. His sadness was now in fight-mode. He promised himself to have resolve, to stay the course until it was done – until he had his revenge.

FIVE

OVER the coming days, Pat was a pillar of strength for Jarrod, just as her daughter had been. Without her, he stood no chance of keeping it together. Struggling to cope with her own loss, she shielded the kids from the nasty business that followed. Jarrod was released from hospital two days later. Still concussed, he was on doctor's orders to take it easy. At first, light-headedness and nausea threatened to drop him every time he got up off the couch. The waves of dizziness subsided, replaced by a gradual sinking to rock bottom as depression set in. Everyone at the station rallied behind him with food drops and well-meaning condolences, but the pain grew with each passing day. His heart was bleeding, and there was nothing anyone could do to stem the flow. He was barely hanging on.

Next came the worst part of all, the business of making funeral arrangements. Decisions about the coffin, songs to be played, photos for the slideshow montage, readers of prayers and tributes. The hardest part was writing the eulogy. Pat helped with that; she had a way with words Jarrod didn't. As they pieced together the highlights of Jayne's life, her story took shape. It was that of a vibrant young girl, good at sports, popular and smart, who blossomed into a capable and independent woman, beautiful inside and out. She was a high achiever, a respected nurse, a loving mother and wife, and a much-loved member of the community. Jarrod and Pat shared tearful smiles as they reminisced over old photos from cute toddler to first day of school, frizzy-haired teenager, university graduate, stunning bride, doting mother. A life well lived but cut way too short.

Jarrod was caught in an emotional cycle of emptiness, grief and despair, but an undercurrent of anger swirled until rage pushed all other feelings aside. His thoughts returned to the other driver who still hadn't been identified. He was out there, going about his life freely while Jarrod's family disintegrated because of what he had done. Jarrod could feel the darkness within him deepening. Fires of fury and hatred smoldered inside him.

Finally, the day of the funeral came. St. Michael's Anglican Church was packed to the rafters during the service, standing room only with mourners spilling out onto the lawns. Wonderful tributes were paid and then it was time for the last goodbye. Jarrod was numb as he and the other pallbearers lifted the coffin into the rear of the hearse. He gripped the brass handle, hoping his trembling knees wouldn't buckle. The long, slow journey to the cemetery followed. His mind wandered any chance it got, anger poking out from its hiding place, seething at the man who was responsible for Jayne's death, still yet to be found.

The day was sweet sorrow, for in the moments of raw pain, when Jarrod's heart screamed in silent anguish, memories of good times blossomed. It was a celebration of Jayne's life and her accomplishments, yet there were no dry eyes. Jayne had left behind her goodness. Jarrod felt it in the loving embrace of relatives and friends, and in the pride of the police family. Huddled alongside Katie, Matty and Pat, Jarrod let the rose petals fall from his hand, lightly coming to rest on the coffin lid as it lowered into the earth. A haunting rendition of Amazing Grace by a lone police bagpiper gave Jarrod the chills. His police comrades, in dress tunics bearing medals, saluted in unison. It was a fine tribute for a remarkable woman.

The mournful melody of the bagpipes echoed around the undulating grounds, floating between headstones and angel statues, and wisping up into the trees. Jarrod absentmindedly scanned the faces of the crowd. His eyes wandered and he gazed off into the distance. It occurred to him he hadn't set foot in the cemetery since the day Vincent Miles took his own life at the grave of his baby girl, not far from where he now stood.

Off in the distance, something caught Jarrod's attention. On the crest of the cemetery's highest hill, a man stood in the shade of an ancient tree. It was too far to make out any detail. The tails of a black coat flapped as they caught a breeze, the man's head concealed beneath a hood. He seemed to watch the funeral from afar. Maybe just a stickybeak, or one of the cemetery groundsmen waiting for the mourners to disperse. Jarrod shielded the sunlight with his hand and squinted to get a better look.

He jumped with a start as someone patted him on the back to give their condolences. The bagpipes wheezed as they exhaled for the last time, leaving behind murmurings of people chatting. The crowd thinned as the service came to an end. His thoughts returned to the man on the hill. By the time he looked back, the man had vanished. He wondered if he'd been seeing things, his unhinged mind playing tricks, a figment of his imagination.

He was distracted by more hugs and kisses from friends and family, telling him to stay strong for the sake of the kids and to let them know if he needed anything, anything at all. Some didn't really know what to say, shaking his hand and saying how sorry they were. He was the same at funerals, awkward and unable to find the right words. Jayne's death had impacted so many people, and it was comforting to know he had such a strong circle of support. She was truly loved by all who had known her, and for the first time he felt the burden of grief was not his to carry alone. Shouldered by so many, the load lessened slightly. Not enough to dull the pain, but it reassured him that in time he might find a way to cope. They said their farewells and would meet soon at the wake at the community centre.

Jarrod had driven to the cemetery in Jayne's Mazda 3 with Pat and the kids. The Forerunner was a wreck and locked in the police holding yard. When they got to the car, he saw a folded piece of paper tucked behind a windshield wiper. He removed the note and unfolded it. Scrawled in pencil in childlike handwriting were the words *Revenge is the only true justice'*. He looked around, expecting to see the note's author waiting for him. The last of the funeral congregation were pulling out in their cars. There was no one else around. Even the strange man on the hill was nowhere to be seen.

'What is it, Daddy?' asked Katie.

'Nothing, sweetheart.' He scrunched the note into his jacket pocket, unlocked the car and opened the back door for the kids to slide in. He scanned his surroundings one last time, but no one was loitering. He had the uneasy feeling he was being watched.

'Let's go,' he said as he buckled the kids in.

Pat gave him a questioning glare.

'It's nothing, really,' he said.

She opened the passenger door, not looking convinced.

His instincts kicked in. The heaviness in his gut told him something was terribly wrong. That man. *Could it really be? No, surely not.* He chastised himself and dismissed the idea as ludicrous.

SIX

ANOTHER week dragged by and still no news of the other driver. Public appeals for information leading to the identification of the vehicle proved fruitless. There had been no sightings or reports of a damaged four-wheel-drive in the local area. The crash investigators speculated the other driver may have been a blow-in and already shot through. That theory didn't sit well with Jarrod. The guy had to be a local. To have gone to ground so quickly, he must have had local knowledge and access to a place nearby to hide the vehicle. There were countless properties within short driving distance of town that could easily conceal a vehicle in a shed or bushland.

It was just a matter of time before they identified the driver, but Jarrod was running out of patience. Still on sick leave, cabin fever had set in. Pat set herself up in the spare room on an indefinite sleepover, an agreed arrangement that gave Jarrod the respite he needed. He welcomed having her around, not that she was taking no for an answer. Baking cakes and pikelets with their nana was a needed distraction for the kids. Pat gladly took care of meals and marshalling the kids with military precision. Since Jayne's dad's passing of cancer two years earlier, Pat had seemed lost. Robert was her soulmate. Now, being there for the kids and Jarrod seemed to give her a renewed sense of purpose.

They did their best to establish a semi-normal routine. Jayne's absence left a cavernous hole in their lives, but they soldiered on with each passing day. Beds still had to be made, school bags packed, rooms tidied, and teeth brushed morning and night. Jarrod took on Jayne's role of chief bedtime storyteller, but he could never get the character voices just right, not like their mummy did. The daily rituals kept them

31

moving forward and held the wolves of grief at bay. Jarrod's body was on the mend, but he feared his heart and soul were broken beyond repair.

He paced the lounge room like a caged animal. Screw it, he had to go searching again, to feel like he was doing something productive.

He grabbed the Mazda keys. 'I need to go out for a drive, clear my head,' he called to Pat, who busied herself in the kitchen. 'I'll pick up the kids from school while I'm out.'

'Okay, love,' she called back. 'Can you pick up a few things for me at Coles? I've written a shopping list.'

Jarrod sighed.

He poked his head into the kitchen.

'The list is on the fridge,' said Pat, churning milk and butter into a floury mix with a wooden spoon.

Jarrod slid the note out from a Bart Simpson magnet. He read the list which extended over the page. He grunted. 'A *few* things?'

She countered with a smile. 'I'll have some warm scones ready when you get back.'

'I hope there's strawberry jam and dollop cream on that list of yours.' He kissed her on the cheek and headed out.

He killed time patrolling the streets of town and outlying roads, scanning for any sign of a damaged vehicle that might fit the profile. Some people averted their eyes as Jarrod cruised the streets, glaring suspiciously at every man he spotted in a passing car or walking along the footpath. Others gave a knowing nod or wave, but most preferred to keep their distance. That suited Jarrod just fine. He only had one thing on his mind – finding the bastard who killed his wife.

Rumours had spread like wildfire about the local detective on the hunt for his wife's killer. He'd heard the whisperings, at the corner store, coffee shop and post office, that he was too unhinged to go back to work. Maybe that was true. It was an apt description for how he felt, and he had been ordered by Benfield to take extended leave. Let them think what they want, he thought. It couldn't hurt to send a message that he was on the prowl, that the driver should watch his back. If it got people talking, kept the bush telegraph in action, then the story would stay in the forefront of people's minds. Someone would talk, eventually.

Despite the innuendos about his mental state, Jarrod sensed the townsfolk were behind him. Even the shitbags and crims seemed to rally to his cause. The tragedy of the hit-and-run which claimed the life of a respected nurse, and copper's wife, had resonated with the community. Tip-offs came in every day, people wanted to help. Brad gave him a daily update of the investigation's progress, or lack of. Apparently, even Thomas Barton came into the station asking after him. Bloody Thomas. The thought made Jarrod smile.

At 3:00pm, as he waited in the car outside the primary school, the bell rang and an avalanche of squealing children burst out the doors and into the playground. Some raced each other to their awaiting parents' cars, some lined up at the bus stop and others dispersed into the streets, riding bikes or dawdling on foot bouncing basketballs. Two forlorn little figures emerged hand in hand, walking slower than most. Katie led Matty along the pathway, seemingly oblivious to the chaos of children around them. They were deep in conversation, and Jarrod wondered what they were talking about.

Matty looked up and his face lit up when he saw Jarrod. Katie smiled and waved. Jarrod hopped out of the car and knelt to one knee as they ran over. He scooped them into his arms, and they embraced. Other parents waiting nearby smiled sympathetically. Everyone knew.

'How's my two favourite little people?'

'Good,' they chimed in unison.

'Did you have a good day?'

'Yeah, it was okay,' said Katie.

Matty held up a strange object, painted green. 'Look what I made in pre-school, Daddy.'

'Oh, um, that looks great. What is it?' Jarrod asked as he examined the clay blob.

'It's a frog, silly.'

'Of course, it is,' he said, handing it back to his little boy.

'His name is Rocket.'

'That's a cool name for a frog,' said Jarrod. 'Make sure you take good care of him.'

Matty nodded. 'I will.'

Jarrod stood and opened the back door. Matty climbed into his booster seat and waited for his dad to buckle him in. Katie opened the front passenger door and slid in, placing her bag at her feet. When she'd turned eight a few months earlier, they agreed she was a big girl and old enough for the grown-up seat up front.

On their way home, Jarrod detoured to the grocery store. The automatic glass doors swooshed open and Matty raced over to his chosen shopping trolley and stretched up his arms, waiting to be lifted into the fold-out child seat. He loved being wheeled around by Katie.

'Righto, try not to crash into too many things,' Jarrod told Katie.

She pulled Jarrod's thumbs to release his grip from the trolley handle. 'I can do this on my own,' she said with a frown. So independent, just like her mother.

They meandered up and down aisles as Jarrod selected the grocery items as instructed in Pat's shopping list. Bopping eighties music echoed around the store from the loudspeakers, disrupted momentarily by a 'clean up in aisle three' announcement from the store supervisor. The intercom beeped and *Girls Just Wanna Have Fun* filled the air waves once more.

Up ahead in the deli section, Jarrod's attention was drawn to the voice of a man ordering three hundred grams of sliced champagne ham. The hairs on the back of his neck bristled. An icy chill ran through him. Jarrod froze midway through placing a jar of Nutella into the trolley.

'What's wrong, Daddy?' Katie asked.

Jarrod ignored her and stared at the man smiling at the attendant as he placed a neatly wrapped parcel into his trolley. Jarrod's eyes followed as the man drew nearer past the bread section. For the briefest of moments their eyes met, a fleeting exchange between two strangers. There was no recognition in the man's eyes. He had no idea who Jarrod was.

Jarrod watched with hatred as the man who killed his wife walked by, grabbed a bottle of milk from the cold section and disappeared down the next aisle.

SEVEN

THERE was no mistaking it. Jarrod would never forget the man's voice. That face had haunted his sleep, vivid nightmares replaying the night of the crash, over and over. In his mind's eye, the man took on a demonic appearance, scowling, eyes squinted. The epitome of evil. After all the searching, there he was, right in front of him – pushing a grocery trolley, peering over the rim of bifocals. Now that he'd found him, Jarrod didn't know what to do. He was numb. A thousand times over, he had imagined what he would say to the coward who had taken Jayne from him, who had run off and left him for dead. He had fantasised about grabbing the man's throat and squeezing the life out of him, watching his eyes fade, just as Jayne's had.

However, in the light of day, in that grocery store, the man was no monster. Far from it. The kind of man who would drift through a crowd unnoticed. Balding, plainly dressed, late fifties with a shuffling gait, he reminded Jarrod of an aging George Costanza caricature.

Jarrod followed him down the canned goods aisle, keeping enough distance to not draw attention. He pretended to inspect a tin of crushed pineapple while surveilling the man who made his way to the end of the aisle.

'Where are you going, Daddy?' Katie whined, struggling to steer the trolley under Matty's weight. 'We've already been down this aisle.'

Jarrod didn't answer and held up his finger in a 'shoosh' gesture. He watched the man place a can of beetroot into his trolley before leaving the aisle and turning towards the checkouts.

'Come on kids, we're done.' Jarrod snatched control of the trolley from Katie and headed for the checkouts.

'But we're not finished, Daddy. What about Nanny's list?' said

36

Katie, folding her arms and stamping a foot in protest at losing her position as trolley pilot.

'We have to go,' Jarrod snapped.

Katie responded to the urgency in his voice and begrudgingly complied, falling in behind. All the while, Matty was oblivious to the drama, mesmerised by a Matchbox car he'd somehow fleeced from a display hook. With his sleight-of-hand skills, the kid had the makings of a magician, or a pickpocket.

Jarrod found a checkout with only one other customer ahead in line, an elderly woman who counted out the exact amount in notes and coins to pay for her half-a-dozen items. Growing anxious and peering through the gaps of an impulse-buy chocolate stand, he maintained a line of sight with the man who was now unloading his groceries two checkouts along. Jarrod hurriedly transferred the contents of the trolley onto the conveyor belt, including the Matchbox car. No time for dealing with a tantrum, a tactical concession had to be made. The wily old lady scrutinised her receipt with a look that said, 'Don't take me for a fool, my girl. I won't be duped.' Satisfied with the accuracy of the bill, she pursed her lips with approval and collected her bags, placing them just so into the compartment of her own two-wheeled trolley, a relic from the nineteen-fifties.

The young attendant waited and fiddled with a u-shaped piercing dangling from the flesh between her nostrils. As the old woman shuffled away, the attendant greeted Jarrod with an insincere smile, not bothering to make eye contact. 'How ya goin? How's your day been?' she said on cue, chewing gum. She couldn't care less how his day had been. Maybe he should share some chit-chat as she scanned items, painfully slow. *Yeah, good thanks. Just the usual. Crippled by grief, drove around town aimlessly, picked the kids up from school, grabbing a few groceries, following the man at checkout five who killed my wife. How's your day been?'*

'Fine thanks. I'm in a hurry, so if you don't mind…' he said instead, gesturing at the idle grocery items and for her to get a move on. She gave him an indignant look. He glanced over and saw the man placing his bags of groceries in his trolley, heading for the exit.

'I'll just have to get a price check on this loaf of bread, it's not scanning,' said the girl, bending down to a microphone. 'Price check please, checkout three.'

Jarrod looked over and the man was gone. 'You know what? I don't have time. Come on kids.' He lifted Matty from the trolley.

'Daddy! What are you doing?' said Katie. 'What about Nanny's groceries?'

'We'll come back. We have to go.'

The checkout girl stopped chewing her gum and glared at him. 'What do you want me to do with all this?'

'I'm sorry. We have to go, something's come up. Can you please finish ringing them up and put them aside? I'll come back for them later.'

He didn't wait for a response and pushed the empty trolley out of the way. Nursing Matty on his hip, he grabbed Katie's hand and hurried from the store. As they walked out into the car park, Jarrod spotted the man placing his groceries into the boot of a white Corolla hatchback.

'Shit! Why did I have to park all the way over there?' he thought, looking to where he'd parked the Mazda several sections over.

He memorised the registration number of the Corolla and hurried towards their car. Katie protested the whole way, trying to pull her hand free of his grip.

'Why are we leaving, Daddy?' she argued. 'We have to get our groceries. Nanny needs them to cook dinner.'

Jarrod lost sight of the Corolla behind rows of cars. He unlocked the doors and placed Matty into his booster seat. He opened the front passenger door for Katie. 'Get in. We have to go. I don't have time to explain.'

'No!' she said, defiant.

He spotted the white Corolla. It was reversing out.

'Katie, do as you're told. Get in, now!' he yelled.

She yielded and got in, buckling herself up without another word. She pouted and huffed, holding back tears. He knew he would have to go into damage control later, but now wasn't the time.

He needed to follow the Corolla to find out where the man lived. He could have approached him inside the store, identified himself as a police officer and arrested him on the spot. But that would have been too easy. He had other plans.

As the Corolla exited the car park onto William Street, Jarrod jumped in and slammed the door. He cranked the ignition and reversed. He reefed the wheel and slammed it into drive with the high-pitched squeal of rubber on painted concrete. He maneuvered his way through columns of parked cars, following arrows to the exit sign. When he arrived at the entrance, he looked left and right. He hadn't seen which way the car had turned. Panicking he may have lost the car, he saw a flash of white as the Corolla changed lanes to turn right at the next intersection. Relief flooded him. Jarrod drove out onto the street and followed, tailing the car as it turned. He sat back, keeping a reasonable distance while they moseyed along well under the speed limit.

Jarrod tried to control his breathing, calm his mind. He thought about the man and the Corolla. The man had access to another vehicle and, if he was a local, Jarrod had never seen him before. Strange, but not impossible. Even Jarrod had to concede he didn't know everyone in town. If people kept to themselves, had no police dealings, then sure, the town's population was big enough for people to go unnoticed. Did he live close by? Jarrod was determined to find out.

Jarrod slowed as the Corolla turned into the drive-through entrance of a bottle shop. He pulled over to the side of the road and watched as the man ordered a bottle of something without getting out.

Still drinking, after what you've done, thought Jarrod. *Bloody mongrel.* His face grew hot with anger.

The man handed over some cash in exchange for a bottle

concealed in a brown paper bag. Leaning down to the car window, the attendant had a good old chat with the driver of the Corolla. He was a regular, Jarrod surmised. The attendant stepped away and waved. The car was on the move again and Jarrod followed as he turned left into Grainger Road. His heart sank as they travelled through the intersection with Kent Road, the scene of the crash. He'd avoided driving through there since that awful night. The kids didn't understand the significance of the location, and he kept it to himself. Matty had unboxed his toy car, and Katie was perfecting her silent treatment, staring out her window.

'Where are we going?' she said, relenting.

'You just have to trust me, sweetheart. Okay?'

She huffed but said nothing.

'Look, I'm sorry I yelled at you. But I have to do something really important.'

They travelled for a few more blocks until the Corolla slowed and turned into the driveway of a small, weatherboard cottage. It was a quaint, well-kept little home with neat gardens. Jarrod pulled over and noticed the single garage behind the house at the end of the driveway. The roller door was closed. The man parked in the driveway and got out, clutching the bottle of liquor. He went to the boot and removed the groceries. He carried them to the front door, unlocked it, and disappeared inside.

All this time undetected, the hit-and-run driver only lived down the road. No wonder it seemed like he'd vanished. Had none of the neighbours heard him drive in? Where was the damaged vehicle now? Jarrod stared at the garage. He noted the address and pulled out, cruising by.

Now that he had an address, he'd soon get a name.

He needed to learn more about the man.

It was time to put his plan into action.

EIGHT

THE kids were restless, so Jarrod dropped them home and watched them run inside with their school bags. He knew Katie would rat on him, so he returned to the store to finish the shopping. When he arrived home with the groceries, Pat met him in the kitchen.

'Better late than never.' She leaned against the sink, eyeballing him.

'Where are the kids?' Jarrod asked.

'Katie's in her room doing her homework and Matty's having a bath. They're fine. It's you I'm worried about.'

'What do you mean?'

'Katie told me what happened this afternoon. What's going on, Jarrod?'

'Nothing for you to be worried about. Everything's okay, really.'

She held her gaze and didn't say another word. The same interrogation technique used by Jayne.

Jarrod forced a smile. 'Listen, Pat. I'm fine, honestly. I thought I saw someone I knew, that's all. It kinda threw me, but it turned out to be a different person.'

Pat wouldn't let him off that easily. 'Who was it you thought you saw?'

'Maybe a ghost from the past.' He chuckled, trying to make light of it.

Pat was unmoved, arms crossed. 'Mm-hmm.' She saw right through him.

Jarrod gave her a hug and kissed her on the cheek. 'It's okay. I promise.'

She waved him away. 'I'm just worried about you.'

'I know. Trust me, I'm fine. So, what's for dinner?'

'Well, if you got everything from my shopping list, we'll be having chicken parmigiana and salad. You go do what you need to do, and I'll let you know when dinner's ready.'

'Sounds good.'

He checked in on Matty, who was lying face down in the bath propped on his elbows, white bum exposed as an island in soap suds. He made a *brom-brom* noise with his mouth as he drove his new car around the walls of the tub. Matty seemed happiest in the bath, so Jarrod let him be. He went down the hall to Katie's room and tapped on her door.

'It's me. Can I come in?'

No response.

He turned the knob and eased open the door. Katie had her back to him, seated at her little homework desk, earbuds in. She was scribbling in her homework book, tongue poking out one corner as her head bounced to the beat of music. Jarrod wondered what she was listening to.

Sensing his presence, she looked over her shoulder and pulled out one earphone. The tinny tune of a pop song Jarrod didn't recognise bleated from the tiny speaker. She tapped the screen of her iPad and paused the music. *When did she stop listening to The Wiggles and start listening to teenage music? Man, things were slipping by him too fast. What else had he missed?*

'Hey Dad,' she said and returned her attention to her homework.

'Hey kid. Everything okay?'

She nodded.

'Need any help with your homework?'

'Nope, I'm all good. It's easy.'

He moved closer, sitting on the edge of her bed.

'What are you working on?'

'It's called geometry. We have to name the shapes of all these different polygons.'

He leaned over her shoulder and pointed. 'What's this called?'

'That's easy. It's a regular pentagon. All the sides are the same length.' She wrote the words under the shape in cursive.

'You're using a biro. When did you get your pen license?'

'Ages ago, Dad. I was the second kid in grade four. Adeline was the first but she's really smart. All the other kids are still using a pencil.'

'Wow. I'm so proud of you.'

'Mummy knew I had my pen license.'

'Oh, I didn't know.'

'You were probably too busy, again.'

A barb jabbed his heart, like a nerve pain. 'I'm sorry, sweetheart.'

'What for? For yelling at me today or for not knowing I had my pen license.'

He stroked her hair and sighed. 'For both.'

She put her pen down and swiveled in her chair to face him. 'Why were you so weird in the shops today?'

'I… I saw someone I thought I recognised. I can't talk about it.'

Katie turned back to her homework book and picked up her pen. 'I know, important police stuff.'

'Sometimes I have to do things I can't tell you about. It's only because I'm trying to keep you safe. You just have to trust me.'

She didn't answer. He didn't blame her for being skeptical after all the poor kid had been through.

'Anyway, everything's okay. Nothing for you to worry about. I'm sorry I got cranky.'

'I need to finish my homework,' she said, staring at her workbook.

He kissed the back of her head. 'Okay. I'll leave you alone. Let me know if you need any help, although you know more about polygons than I do.'

'Probably,' she said in a sassy tone. She put her earbuds back in and tapped the play button on the iPad screen.

He got up and left her alone, feeling like a real arse.

He skulked into his study and closed the door. Sitting at his desk, he stared at the blank screen of his laptop. His thoughts returned to the man in the Corolla. He needed to find out more about him and to locate the vehicle used in the crash. However, he had to rely on unconventional methods. Using his laptop to log into the police criminal and traffic databases wasn't an option. Every key stroke could be tracked against his user ID. There had to be no digital trail. No one could know he was conducting his own surveillance. No one could know what he planned to do. He no longer had faith in the court system to administer true justice. No, that would never do. Jayne deserved so much more. This time, he was taking matters into his own hands.

He sat in silence, lost in his thoughts until Pat called him for dinner. Now dressed in his pajamas, Matty insisted the clay frog should have his own setting at the table. The green blob served as a distraction and talking point during dinner. Katie was still milking the silent treatment for maximum effect. There was not much else to talk about, so they quietly ate Pat's parmi. Their routine of dinner chit-chat and laughter had died along with Jayne. His mind was lost in a dark void and all he could think about was his plot for revenge.

After dinner, he snuggled with Matty in his bed, together flicking through the pages of a Monsters Inc. picture book. In minutes, he was out like a light, still holding his clay frog. Jarrod prised it from the grip of his little fingers and placed it on his bedside table for him to find in the morning. He turned off the lamp and tiptoed into Katie's room. She'd put herself to bed without saying goodnight and lay on her side facing the wall. Unsure if she was asleep, he flicked off her lamp and let her be. He feared they were growing more distant with each passing day and neither knew how to bridge the gap. He ached for everything to be back to the way it used to be.

He helped Pat with the dishes, and she headed off to bed. She had taken charge of running the household and was exhausted at night. The business of pretending to get on with life was mentally and physically draining.

The house fell quiet, and he felt lost. Lingering in the kitchen, he stared at his reflection in the window above the sink. A stranger looked back at him with sunken eyes and a drawn face. He grabbed a beer from the fridge and went out onto the veranda and sat on the top step. The spring air was warm and crickets chirped. Moths fluttered around the porch light and geckos chatted. He scratched at the bristles prickling his neck, contemplating whether he should let it grow into a beard. He'd been clean shaven ever since he joined the police academy a lifetime ago. Maybe. Yeah. Why not? He couldn't be bothered shaving. He didn't have the energy to think about it, only one thing consumed his thoughts. His mind raced, a revenge plot taking shape.

His mobile phone vibrated in his jeans pocket. He put the beer down and fished out the phone, checking the caller ID to see who was calling that time of night. CALLER UNKNOWN appeared. He paused, considering whether he should answer it or let it go to message bank. For weeks he'd been screening his calls. He sighed and swiped the screen with his thumb.

'Hello, this is Jarrod O'Connor,' he answered.

Silence.

'Hello? Who is this?'

Someone breathing on the other end.

'I don't have the time or patience for this bullshit. You picked the wrong person to prank call, arsehole. I'm hanging up.'

'Don't hang up, *Jarrod*,' came a reply, coarse and hushed. It was a voice he immediately recognised.

NINE

KALEB Carmichael whispered into the phone. 'Revenge is the only true justice.'

Jarrod was stunned, mouth agape. Fear welled inside him.

'Lost for words, Jarrod?'

'How… how did you get this number?' Jarrod tried to keep his words even, to mask his anxiety. He cleared his throat.

'Oh, I've known it for a long time, seared it into my brain. I've been waiting for the right time to call, to phone a friend,' Carmichael said, his voice relaxed, casual.

'What do you want? Why are you calling me?'

'Well, that's just the thing, my friend. I want nothing from you, not yet anyway. In fact, I can help you.'

'How could you possibly help me?' Jarrod's voice was a low growl.

'With insight. With redemption.'

'Redemption?' Jarrod scoffed. 'Found your redemption, have you? Found your inner peace, even after what you've done?'

Carmichael paused, considering. 'Yes. I have, thanks for asking. I can live with my decisions. I have no guilt.'

'That's what makes you and me different.'

'Different? We're no different, Jarrod.'

Jarrod waited before he spoke again. He wouldn't be lured into Carmichael's games. 'What do you want, Kaleb?'

'I'm sorry to hear about your wife. It was such a sad funeral. Jayne was her name, wasn't it?' He feigned sincerity.

Jarrod gritted his teeth, seething. 'You don't get to say her name.'

'Don't be like that now, Jarrod. I want to help you.'

'You want to help me? How about you walk into the closest police station and hand yourself in? Or better yet, step out in front of a moving bus. That would help me. That would make my fucking day!'

'Ah, that's the spirit,' laughed Carmichael. 'But no, I won't be handing myself in – I still have too much to live for.'

'What do you have to live for? Hiding in the shadows, stalking your next prey?'

'Now you're catching on.'

'Who's next on your kill list?'

'You are, of course. But when, well, that's up to you.'

'Up to me? What the hell are you talking about?'

'All in good time, brother.'

'I'm not your brother!' Jarrod's voice rose. He caught himself, conscious of not waking Pat.

'Oh, but you are. You and I are kindred spirits. We're driven by the same desire for revenge, to right the wrongs of this world. You and I *are* the same, Jarrod.'

Jarrod held his breath and closed his eyes, calming himself. He decided to change tack. 'Those words you said earlier. You left that note on my car. How long have you been following me?'

Carmichael chuckled, high-pitched and humourless. 'Don't worry. If I wanted you dead, I could have taken you and your little family out long ago. Mind you, I've been tempted. After all, you did shoot me. Twice. But no, you're safe, for now. Things have changed since your wife's death.'

'How have things changed?'

'That pain inside you, that need for revenge. I know how that feels. It can destroy you if you let it, or it can bring you salvation. All this has happened for a reason. It's a chance for you to open your eyes, to truly understand the ways of the universe. It's the same choice Vincent gave me.'

'Is that right? And how did that turn out for you and Vincent?'

Carmichael chuckled, followed by a drawn-out silence.

'What's it to you?' Jarrod said. 'How does what I do affect you?'

'You and I are connected. I see that now. Your salvation is my salvation.'

'That doesn't make sense.'

'It will in time.'

Jarrod peered out onto the dark street. 'Where are you?'

'I'm closer than you might think.'

'Enough of the games. Either show yourself and you and I get this over with, or you tell me what you really want.'

'Be patient, my friend. All in good time. There are greater powers at play here, you have no idea. You see, I'm offering you a chance for salvation, to right the wrong of your wife's death. I can help cleanse your soul.'

'And what do you want in return?' Jarrod asked.

'We'll get to that when the time is right. For now, I have something for you, a gesture of goodwill. Now listen carefully. You'll need to contact your colleagues in Sydney. There's a dead body.' He paused, letting his words linger, enjoying the suspense.

'Where? Who?'

'No one important, just someone who needed to pay for his sins. He lost the right to live. I rid the world of that scum. Let's call it my gift to you. You'll find him in unit fifteen on the third floor of an old block of apartments, twenty-three Highgate Street, Kings Cross. Good luck, Jarrod. I'll be in touch soon. I'll be watching.'

The line went dead. He was gone. Only then did Jarrod realise his heart was thumping inside his chest, his hands shaking.

He dialed Brad's mobile.

'Hey mate?' answered Brad after two rings. 'What's up?'

'Sorry to bother you this time of night, but it's important.'

'No problems. I'm still at the station, on the late shift. What's going on?'

'Kaleb Carmichael just called me.'

'You're shitting me! What did he say?'

'He rambled on about revenge and redemption. Said there was a dead body in an apartment building in Kings Cross. He could be playing games, but can you contact the Sydney Metro police to get them to check it out?'

'Sure, I'll get straight on it. What's the address?'

Jarrod recited the details.

'I'll get our intel guys to run a reverse CCR on your mobile phone to track where the call came from,' said Brad.

'Good idea. One other thing. He's in Lockyer, or at least he was. I need to get my kids somewhere safe, just in case. I think he's been following me.'

'Oh, shit. Are you sure? You didn't think to share that with me?'

'I'm telling you now. Besides, I've only just joined the dots. I found a note on my car at Jayne's funeral. I didn't think much of it at the time, but he used the same words in the phone call just now. There was a guy up on the hill at the cemetery, watching. I thought my mind was playing tricks, but it was him, I know it.'

'I'll send a patrol car around to your house straight away,' said Brad, urgent.

'No, that's okay. I have a place in mind. I'll let you know once I've confirmed the arrangements. No one can know.'

'Righto, I'll trust your judgement on that, but I have to tell Benfield that Carmichael might be back in town. He'll lose his shit. He'll have to tell the brass in the city, and you know what that means.'

'Yeah, the circus will be back in town.'

'You just get your family somewhere safe. I'll handle the rest.'

'Thanks mate. Let me know when you hear from the Sydney coppers.'

They ended the call. Within an hour, Jarrod had Pat and the kids packed up and in the car. He was taking them somewhere out of Kaleb Carmichael's reach.

TEN

IT was 11:00pm. Detectives Travis Jones and Will Scholes of the Metro Homicide Squad were cruising the sordid streets of Kings Cross when they received the 501 'sudden death' job to attend an apartment building in Highgate Street.

'Please call Coms by phone for more information,' crackled the female dispatch operator's voice over the radio. The information was too sensitive to relay via police radio, which they knew could be monitored by media and ambulance chasers.

Scholes made the call and jotted down the details as he fumbled with his notebook. 'Roger that, show us proceeding to that address now.'

He hung up and turned to his partner. 'Apparently, this might have something to do with that wanted freak, Kaleb Carmichael. Info from the coppers at Lockyer Station.'

Jones raised one corner of his mouth, as if tugged by a fishhook. 'Do you reckon there's anything in it? Did it sound legit?'

'Who knows?' said Scholes. 'Probably another red herring. Those country coppers have been jittery ever since they let that nutcase Carmichael escape. We better check it out, though. Besides, you got somewhere better to be right now?'

'I'd much rather be home in bed for starters,' said Jones dryly as he steered the unmarked police vehicle into a U-turn.

In ten minutes, they were pulling up out the front of the dull apartment building, a featureless rectangle. They got out of the car and headed to the front entrance. The glass door to the foyer was locked.

Scholes pressed the intercom button. Jones held up his badge in the direction of the overhead security camera.

'Yeah, what do you want?' came a man's gruff voice through the intercom speaker.

'Police,' said Scholes, pressing the intercom button with his thumb. 'We've been sent here to do a welfare check on the guy who lives in apartment fifteen.'

'Welfare check, my arse. I'm getting tired of your police harassment.'

'Just let us in,' said Scholes.

A muffled grunt came through the speaker. 'Take the stairs to the third floor. Lift is busted.'

A buzz followed by a click. Scholes pushed the door open. They made their way into the foyer, past the elevators with an "out of order" sign, towards a narrow, internal staircase. The air was thick and musty, the smell of stale cigarette smoke lingered. The younger, fitter Jones reached the third floor ahead of Scholes, who wheezed two flights behind. As Jones waited for his partner, he studied the brown swirling patterns of the wallpaper. It was peeling from the rising damp seeping up the walls. He wondered if the place would pass a fire inspection.

'I gotta give up those smokes,' panted Scholes as he lumbered up the last few steps. He met Jones outside door number fifteen, the first unit on the left. Jones showed no signs of physical exertion.

'Smart arse,' grumbled Scholes.

'What? I didn't say anything.'

'Well? What are you waiting for? Knock on the door then.'

Jones complied and after several raps on the door there was no answer.

'Go and get the manager. He'll need to let us in,' ordered Scholes.

Jones strode down the stairs and returned a few minutes later, followed by a dishevelled man jingling a set of keys. 'This is Nigel Withers, the caretaker.'

'Have you blokes got a warrant?' asked Withers, a lit rollie dangling from the corner of his mouth, his eyes squinting from the smoke.

'We've had a report of a possible dead body,' said Scholes. 'We're happy to leave you to sort it out. Give us a call if you find it. Can't guarantee how long it will take to come back.' He turned, motioning to leave. 'Come on Jones, let's stop harassing this good man.'

'Hold up,' said Withers. 'What makes you think there's a dead body?'

'We got a call,' replied Scholes, stopping at the top of the stairs. 'Who lives here?'

Withers raised nicotine-stained fingers to his lips in a V and drew on his smoke. 'A guy named Kevin De Vries,' he said, and then blew out smoke through his nostrils. 'He gives me no trouble. Works nights as a security guard in the city. He's probably at work now.'

'When was the last time you saw him?' asked Jones.

'Let me think. A few weeks, maybe. He pays his monthly rent in cash up front. Other than that, he doesn't bother me, and I don't bother him.'

'Are there any other residents on this floor we can speak to?' asked Scholes.

'Nope. Asbestos. It's an old building. Owners started ripping out the sheeting in the other apartments but it's taking them forever to get the reno work finished. They're all vacant on this floor, except for this one. De Vries was happy to pay the cheap rent. He didn't seem to mind.'

Jones took notes in his police notebook. 'Which security company does he work for?'

'Waltons Security, I think it is.' Withers nodded, now surer. 'Yeah, that's it, Waltons. I've seen him coming home from work in his uniform.'

Scholes turned to Jones. 'Make a call with the security company. Let's find out first if he's been attending work.'

'On it,' said Jones, eager. He slid out his mobile phone and searched for the company's contact number. He dialled and paced the hallway as he spoke to someone on the other end.

Withers waited, growing more agitated by the minute.

'Okay, thanks so much for your help,' said Jones and he ended the call. 'That was the security company night supervisor. He says De Vries hasn't been to work in over a week. He sent a text out of the blue saying he was sick and needed to take some leave. The guy I just spoke to was the one who received the message. He said he didn't think too much of it.'

'No one thought to check in on him?' asked Scholes.

'Apparently not. He only works casual, so they found a replacement soon enough. Apparently, he said he'd call in when he was ready to return to work.'

Scholes looked at Withers and gestured with a nod at the bunch of keys in his hand. 'Well, after you. We have reasonable grounds to go in.'

The scruffy man sighed and worked his way through the keys until he found the right one. He inserted it into the lock and jiggled it like a safe cracker to find the sweet spot. The key turned with a clunk. He gripped the knob, but the door resisted, sticking in the sagging door frame. He nudged it with his shoulder and the door gave way and creaked opened.

The three men recoiled and gagged, hit by a wall of foul air.

Scholes covered his mouth with his handkerchief. 'You better wait outside,' he told Withers, who retreated to the top of the stairs.

Jones opened his jacket and drew his Glock from a shoulder holster. Scholes nudged the door open with his knuckles as the putrid air escaped past them. The apartment was in darkness.

'This is the police. Mr De Vries, are you home?' called Scholes. The eerie silence was broken only by echoes of a dripping tap.

Jones switched on the light source mounted to his Glock, the bright beam catching unsettled dust particles. He scanned the gun in an arc, following the light as it lit up the hallway leading towards a cluttered sitting room. Beyond that, he made out the features of a small kitchenette. He ran his fingers down the wall inside the doorway until they found a light switch. With a flick, a fluorescent bulb in the hallway flickered to life with an electric hum. Jones and Scholes squinted as their eyes adjusted to the sudden brightness. Up ahead, on either side of the hallway, were two closed doors. Jones moved forward, hugging the left side wall, followed by Scholes who covered the right. They slid past the closed doors and canvassed the sitting room and kitchenette. The foul stench was now much thicker. Jones gagged, pulling out his handkerchief to cover his face. Scholes reached into his jacket pocket and produced a menthol vapour stick which he smeared under his nose. He offered it to Jones.

'Thanks, but I'm good,' Jones whispered.

Scholes shrugged and placed the stick back into his pocket.

Scholes found the light switch to the sitting room, but the bulb was blown. Jones shone his light around the room. An old television set was propped on a rickety stand and beside it, a stack of magazines and newspapers were piled on the lino-covered floor. A vinyl recliner with torn armrests was positioned in front of the TV in the middle of the room. The headrest was stained with a greasy patch. Beside the recliner stood a TV dinner stand. A dirty plate with knife and fork rested on top alongside the TV remote and an empty bottle of whiskey. Clearly, Kevin De Vries rarely hosted dinner parties in the drab little apartment. The kitchenette benchtop was cluttered with assorted fast-food containers and more dirty dishes and cups. The tap dripped hypnotically into a plastic bowl in the sink.

With the sitting room and kitchenette cleared, they turned their attention to the closed doors in the hallway. Scholes nodded towards the first door. Jones held the doorknob, his Glock pointed down in the Sul position. He gave Scholes a nod and mouthed 'one, two, three'. With a twist of the knob the door creaked open. Jones swivelled into the opening, his torch light flickering inside the room. He flicked on a light. 'Bedroom clear,' he announced, before returning to the hallway. 'Just an unmade bed and a pile of clothes on the floor.'

'This one must be the bathroom,' said Scholes, looking at the other door.

Jones grinned. 'Your lead. After you.'

Scholes shot him a look and smeared more menthol on his top lip. He gripped the doorknob and leaned his heavy frame against the door. Jones shone his torch at the door, ready to cover his partner. Scholes turned the knob and heaved the door open. Rancid air poured out into the hallway – the stench of decomposition. Scholes tucked his nose and mouth in the crook of his arm. It was his turn to gag. Jones aimed the gun torch into the bathroom. Scholes reached in and flicked on the light. A dim bulb with no shade hung low from the ceiling. A quick scan revealed a toilet with rust stains at its base and a handbasin with mould dotted along the tile grout. Above the bathtub hung an opaque plastic shower curtain drawn closed. The word "father" was finger painted across it in what looked like blood, drips from each letter now dry.

Jones trained his weapon on the tub as Scholes stepped forward and gathered the shower curtain. He looked at Jones who gave a nod, and then slid the curtain open. They both reeled from the grotesque figure in the bathtub. The body of a man in a security uniform lay on its side, hands bound with nylon rope, hog-tied to his boots. The hands were bloody, the skin marbled with purplish blotches. The man's face and neck were bloated, the skin blackened.

'Oh, God,' Jones gasped.

Scholes bent down for a closer inspection. The body lay in a pool of congealed blood. 'His throat was cut,' he said. 'More stab wounds to the chest. Poor bastard was tortured.'

'How do you figure that?' said Jones.

'Look at the hands. Stab wounds through the palms. There's a finger missing.'

Jones studied the dead man's face. 'Christ, his own mother wouldn't recognise him.'

Scholes looked up at the word scrawled on the shower curtain. 'Or maybe even his own son.'

ELEVEN

JARROD doubled back to be certain he wasn't being followed. After making a few last-second turns into various side streets, he zig-zagged through town until he reached the old highway. There were no headlights in the mirror as he sped away from town. Trance-like, Pat stared out at the car's headlights cutting through a veil of darkness. When Jarrod had explained to her the phone call from Carmichael, she needed no convincing. She helped him bundle the kids into the car after packing clothes and essentials into suitcases. Despite Jarrod's erratic driving, Katie and Matty slept soundly in the back seat, buckled in with their teddies, blankets and pillows. It was nearly midnight, and they were now heading along a dirt road in the countryside.

His mobile phone rang, and Pat picked it up from the centre console and read the caller ID. 'It's Brad,' she said. 'I guess you need to take it.'

He nodded.

She swiped the screen to answer the call and handed him the phone.

'Hey mate. Any news?' he said.

'Sydney Metro Homicide called. There was a body at the address Carmichael gave you. A security guard with his throat cut and multiple stab wounds. He'd been tortured and tied up in the bathtub,' explained Brad.

'Tortured? How?'

'Finger cut off.'

'Jesus.'

'Looks like he's been dead for about a week.'

'Do they know who he is?'

'A guy named…' Brad flicked through his notes. 'Here it is. Kevin De Vries. Ever heard of him?'

'No. What's his connection to Carmichael?'

'There was one pretty obvious clue. The word "father" was written in blood on the shower curtain.'

'Interesting. There was nothing on his file about his biological father, no record at all. We all know what happened to his stepfather.'

'Yep, he incinerated that poor bastard,' said Brad. 'Also, I have other news,' he continued. 'We had no luck running the reverse CCR on the call you received from Carmichael. Untraceable. Probably one of those cheap burners.'

'He's not far. I know it. He's reaching out to me for some reason, toying with me.'

'Of course, he is. That's his M.O. Where are you now?'

'I'm on my way to Julie and Darren Sommerville's place. Remember the young foster couple who took in baby Zalia last year? Karl Mundy's little girl.'

Mundy was a drunken lunatic who jumped Jarrod one night outside the police station, nearly killing him. Jarrod had blown a hole in him.

'I remember. Nice young couple. They still live in that farmhouse out of town?'

'Yeah, that's where we're heading now. We'll be there in a few minutes. And Brad, you can't tell anyone where we've gone. Not even anyone at the station. I can't risk any leaks, not this time.'

'I understand.'

'If you hear anything new, give me a bell. We'll stay here tonight until I work out my next move.'

'Roger that. Benfield has already called in the cavalry. SERT's on standby and detectives from the Carmichael Taskforce in the city will be in town first thing in the morning. You'll be the first to know if there's any news. Stay safe, mate.'

'You can count on it.'

Jarrod hung up just as he turned off into the long driveway of the Sommerville's farmhouse. As he pulled up in front of the renovated cottage, the veranda light came on and Julie and Darren came out in their pajamas. He'd called ahead, explaining his family needed somewhere to hide out, somewhere he couldn't be traced back to. He had gotten to know Julie and Darren as friends, regularly calling in on them to check on little Zalia. They were now bonded, a mutual connection forged by inexplicable circumstances that had brought the little girl into their lives. When the couple learned of Jayne's death, they offered to help in any way they could.

Pat and Jarrod carried Matty and Katie inside and Julie showed them to a spare room with two beds already made up. Tucked under the covers, the kids snuggled and hardly murmured.

Jarrod gave Julie a hug. 'Thank you so much for taking us in. I didn't know who else to call.'

Darren gave him a firm handshake. 'Don't mention it, Jarrod. Anything for you and your family. You've always been there for us, time now for us to repay the favour.'

Jarrod introduced Pat.

'So pleased to meet you,' said Julie as she gave Pat a warm embrace. 'We were so sorry to hear about Jayne. We didn't get to speak to you at the funeral. Wanted to give you space.'

'Thank you, my dear,' said Pat with a sad smile. She looked exhausted.

'Where's that little one of yours?' Jarrod asked.

'Zalia's asleep. Come and see,' said Julie.

Jarrod followed her down the hallway where a bedroom door was ajar. The melody of a nursery rhyme played quietly as the rotating night light projected stars onto the walls and ceiling. Inside a cot lay a plump infant with fluffy hair. She grunted as she sucked her thumb contently, tucked under her blanket.

'So beautiful,' Jarrod whispered. 'How old is she now?'

'Just gone twelve months.'

'Already? Wow, how time flies.'

They crept out of the room, leaving baby Zalia to her dreams.

Jarrod gave Julie and Darren an overview of why he needed to hide his kids. He didn't want to alarm them, but they took it all in their stride. They were more than happy to open their home for as long as they needed. Pat was shown to another spare room where she settled in for the night. Jarrod was offered the couch with a blanket and pillow. Julie apologised profusely, but he told her not to be silly, thanking her again for their unquestioning hospitality.

After everyone settled and the lights turned off, Jarrod lay on the couch and stared at the ceiling. Restlessness getting the better of him, he tiptoed out the front door and sat under the stars on the top step of the veranda. A full moon hung high in the night sky. The stars were dazzling out in the country, away from the artificial haze of the town lights. He'd forgotten how peaceful the sounds of the bush could be, so quiet. His thoughts swirled. Anxiety had become a kind of background noise, as if it were traffic on some unseen road. He told himself that grief was natural, part of the system that evolved to keep humans safe and well. It is an alarm system of sorts, one that should be heeded. For when we are stressed, it impacts both the functioning of the brain and the body. The key is finding the actual cause, addressing it, and the symptoms should fade. Well, that was the theory he had read on a Facebook post by some life coach. His thoughts returned to the man responsible for Jayne's death and Kaleb Carmichael's taunts. Bitterness rose like bile into his mouth.

He jumped when his phone vibrated in his jeans pocket. "Caller ID unknown" appeared on the screen. His stomach churned and the base of his neck tightened.

He answered and the voice at the other end chilled him to the bone.

'Hello, Jarrod. You *were* expecting my call, weren't you?' said Kaleb Carmichael.

'So, you knifed some poor bastard in his bathtub. Good for you.'

Jarrod tried to conceal the quiver in his voice.

'Do I have your attention now?'

'Sure. What now?' Jarrod refused to fuel his delusions of grandeur.

'Let's talk about you, shall we?'

'What's there to talk about?'

'Let's start with revenge. You should know by now that everything I've done, all the people I killed, I was driven by revenge. It can be powerful if you let it.'

'What's that got to do with me?'

'They haven't found the driver who killed your wife, have they? It must be driving you mad. The anger. The need for revenge. You must feel so helpless.' Carmichael was trying to get a reaction, but Jarrod refused to bite.

'What do you suggest, Kaleb?'

'Patience, my brother. Seek the truth and take your revenge.'

'Why are you taking such an interest in me? I'm the one who shot you and locked you up.' It was an answer Jarrod needed.

'True. It would be fair to say I was a bit pissed about that at the time. The pain in my shoulder has never left me, it's unbearable at times. Do you know the damage a bullet does when it tears through the human body? But you know what they say, "what doesn't kill you makes you stronger". I am stronger now, much stronger. Pain reminds us we are alive. I've lived with pain all my life.'

Images of Carmichael's horrific burn scars flashed in Jarrod's mind.

'So, am I still on your kill list?'

'Maybe, maybe not. The universe seems to have brought us together for a reason. I respect your courage. You were the only one who could take me down. Don't get me wrong, it won't ever happen again, and I won't hesitate to kill you if you get in my way. You see, I don't get emotionally attached to people. Never have, never will. That part of me is, how would you say, broken. Benefits of being a sociopath, I guess,' he said with a satisfied chuckle.

'What do you want from me then?'

'I know what a man can be driven to do in the name of revenge. I also know the healing power of retribution. I can feel it in your voice, Jarrod. You're broken. Let me help you.'

Jarrod clenched his jaw. 'How can you help me?'

'By giving you the courage to seek retribution, to heal your soul before the day of final judgement.'

'Who's final judgement?'

'Yours, Jarrod. That day will come soon.'

'And how do you plan on doing all this? Healing my soul?'

'By giving you some incentive.'

'Incentive? Go on.'

'Kill him, Jarrod. Kill the man who took your wife. Once you cross that line, your mind will open to all the possibilities.'

'And if I don't?'

'I'll kill you. You choose, Jarrod.'

The line went dead.

Jarrod didn't move. He lost all sense of time as a million thoughts raced through his mind. Carmichael's words resonated with him and replayed over and over. He kept talking about revenge, willing Jarrod to seek retribution for Jayne's death. He wondered just how much Carmichael knew. Had he been following him when he tailed Jayne's killer back to his house? Did he know about the man in the Corolla?

Kaleb Carmichael was getting inside his head, and it scared the hell out of him.

TWELVE

JARROD managed a few restless hours sleep on Julie and Darren's lounge room couch. The morning sun finally broke through the tall ghost gums surrounding the farm, and the household came to life. Julie tinkered in the kitchen and the rich aroma of freshly brewed coffee filled the house. Darren appeared with Zalia in his arms, the baby grinning from ear to ear and legs kicking with excitement. He lowered her to the floor, and she took a few wobbly steps towards the couch where Jarrod lay. He turned his head and she held onto the armrest for stability. She took an instant shine to Jarrod and poked his unshaven face with her plump little fingers. She gave a gummy smile that warmed his heart. Memories flooded back of the day they rescued her from near death from dehydration and neglect. She was now thriving in the care of her foster parents who loved her like their own.

Jarrod went into the spare room where Katie and Matty were stirring. He had no idea how he was going to explain all this to them. They would be so confused.

'Where are we, Daddy?' said Katie as she sat up in the strange bed. He sat down beside her and tried to find the right words. Matty jumped out of his bed and ran over, embracing him with a morning hug.

'Hey big buddy, how did you sleep?'

'Good,' Matty said, rubbing his sleepy eyes. 'We went for a drive last night?'

'Yes, mate. We've come to visit some special friends. We slept here last night. They have a little baby called Zalia who you can play with today.'

'What about school?' Katie asked. She knew something was up.

'You guys can have a few days off from school while I try to work out a few things.' It was an inadequate response, but the best he could come up with.

Pat peered into the room and smiled. 'Good morning, my little darlings.'

Matty padded over and hugged her legs.

'Morning Pat,' said Jarrod. 'Would you mind taking Matty out and introducing him to Julie, Darren and Zalia? I need to talk to Katie.'

'Sure,' she said. 'Come on big man, let's meet our new friends.'

'Okay,' he said and took Pat by the hand. Pat led Matty down the hallway. He heard Zalia squeal with delight while Matty giggled. Jarrod knew Katie wouldn't be so easily distracted. She would demand answers.

Jarrod inhaled and started his pitch. 'I'm sorry, sweetheart. There's some stuff I can't tell you, but we needed to come here to make sure you guys are safe. No one can know where we are.'

'What do you mean? What's wrong, Daddy? I'm scared.' Her eyes moistened, tears forming.

'Don't be scared. I won't let anything happen to you. You're perfectly safe here. I need you to stay here and look after Nanny and your little brother while I go and sort out a few things.'

'Please tell me what's going on, Daddy!' she insisted.

'Look, it just might not be safe at home until that bad man is caught. I don't want to take any chances, so I decided we need to stay somewhere secret for a while.'

Katie squeezed his hand and a tear fell down her cheek. 'I want to go home. I don't want to stay here.'

'I know. I'm sorry I didn't get a chance to explain it to you first, but I found out something last night and we had to leave home quickly.'

'What did you find out? Why did we have to leave home?'

The renewed anguish on Katie's face almost killed him right then and there. A child shouldn't have to endure what Katie had. What irreversible damage had already been done? Guilt rose inside him. It was all his fault. The poor kid was grieving for her mother, and now he was uprooting her from the one place she felt safe. His family was exposed to danger. He'd let the wolves in again. All because of *the job*. He was at breaking point, something had to give.

He rubbed her shoulders and looked into her eyes, her mother's eyes. 'I need you to be strong, to trust me. Will you do that for me?'

She considered and wiped a tear away with the back of her hand. She sniffed and nodded, resolute.

'That's my girl. Now come and meet my friends. They are really nice, and you'll like it here on the farm. They have animals.'

Her eyes lit up. 'What kind of animals?'

'They've got chooks, cows and horses. They even have a goat tied up around the back.'

A hint of a smile emerged.

'Come on,' said Jarrod. 'Let's come and say hi.'

He led her by the hand to the lounge room where she met Julie and Darren. Katie melted when she saw Zalia. Her face beamed at the baby who stood beside a coffee table, leaning against it for support.

'She's so cute.' Katie flopped onto a shagpile rug beside Zalia, who blew bubbles of drool and giggled gibberish. There was an immediate connection, and for a moment Katie's worries seemed to evaporate.

The distraction was a godsend. Jarrod sensed a strange destiny that had brought this bundle of joy into all their lives.

After a hearty breakfast of bacon and eggs, Jarrod gathered his thoughts with a coffee on the veranda, energised by the warmth of the morning sun. Pat joined him and leaned against the railing, blowing steam off her coffee as she stared out towards the rugged beauty of the valley beyond.

'What are you going to do?' she said.

'I have to go back into town tonight. There's something I need to take care of.'

She gave him a look.

'You'll just have to trust me,' he added when he saw the skepticism on her face.

'I do trust you, Jarrod. I know you've got a lot on your mind. Do what you have to do. But spend some time with the kids today. They need you more than anyone.'

As usual Pat was right. They had a lovely day on the farm, milking cows and feeding the chickens. The kids seemed to adjust to their new surroundings and the country air brought with it a renewed sense of optimism. However, as the day's end came, a wave of anxiety fell over Jarrod. He had decided what he needed to do next, to start righting the wrongs of his world.

Kaleb Carmichael's words had replayed in his mind all day. He was right, the need for revenge is a powerful motivator. It was pulling him in, drawing him towards the darkness. It was time to act, time to set himself free of the hatred, whatever it took. It might damn him to hell, but he no longer cared.

THIRTEEN

IT was after 11:00pm when the lights of the farmhouse disappeared in the mirror as Jarrod drove along the dusty road towards town. They had enjoyed a nice barbecue dinner and the kids were tucked in for the night, sleeping soundly. Pat promised to keep a close eye on them as he skulked away into the night. He told her he needed to check in on the house and pick up a few things, which in part was true. He didn't tell her about his other plans.

When he arrived in his street, he parked a few houses away from the house to not arouse any attention to his arrival. He crept along the fence line of houses until he came to his front yard. He slunk along the side of the house and unlocked the laundry door at the rear. Using his phone torch, he crept through the house like a burglar, paranoid Kaleb Carmichael was staking out his home. The house was in darkness and the windows and doors were all still locked and secured just as he had left them.

He filled a suitcase with extra clothing and essentials he had forgotten to grab in their rush the night before. He went to his study and shone the light around in the darkness, sitting in his swivelling desk chair and savouring the familiar smell of its leather. The chair was contoured to his body shape and welcomed him home like an old friend. He checked the phone message bank. No messages, that was a good sign. No one was looking for him. In the bottom drawer he found a lithium battery pen torch and pressed the button with his thumb, fully charged and nice and bright. He found a pair of protective gloves he used to carry when he was a uniformed patrol officer, designed to protect against sharp objects when searching offenders. They would do nicely for what he had planned.

He grabbed an empty duffel bag from his shelf in the walk-in robe and on his way out he rummaged through the laundry cupboard. He found the rope he'd bought from Bunnings, never used but he always knew it would come in handy one day. He found his toolbox buried beneath two sleeping bags, and selected the tools he needed. A roll of industrial masking tape and a garbage bag were the last items he shoved into the duffel bag.

As he went to leave, he took one last look around the house. Everything was in order, but he felt sad to be deserting their home. He yearned to turn the lights on and pretend everything was back to the way it should be, that Jayne was alive, and Carmichael was behind bars. He shook away the fantasy, furious that Kaleb Carmichael had taunted him out of his own home. Despite this, he had no choice. Carmichael had given him fair warning and Jarrod had to protect his children. He was powerless to do anything about finding Carmichael. Every police force in the country had dedicated enormous resources to tracking him down. Cops from the city would have already flooded into Lockyer to tighten the net in case Carmichael reared his head. As much as he had faith that his colleagues were working around the clock to find the county's most wanted man, he knew Carmichael would only appear on his own terms, when he was good and ready.

He had to focus on what was still in his control. One thing at a time. He had other priorities, his own agenda. The pain of Jayne's death was getting worse with each passing day, like an infected wound. The senselessness of it all was overwhelming and the bitterness inside him grew.

He locked the door behind him and returned to the darkness outside, skulking back down the street to his car. Sliding into the driver's seat, he eased the door closed. He drove away with the headlights off. Ten minutes later he was parked down the street of Jayne's killer's house. The entire street was lifeless. A few houses down, the white Corolla was parked in the driveway and the house was in darkness. He watched the house for a few minutes until he was confident he could move down the street without being seen. Making sure the interior light was off, he quietly opened and closed the car door and slung the duffel bag over his shoulder. He approached and waited in the shadows of a hedge dividing the house from the side neighbour. He entered the front yard and slid along the hedge line. A dog barked from a nearby yard. He stood like a statue, concealing himself within the foliage of the hedge. The dog stopped barking, and all fell quiet again.

He sidestepped along the fence line with the hedge brushing against his back until he came to the garage. The gap between the side of the garage and the hedge was only a few metres. Making a quick dash he pressed his back against the side of the garage, shimmying his body along the wall until he came to a sliding window. Confident he was sufficiently concealed within the shadows, he moved with more urgency and purpose. He tugged the window frame, however it was latched from the inside. He shone his pen torch through the glass. A blanket hung inside the window like a curtain. He pressed his face and gloved hands against the window. He found a tiny gap between the window frame and the edge of the blanket and angled the torch light through the opening. The light caught the bull bar of a vehicle. He reached into the duffel bag and found the screwdriver.

Holding his breath, willing himself to make no noise, he positioned the screwdriver in the aluminum frame and jimmied with just enough force for the window to pop from the frame. Looking around to make sure no lights had come on in any of the houses, he slid the window open. He drew the blanket across and shone the torch on a white Toyota Landcruiser four-wheel drive. With all his strength, he pushed himself up and slung his feet into the window. With some effort he squeezed both legs and his body through the opening. He lowered himself until his boots found the concrete floor of the garage. It was the point of no return. He shone the pen light around.

Along the walls were neatly organised shelves holding storage boxes and assorted gardening tools. The Landcruiser took up most of the space inside the pokey single garage. Jarrod slid around to the front of the vehicle. What he found confirmed what he already knew. The bull bar was bent back against the dented bonnet. The right-side front wheel guard panel was a twisted mess, and the headlight assembly was shattered. A single light bulb dangled from wires. He bent down and shone the light on the floor beneath the engine bay to find a green stain from leaking radiator coolant. A pool of oil had formed where it had dripped from the engine block. He was surprised the wrecked vehicle had made it home in this state. Clearly, it was no longer in a drivable condition and had been hidden out of sight of the prying eyes of neighbours – and police.

He inspected the bent bull bar closer with the torch. His heart sank when he saw the flecks of dark blue paint from his Forerunner seared into the aluminium surface. He remembered Locard's Exchange Principle "Every contact leaves a trace". It was the fundamental theory of forensic crash investigation. He had all the evidence he needed. A surge of bitter sadness was followed with intense anger for the man who had concealed evidence of his crime.

He moved to the front passenger door and pulled the handle. With a creak the door opened, and he popped open the glove compartment. He rifled through old service records and assorted documents until he found the registration certificate. The vehicle was registered to a Mr and Mrs George and Audrey Willmott. George Willmott – a name that would be etched in his brain forever. The name of the man who recklessly killed his wife.

An envelope fell out of the glove compartment onto the passenger floor, landing near an empty bottle of rum. He shone the torch onto the white envelope and picked it up so he could make out the insignia and writing on the front, "St. Stephens Private Hospital". It was addressed to Mrs Audrey Willmott. The envelope had been opened and contained a letter. He slid out the folded sheet of paper and read through a doctor's report. He stopped reading when he came to a sentence saying, "*It is with regret I confirm the tumor is non-operable and terminal. The patient will be provided with palliative care and pain relief. Life expectancy is estimated to be from three to six months from this date."* He wondered what became of Mrs Willmott. Was she still alive? The letter was dated ten months ago.

He placed the items back in the glove compartment and left the vehicle as he found it. He took photos with his mobile phone, capturing the evidence if he ever needed it as a fallback. Somehow, he knew the photos would never see the light of day. There would be no need for traditional "justice", such a joke that concept was. No, he had made up his mind. There was only one true form of justice.

Kaleb Carmichael called it "revenge and retribution".

All in good time.

FOURTEEN

WHEN Jarrod drove out of George Willmott's street, he knew where he was heading next. He'd had a gutful of running from Kaleb Carmichael. It was approaching 1:00am and the streets were deserted. The station's illuminated police sign came into view, and he swung the car into the driveway, parking in the nearly empty staff car park. He got out and hurried to the station back door, watched over by a security camera. When he swiped his badge on the sensor panel, it beeped and the door unlocked.

The station sergeant on the graveyard shift, Paul Richardson, gave him a wave as he spoke on the phone in the communications room. It was common for Jarrod to come and go at odd hours, so Paul hardly paid attention. At the end of the hallway, Jarrod turned and headed up the stairs to his office. He flicked the switch on the wall and the fluorescent tube lights blinked to life. Brad had been running the office in his absence and his partner's desk was scattered with unfinished court briefs and crime reports. Jarrod's desk remained untouched.

Avoiding the temptation to check his messages, he headed straight for the gun safe. The muscle memory in his hand expertly worked the combination dial clockwise and anti-clockwise until the lock clicked. He tugged the lever and heaved the door open, unlocking the padlock and sliding the Glock from the peg. He closed the safe door and spun the dial. No one would check the safe to notice his gun missing, not straight away. Carrying a Service firearm while off duty was prohibited by policy. *Screw that.* The safety of his family came first. He'd cop the slap when it came. He unlocked his locker and grabbed two loaded magazines, thirty shots in total. He loaded and slid the gun behind his belt, concealed under his T-shirt. The spare mag fit nicely into his jeans front pocket.

He gave the office a long last look, turned the lights off and dashed down the stairs. The station sergeant was still on the phone and didn't notice him leaving. The back door closed behind him and soon his tyres were screeching as he accelerated out the driveway. The blue and white checkered sign grew smaller in his rear-view mirror. A thought occurred to him. *I wonder if I'll ever go back.*

Rather than heading back out to the farmhouse, he decided to go home to clear his mind in the quietness of familiar surroundings. Pat promised to call if the kids had trouble sleeping, so he assumed no news was good news. They were tucked away, safe and sound. He pulled into the driveway and killed the engine, pondering in the early morning silence. Right then and there he decided. He was done hiding and refused to be intimated by Kaleb Carmichael. Now armed, the odds had shifted. Even playing field.

He unlocked his front door and turned on the porch light. Moving about the house, he flicked on light switches as he went. If Carmichael was watching, Jarrod wanted him to know he was no longer in hiding. Game on. *Come and get me.* He grabbed a beer and sat in his recliner in the lounge room. The cold fizz soothed his dry throat and his body relaxed as he melted into the comfy chair. His other hand rested on the handle of the Glock, still tucked under his belt. The first beer was gone in seconds. Four empty bottles soon lined the floor at his feet. His eyelids drooped so he reclined the big old chair and drifted into a light sleep. As he dozed, he lost all sense of reality. His body lingered in a strange void, somewhere between consciousness and sleep. Sensing he was being watched through the front windows, his eyes snapped open. Nothing. Was his mind playing tricks? Was he dreaming? A buzzing sound grew louder, persistent. His mobile phone vibrated across the coffee table. It stopped ringing as he grabbed it. "Missed call from unknown caller".

As he stared at the screen the phone chimed and a text message appeared. "*Glad to see you back home, brother. I've been watching you. You've been busy."* He jolted to his feet, sending the coffee table and empty beer bottles flying. Bare-footed, he ran out the front door with the Glock raised, scanning the front yard. He crossed the lawn, leaving dewy footprints behind him. He moved out onto the street, the bitumen still warm under his bare soles. The street was ghostly quiet. His peripheral vision caught a slither of movement at the T-intersection at the end of the street. He turned his head and squinted. A shadow moved beneath the dim light of a streetlamp and scurried off. Jarrod blindly gave chase, the weight of the Glock heavy in his hand. His feet screamed from the biting bitumen. When he arrived at the intersection, he aimed the gun in both directions but had no idea which way the person had run. Lowering the gun, he gulped cool night air to catch his breath.

Carmichael was taunting him, all part of his game. He was daring Jarrod to come find him. Did he want to get caught? Or was he luring Jarrod into a trap?

Jarrod decided to not call it in. This was between him and Carmichael. 'Come and get me, mother fucker!' he yelled. 'I'm waiting.'

Nothing but silence.

He turned and headed home. As he approached the front gate, he noticed a piece of crumpled paper poking out of the mailbox slot. He must have missed it when he'd raced out of the house. He slid out the note and carried it to the light of the front porch and unfolded it. Handwritten in red colouring-in pencil, it read, *"Take your revenge. KILL HIM! Set yourself free."*

Jarrod stared out into the night and waited for what seemed like eternity before going back inside and locking all the doors and windows. He figured Carmichael's games were over for the night. He was left alone with his thoughts, the seed of revenge growing inside him.

Kaleb Carmichael was enticing him to seek retribution for Jayne's death. What could Carmichael possibly gain from that? Was it just a sick, twisted game to him? Did he get off on manipulating him?

Perhaps it gave Carmichael a sense of power and control. Had he been sent from the shadows by a dark force to test Jarrod's resolve? Did he have the stomach to do what needed to be done to avenge his wife?

Only time would tell.

FIFTEEN

AFTER a few hours of restless sleep in his own bed, Jarrod rose just as daylight broke. He needed to get back to the farmhouse to be there when the kids woke up. The new day was destined to change him forever, but he was prepared for the consequences. By day's end he would be confronting his inner demons, one way or another. He locked up and headed back out of town, making sure he wasn't being followed. His mobile phone rang. "Brad Harding" appeared on screen as the caller. Jarrod put the phone on speaker as he drove.

'Hey Brad, what's up? You wet the bed?'

'Benfield's got us starting at six am. Came in early to get a jump on things. Thought I'd check in with you before the daily shitstorm fires up. Sorry if I woke you.'

'Nah, all good. I'm up.'

'Thought so. How are you and the kids holding up?'

'Yeah, they've settled in as good as can be expected. Farm life is a real novelty for them.'

'Are you there now?'

'Yeah, I've just gotten out of bed,' Jarrod lied.

'I have some news about the homicide in Kings Cross. You ready for it?' Brad said with a hint of excitement.

'Fire away.'

'They confirmed the identity of Kevin De Vries. They also ran a DNA check on some foreign hair fibres found at the scene and it came back with a match. Kaleb Carmichael. No great surprises given he was the one who led us to the body. But here's the humdinger. They followed a hunch because of the word "father" written on the shower curtain and ran a comparison of the victim's DNA with Carmichael's.

They matched. The victim was Carmichael's biological father.'

It took a few seconds for Jarrod to process this new information.

'Holy shit. There's been no mention of his biological father on his records, only references to his mother and stepfather. I wonder how he tracked the guy down?'

'Who knows. He's a resourceful bastard. Extreme daddy issues, I'd say,' Brad said, chuckling.

'Revenge,' said Jarrod.

'Huh?'

'Revenge. He's driven by revenge,' Jarrod said, thinking out loud.

'Well, if anyone knows how that freak thinks, it's you. Speaking of which, has he been in contact with you again?'

'No, I've heard nothing,' Jarrod lied.

'Strange. It's only a matter of time before he turns up again. The taskforce is working around the clock. If he's still in the area, we'll get him.'

'Yeah, I suppose,' said Jarrod, his words laced with doubt. 'Anyway, I better go. Let me know if you hear anything new, will ya?'

'Sure thing. You take it easy.'

'You too, mate.'

Jarrod's phone beeped and Brad was gone. He thought about the possible motive for the Kings Cross homicide. Carmichael had come after his own flesh and blood. Were there no lines he wouldn't cross? He wasn't to be underestimated. Jarrod reached for his Glock in the centre console. Gripping the handle reassured him.

Soon he was driving back along the dirt road towards the farmhouse. He'd backtracked to ensure he wasn't followed. As he pulled up in front of the house, he could see into the kitchen window. Pat and Julie were chatting as they prepared breakfast.

'Ah, look who's showed up,' said Pat as he closed the flyscreen door behind him. 'Should I ask where you were all night?'

Jarrod shook his head. 'Best you don't.'

Pat sighed. 'The kids have just woken up. You should go in and see them.' It wasn't a suggestion.

He kissed her on the cheek and obeyed. She had let him off the hook for now, no interrogation. Best he didn't ride his luck.

He enjoyed morning hugs with the kids, who thankfully hadn't noticed he'd been away all night. During breakfast, baby Zalia was the centre of attention. Jarrod and the kids spent the morning together, but his thoughts drifted.

'What's wrong?' asked Pat.

Jarrod leaned against a fence, staring off into the distance while the kids fed the chickens.

'You were miles away just then. What's going on in your mind?' she persisted.

'Just missing Jayne, I guess,' he said. In part, that was true.

'There's something else going on, Jarrod. What is it? What are you up to?'

He faced his mother-in-law. He loved her as though she were his own mother. Placing his hands on her shoulders, he said, 'Don't worry about me. Really. It's just… there's something I need to do. I need to make it right.'

'What do you mean? Make what right?'

'I can't explain it, you'll just have to trust me.'

'I'm worried about you, Jarrod. You haven't been yourself ever since news of that Carmichael man resurfacing. Are we in danger? Please, I can handle it. I just need to know what we're dealing with.'

He admired her courage and resolve. 'There's no way he could know we're here. You and the kids are safe. Coppers from all over the state are working around the clock to find him. Brad is keeping me updated.'

Guilt gnawed at him. He'd let Carmichael get away, didn't call it in. He'd betrayed everyone Carmichael had harmed; he had undermined his colleagues who still hunted him. Yet, some warped notion, a subconscious whisper, told him that Carmichael was the key to finding balance in his off-kilter world.

'Then what is it, Jarrod?' asked Pat. 'I can tell something is eating away at you.'

'What if there was a way to make the man responsible for Jayne's death pay for what he's done? I'm talking about being held accountable for his actions, not so-called court justice. Real justice.'

Pat's expression told him he'd said too much. She put her hand to her mouth. 'No, Jarrod. Only God can dispense that kind of justice. Let it go, please.' She took his hand in hers and squeezed.

'I'm sorry,' he said, turning away. 'I've lost my faith in your God.' He looked over at the kids who giggled as they chased chickens around the pen. 'I need to go now. I'll be home tonight, I promise.'

Pat held his hand tight. 'Listen to me, Jarrod. Don't do anything stupid. If Jayne were here, what would she say?'

'Jayne can't say anything because she's dead!' he snapped. 'It's up to me to speak on her behalf. I'm sorry, I have to go.'

Pat released his hand. The look of sad disappointment on her face nearly killed him. He walked away without turning back. If he didn't leave then, he never would. He knew he would regret the decision to stay. It had to be done today.

He drove away from the farmhouse, heading back towards town. The weight of guilt and sadness was almost more than he could bear; sadness for losing Jayne, and guilt for what he was about to do.

But there was someone he needed to visit first.

SIXTEEN

AS Jarrod approached the main gate to the cemetery, he pulled the car over beside a pop-up flower stand. A woman with a mop of grey hair sat in the shade of a marquee behind generous bouquets soaking in buckets, each wrapped in clear cellophane. "$15 a bunch" advised an A-frame blackboard, the sign written in chalk.

'Hello,' he said as he examined the offerings.

The old woman acknowledged him with a courteous smile and a nod.

He selected a nice bunch of white daisies from an array of vibrant colours and offered her a twenty-dollar note. She leaned forward and reached for the money. He noticed she was wearing fingerless woolen gloves, the grooves around her fingernails soil stained. Wiry fingers took hold of Jarrod's, the strength of her grip belying her frail appearance. She cupped Jarrod's hand with both of hers. The gesture was strangely warm and comforting. She closed her eyes and held on for a few seconds. Her eyelids opened, her head tilting upward to his face, and her eyes slid into focus. Her wizened face stared at him – no, she stared *through* him, like his head was transparent and she was fascinated by an object behind his skull.

'She'll love these. Beautiful choice,' she said. Her smile faded. 'Is it forgiveness you're seeking?'

He slid his hand away, leaving the money in her grasp. Her stare intensified, a gaze of a stranger, aloof judgement.

Jarrod's brain stuttered for a moment, every part of him on pause while his thoughts caught up. 'Keep the change,' he said as he backed away.

He turned and headed for the car. He got in and placed the

flowers on the front passenger seat. As he pulled away, his eyes met the woman's, her stare unfaltering. 'Weird,' he said out loud.

He turned into the entrance and drove beneath an ornate archway. The main road was lined with ancient oak trees. Branches arched overhead and interlinked like extended fingers, forming a natural tunnel that blocked the sun. As he ventured deeper into the cemetery, the gardens, headstones and lawn plaques created a calming sense of reverence. He found the row he was looking for and parked the car. As he got out, he breathed in air cooled by shade.

Memories from Jayne's funeral flooded his mind. He looked around to get his bearings and spotted the distant hill, remembering the hooded figure standing beneath the lone tree. He strolled past graves until he came upon one covered in bare soil, no time yet for grass to grow.

A simple granite headstone, yet to suffer the ravages of time, bore a familiar name. He read the plaque. *"In loving memory. Wife – Mother – Daughter – Friend. Jayne Patricia O'Connor. In God we Trust."*

He got down on his haunches and pulled out weeds that had crept across the base of the headstone. He placed the flowers on the grave and knelt in silence, allowing tears to well. The lump in his throat returned, restricting his attempts to swallow. He wanted to stay there forever with his wife. If it wasn't for the kids, he could just lay down and die.

'Hello, my love,' he whispered. He gave in to despair and a dam of tears burst. 'I miss you so much,' he sobbed. He had never felt so alone.

'The kids miss you, but they send their love. They're so strong. You'd be so proud of them. It's been hard for Pat, but she's been my rock.'

He didn't know what else to say and thought about the real reason for his visit. 'I have some news. I found the man who did this to you. I know where he lives. No one else knows. I hate him so much. I can't ask for your permission or forgiveness, but I need to do something you won't like. I don't know what else to do. I need him to suffer like I've suffered. I need to take my revenge, your revenge. I'm so sorry, my love. Please forgive me.'

More tears came as his face fell into his hands. A gentle breeze blew and the tree branches above swayed. Leaves danced in harmony with the wind. He so desperately wanted to hear Jayne's voice, but there was only the rustling of leaves.

He curled into a ball on the grass beside her grave, knees tucked into his chest, arms wrapped around his knees. He waited for a sign from Jayne, but there was nothing.

Eventually, he lifted himself to his knees and said goodbye. He kissed his fingers and dabbed the headstone. He rose to his feet and trudged back to the car, each step from Jayne heavier than the last. He was now ready. It was time.

Once it was done, he would deal with Kaleb Carmichael.

SEVENTEEN

AS the last light of the day drained away, Jarrod watched from his car. George Willmott's house was in darkness. The residents of the quiet street had hunkered down for the evening. The glow from television sets flickered from lounge room windows and the aroma of home cooked dinners wafted through Jarrod's window. He was parked in front of a vacant house further down the street. Faded FOR SALE signs competed for space in the front lawn with knee-high weeds. No one had lived there for a long time. He was confident he had gone unnoticed as he waited. Just in case, he had obscured his number plates with masking tape before he arrived.

Just after 7:30pm, a set of headlights came around the corner and grew brighter in Jarrod's rearview mirror. He slid down in his seat as the car passed. A white Corolla turned into Willmott's driveway and parked in front of the closed garage door. The prick was going about his life like nothing had happened. New anger boiled up inside Jarrod. He reminded himself that he was the only one who knew the man's dirty little secret hidden inside that garage. He had the initiative.

Willmott climbed from the car carrying a grocery bag in one hand, and a brown paper bag the shape of a liquor bottle in the other. He fumbled with the items and shuffled up the porch stairs and unlocked the front door. He disappeared inside and closed the door behind him. The porch light came on, followed by more lights as he moved about the house. Jarrod recalled the medical report and wondered what had become of Willmott's wife. He decided he didn't care; he had no capacity to sympathise. That part of him had died with Jayne.

He gave Willmott time to settle in with his bottle of booze, to tilt the odds in his favour. To pass the time he checked the rope coiled in the duffel bag and tied and retied the knot to get it right. It had to be perfect. Satisfied the rope was ready, he reclined his seat and waited. Exhaustion took hold and he allowed himself to doze. Phone calls nor texts disrupted him, he had made sure of that. He'd powered down his phone hours ago while he was still at Jayne's graveside. He couldn't risk any phone tower pings placing him near Willmott's house. He had to be a ghost.

He waited until 10:00pm, pulled the balaclava down over his face and checked himself in the mirror. He'd used it once for a trip to the snow with Jayne before the kids had come along, no need for it again, until now. With just eye and mouth holes, he looked like a bank robber. *If only that's all I was up to,* he thought to himself. He slid on his gloves and checked the items in the duffel bag. Everything he needed was accounted for. He locked his Glock in the glovebox. He wouldn't be needing it. Grabbing his black hoodie from the back seat, he opened the door and got out, easing it closed.

He made his way on foot towards Willmott's house, pulling the hoodie over himself as he walked. He followed the same path as the previous night, concealing himself in the shadows of the hedges. Entering the yard, he snuck down the driveway and pressed his body against the side of the house. Light from the kitchen window fell to the ground. He slid along the wall until he was beneath the kitchen window. There was no sound of movement, so he craned his neck and peered in. The kitchen was empty. He ducked under the window and moved down the wall and around the corner to the back of the house. It was much darker in the backyard away from the residual glow from streetlights. He came to an open window, the glow from a lamp filtering through swaying curtains. Careful to remain in the shadows, he peered up into the window for a quick scan before dropping below the window line again. Willmott was alone in the lounge room, lying back in a recliner, eyes closed.

Jarrod risked taking another look and peered inside. A half empty bottle of liquor stood on the floor at Willmott's slippered feet. His hands rested in his lap, nursing an empty scotch glass. A reality show played on the TV, the volume low. Willmott's round belly rose and fell under a white singlet, a dressing gown splayed open. Baggy sweatpants covered his bottom half. Jarrod watched him sleep. Now was the time to go in.

Jarrod moved to the back door. He checked the doorknob but it was locked. It was an old lock and wouldn't put up much resistance. He unzipped the duffel bag and selected a pair of multi-grip pliers, adjusting them wide to fit the doorknob. Applying pressure, he squeezed and pushed down with his body weight until the lock gave way with a pop. He held his breath and waited. No sign of movement inside. The door opened easily with a slight creak of the hinges. He returned the pliers to the bag and stepped inside the laundry and waited silently in the half dark. He'd never broken into anyone's house unlawfully before. It signalled a turning point in his life. Screw it. There was no hesitation in his mind.

He crept up the steps leading to the kitchen and placed the duffel bag on the floor. He pulled out the garbage bag and took slow, deliberate steps towards the lounge room entrance. When he came to the doorway, the recliner had its back to him. Willmott's bald patch and tufts of hair peeked over the headrest. Jarrod entered the room and approached Willmott from behind. Surprise was the key. Now or never.

Willmott roused, maybe sensing Jarrod's presence. In two bounds Jarrod was on him, slipping the garbage bag over the man's head and twisting it tight. Willmott squirmed and clawed at the bag. A guttural sound escaped his mouth, something between a groan and a yelp. Jarrod moved to his front and pinned his wrists against his chest. Anticipating a struggle, he knew he could overpower the man in his pickled state.

Pulling Willmott's wrists, Jarrod yanked him from the chair and onto the floor. Jarrod rolled him onto his stomach and pulled his arms behind his back, pinning him with his knees. He crossed Willmott's wrists and applied the first zip tie. Willmott cried out when Jarrod zipped it tight. He attached a second zip tie for good measure. Selecting the masking tape and a pocketknife, he peeled off a good piece and sliced it free. He pulled the plastic bag from Willmott's head and secured the tape across his mouth, pressing it hard to make sure it stuck. For good measure, he peeled off a much longer length of tape and wrapped it around Willmott's mouth and head.

Jarrod rolled him onto his back. Willmott pushed himself along the carpet with his heels in a futile attempt to escape. His cheeks puffed and he snuffled through his nose, his mouth bound tight by the tape. Jarrod stood over him and the man froze, eyes wide.

'It's time you and I got to know each other, *George*.'

EIGHTEEN

JARROD was jacked up on adrenaline, his hands shaking. He stepped over George Willmott and retrieved his duffel bag from the kitchen. Back in the lounge room he took the hammer from the bag. He raised it poised to strike, arm trembling. 'Make another sound and this hammer hitting your face will be the last thing you ever see. Do you understand?' He could hear the tremor in his own voice.

Willmott's body recoiled. He nodded, eyes blinking rapidly. Jarrod sat on the recliner and calmed his breathing. He stared through the eyeholes of the balaclava at the pathetic figure on the floor. Willmott stared back, fear in his eyes.

Jarrod tapped the face of the hammer into his palm. 'Now pay attention, George. You don't know me but clearly, I know you. Do you know why I'm here?'

Willmott shook his head, confused.

'Are you hiding any secrets, George?'

His expression changed, his eyelids drooping.

'No? What about what's hiding in your garage? Does that ring a bell?'

Willmott turned his head, diverting his eyes.

Jarrod leaned forward and grabbed his plump chin with a gloved hand. He turned Willmott's head, forcing him to face him. Their eyes met. 'Are you living with guilt, George?'

Willmott's shoulders slumped. He nodded slowly and tears welled. His eyes dropped.

'Look at me, George!' Jarrod yelled.

He looked up and held Jarrod's gaze.

'Do you think it's time to pay for what you've done?'

He frowned as if he didn't understand the question.

'Got nothing to say, huh? Well, let's let fate decide. Get up!' Jarrod stood and grabbed Willmott under his armpits, heaving him to his feet. 'We're going for a walk. Where are the keys to the garage?'

Willmott gave a muffled answer behind the masking tape and nodded towards the kitchen. Jarrod slung the duffel bag handles over his shoulders, carrying it like a backpack. He led Willmott into the kitchen by his arm and grabbed a set of keys from a hook. Jarrod marched him down the stairs through the laundry and headed out the back door towards the garage.

'Remember, make a sound and I'll cave your skull in,' Jarrod whispered.

He tugged at Willmott's arm as he reluctantly walked alongside. When they reached the garage door, Jarrod slid the pen torch from his pocket. He shone light on the keys dangling in front of Willmott's face. 'Nod yes when I hold up the right key.'

One by one, Jarrod held up keys until Willmott nodded. Jarrod inserted the key and turned it to release the roller-door lock. He pulled it open and led Willmott inside, closing the door behind them. His torch light bounced off the walls until he found the light switch. He moved down the narrow space between the wall and the side of the Landcruiser and flicked the switch. A bright fluorescent bulb came to life, illuminating the garage. The blanket still fixed to the window gave him all the privacy he needed.

'Come here,' Jarrod said.

Willmott hesitated at first, then squeezed along the wall to where Jarrod waited in a pocket of space between a workbench and the front of the vehicle.

Jarrod pushed him against the bent bull bar. 'Don't move.'

He placed the duffel bag on the floor and took out the rope. Willmott looked at him in horror, the whites of his eyes prominent. A muffled whimper escaped from behind the tape. Jarrod slung the rope over a wooden ceiling beam and caught the other end as it dropped.

Willmott's eyes widened when he saw the noose.

Jarrod grabbed Willmott's arm and pulled him over, placing the loop over his head. He adjusted it and pulled the slip knot so the noose fit snug around Willmott's throat. The man just stood there, dumbstruck. Jarrod dragged over a milk crate and upended it. Spanners and screwdrivers clattered on the concrete floor. He positioned the crate near Willmott's feet.

Jarrod raised the hammer. 'Don't even think about yelling out for help. Understand?'

Willmott nodded, his eyes saying he understood.

Jarrod lifted an edge of the masking tape with his thumb nail and peeled it off Willmott's face. His eyes clenched and he grimaced from the sting of the tape pulling on his skin.

Willmott wiped away drool using the shoulder of his dressing gown. 'Who are you? What do you want?' he spluttered.

Jarrod looked at the damaged front end of the vehicle and shifted his eyes, staring at Willmott through the holes in the balaclava for a long time. 'I'm the Grim Reaper. I've come for you. A soul for a soul.'

Jarrod tugged the loose end of the rope.

Willmott flinched as the noose tightened. 'I'm so sorry. I didn't mean to hurt anyone. It was an accident.' His voice was childlike.

'You were drunk. You left her to die. You killed her!'

'I wish I could take everything back, but I know I can't.' Willmott rambled, his words spewing out of him. 'My wife died in hospital that day and I hit the bottle hard. I was driving home when it... when the crash happened. I didn't see the other car until it was too late.'

Jarrod pulled harder on the rope. 'I'm not interested in your excuses. Stand on the crate.'

Willmott clumsily stepped up onto the crate. Jarrod tugged the rope so there was no slack and tied it off to the bull bar of the Landcruiser. He had already estimated the ceiling beam would hold a man's body weight, factoring that in when he made his plans.

Willmott's legs quivered and a wet patch appeared in the crotch and down the leg of his sweatpants. The crate nearly toppled as he struggled to keep balance.

Jarrod moved behind him and sliced the zip ties with his knife. He raised the blade to Willmott's throat. 'Slowly, move your hands to your front. Don't try anything stupid.'

Willmott stood frozen, dumbstruck.

'Hands to the front. Now!'

Willmott jumped, snapped out of his daze and complied.

Jarrod secured a fresh zip tie to his wrists. He picked up the discarded ties and placed them in his pocket. He would leave no trace that he was ever there.

'Suicide,' said Jarrod matter-of-factly.

Willmott looked confused. 'What?'

'That's what the police will think when they find your swollen body hanging from this beam. But they won't find you for a week or two, not until the neighbours complain about the smell. No one will miss you, will they?'

Willmott just stared, the reality of his situation sinking in.

'You see,' Jarrod continued, 'it's easy for a person to put a zip tie on their own wrists using their teeth to pull it tight. They'll think you tied your own hands before you stepped off the crate. People sometimes do that, you know, before they hang themselves, to make sure they do the job properly, not change their mind after they step off. Funny how the survival instinct kicks in when you know you're about to die. It'll explain the marks around your wrists, but I reckon your skin will be so decomposed by then it will be hard to tell. It'll be written off as a clear-cut suicide. No need to investigate further.'

Jarrod looked at the damage to the vehicle. 'They'll see this and will put the pieces together. They'll figure you did yourself in, couldn't handle the guilt.'

Willmott stared at Jarrod and his expression hardened. 'Do you think I haven't thought about taking my own life? I have nothing to live for. I'm all alone and I can't bear the grief and the guilt. I have no family, no friends, no job, no life. If this is to be my end, then let it be.'

'Then go ahead, step off. I won't stop you. Put yourself out of your misery.'

Willmott glanced down at the floor and then up at the rope slung over the ceiling beam. He closed his eyes and stood perfectly still.

Jarrod waited for fate to decide.

NINETEEN

'DO it!' said Jarrod. 'What are you waiting for?'

Willmott teetered on the edge of the crate for what seemed like an eternity. Jarrod had already decided that if he stepped off, he wouldn't save him. The man's destiny was in his own hands.

Willmott blubbered and raised his bound hands, smearing tears and snot across his face. His cheeks became hot and red, veins protruding from his temples. He looked more likely to die on the spot from an aneurism. Swaying, he almost lost his balance on the crate. He stooped, shoulders slouched, and the rope tightened around his throat. 'Why are you doing this to me? Who are you?' He clenched his eyes closed, shaking his head, willing himself out of the situation he now found himself in. 'No, no, no. This isn't happening.'

Jarrod stepped closer and slapped him in the face. 'Wake up, George.' He grabbed Willmott's jaw and turned his face towards the damaged vehicle. 'Open your eyes.'

'No, I won't!'

Jarrod slapped him again. 'Open your eyes or God help me, I'll slit your throat!'

Willmott opened his eyes.

'Look at it. See that mangled metal, the smashed headlight? That's real. What you did was real. You can't hide from it any longer, pretend it never happened. It's time to pay for what you've done, for what you've taken.'

Willmott stared at the broken Landcruiser. His eyes lifted and he looked hard at Jarrod. 'What do you want from me?'

'I want you to suffer.'

'Who was she to you?'

Images of Jayne's smiling face flashed in Jarrod's retinas. He heard her laughter, felt the warmth of her breath on his neck, the tingle in his scalp as she ran her fingers through his hair. The happy image was replaced with another, one of pain and despair, her body slumped and blood seeping from her ears and nose, her eyes lifeless. Jarrod felt giddy, his legs jelly. He stumbled backwards and leaned against the bent bonnet of the Landcruiser. Gathering himself, he straightened the balaclava so he could see clearly through the eye slits.

He stepped forward and pressed his face against Willmott's ear. 'Who was she to me? Who was she to her children? Her husband? Her family? Her friends? Who was she, George?'

'What? I don't understand.'

'Say her name.'

'I don't know her name.'

'Jayne. Her name was Jayne. Say it.'

Willmott closed his eyes again, shaking his head like a child, refusing.

'Say her name, George,' Jarrod whispered.

He shook his head, defiant.

Jarrod stepped back and pulled on the rope.

Willmott gagged and his neck stretched. As the rope was pulled harder, he rose to his toes and the crate wobbled.

Jarrod released the rope and Willmott gasped. 'Say her name, George.'

The skin on his face sagged as his head dropped. 'Jayne. Her name was Jayne.'

'Ask for her forgiveness.'

Willmott sobbed, his shoulders heaving. 'I'm sorry, Jayne. I'm so sorry.'

Jarrod stepped away and studied him. 'You lost your wife. You understand grief, don't you?'

Willmott nodded, his eyes lowered.

'Yes, you do. I know it. You understand there's no pain greater, the torture of it. You know how it tears your heart out, you've felt it. But you can never make things right, never take back what you did.'

Willmott lifted his head, looked Jarrod in the eyes. 'I know! Don't you think I know that? I can't take this anymore.'

'Then step off that crate, and it will all be over.'

Willmott shook his head. 'I can't,' he finally said. 'Please, let me down. I promise I'll turn myself in to the police. Going to jail is what I deserve but I'm not ready to die. Not like this. Let me do what's right, for once in my life. Please.'

Jarrod folded his arms and let out a long breath as he considered his next move. 'How can you be trusted to do what's right?'

'You know where I live. I've got nowhere else to go. I won't run. I won't hide. Not anymore. You have my word.'

Jarrod stood beside him and pressed the blade of the knife against his wrists. 'I could just slit your wrists. Then you could decide to either bleed to death or jump off this crate. Either way, once you pass out from blood loss you'll fall and dangle by the neck until you choke to death.'

Willmott raised his chin in defiance. 'Do what you must. Either kill me now or let me go. You have my word. I'll call the police straight away and hand myself in.'

'You know I'll hunt you down if you say a word about what happened here tonight?' Jarrod whispered into his ear.

Willmott closed his eyes and nodded.

Jarrod ran the blade of the knife along Willmott's wrists. With a sudden tug he cut the zip tie.

Willmott flinched and exhaled with relief.

'What happens next is up to you,' said Jarrod. 'Do the right thing, or I'll come for you. I'm watching from the shadows. Keep the rope in case you decide to use it.'

Jarrod zipped everything into the duffel bag and slung the straps over his shoulders. Their eyes locked one last time before he turned and slid down the side of the vehicle. Pulling the roller door open to waist height, he ducked under and closed it behind him. He ran into the night, sprinting as fast as his legs would carry him. He kept running through the shadows and down the street until he came to his awaiting car. Water ran to his mouth, and he felt the urge to be sick. He pulled the balaclava off and made it to the footpath where his knees buckled, vomiting on his hands and knees. He spat and gagged until the wave of nauseousness passed. He rose to his feet and tossed the duffel bag into the boot. When he sat in the car, he pulled off his gloves, his hands clammy and shaking. He wiped them on his pants legs and started the ignition, pulling the Mazda out onto the street and away from there as fast as he could.

As he drove out of town, his mind processed the insanity of what had just unfolded. He'd reached his breaking point, crossed that line to where he was willing to take another life – in the name of revenge and retribution. Grief had led him to the brink, to the point of no return. He'd lost control, and that terrified him.

The trip back to the farmhouse was a blur. Before he realised it, he was pulling into the driveway. He parked and sat in silence to collect himself. He got out and walked towards the house. Pat was waiting. She met him on the top of the stairs to the veranda, arms folded.

'Are you okay, Jarrod? You're white as a ghost.'

'I'm fine. Everything's okay, I promise. Why are you still up? It's late.'

'Exactly! It's late and you're out doing God knows what until all hours. I've been worried sick. Where have you been? What have you done?'

'I've done nothing, I promise,' Jarrod lied. 'I spent the afternoon at the cemetery by Jayne's grave. I drove around to clear my head. I lost track of time, that's all.'

Pat looked far from convinced.

'How are the kids?' he asked.

'Fine. They're asleep. They wanted to know where you had gone. I didn't know what to tell them.'

'I'll spend time with them in the morning. I'll make it up to them. Come on, let's go inside and get some sleep.'

Pat hesitated. 'When will all this end, Jarrod? All the sneaking around at night, the secrets.'

'Soon, I promise. I've given it some thought. I'm ready to go back to work.'

'Are you sure?'

'As long as Carmichael is still on the loose our lives will be upside down. I need to get back in the game. I can't sit on the sidelines anymore. I'm ready.'

'And what about the business with the crash? That other driver is still out there. You can't get involved in that. You have to leave it to your police colleagues.'

'I know. They'll find him soon. I'm certain of it.'

Pat's eyebrows raised. 'And how can you be so sure?'

'I just do, trust me.'

Pat's hardened expression softened. 'Do what you need to do, Jarrod. You know I'm here for you and the kids.'

'I know.' He embraced her. She seemed so frail in his arms. The stress of everything had taken its toll on her.

'Come on, tomorrow is a new day,' said Jarrod. 'Let's get some sleep.'

They went inside and Jarrod turned off the veranda light. As he went to close the door, he took a last look out into the darkness. He stared up at the sky. The stars shone brighter than he'd noticed before.

TWENTY

AT 7:00am the next morning, Jarrod jolted awake when his mobile phone came to life. He lay in a momentary daze until he found his bearings. The ceiling's exposed beams came into focus and the familiar surroundings of the farmhouse became clear. He rolled over on the couch and fumbled through a pile of his clothes on the floor for his vibrating phone. As his fingertips found it, the phone eluded his grasp like a freshly caught fish. He grabbed it and squinted at the caller ID. Brad Harding.

'Sorry for calling so early, Jarrod, but I thought you'd want to know.'

Jarrod's heart raced. 'Know what?'

'We got him! The other driver from your crash. We have him!'

'How? Who is he?' Jarrod said, feigning surprise.

'Well, you wouldn't believe it. This fella, George Willmott, just wanders into the front counter of the police station last night in a daze. He's this harmless bloke in his mid-fifties. He was rambling but as soon as the uniform guys worked out what he was talking about they called in Steve Jackson from FCU. They called me in as well and I sat in on the interview. He made full admissions. He admitted to being the driver and kept saying how sorry he was. It was strange though, he kept repeating the same thing over and over.'

'What was he saying?' This time, there was nothing contrived in Jarrod's tone. He was dying to know what Willmott had said. *Did he talk about the man in the balaclava and the threats? Had he recognised him?*

'The Grim Reaper came for me. That's what he kept saying. He said he couldn't live with his guilt anymore and that the Grim Reaper gave him a choice.'

'What choice?' Jarrod asked, but he already knew the answer.

'He could either choose to die or confess. He kept talking about salvation. The guy's pretty unhinged. It turns out his wife had just died, and he hit the bottle hard. He said he panicked after the crash.'

'Did you find his car?'

'Yeah, he had it hidden in his garage. He was here under our noses the whole time. We've seized the vehicle for forensic testing, but the damage and paint scrapings are all consistent. He was driving a Landcruiser with a bull bar. Poor Jayne didn't stand a chance. It was pretty banged up, but he was able to drive it to his house straight after the crash. We'll canvass the neighbours this morning to see why no one reported anything suspicious.'

'Did he say anything else? Did he say why he decided to come in last night?' Jarrod pressed, trying not to raise Brad's suspicion.

'No. The bloke was pretty messed up. He'd been drinking but he just kept raving on about how the Grim Reaper visited him last night. I'd say the booze and his own guilt scrambled his head.'

Jarrod decided not to press with more questions. He had the answers he needed. 'So, what now?'

'Well, he's been charged with dangerous driving causing death and failing to remain at the scene of a crash. We've kept him in custody because he's on suicide watch. He had rope burns around his neck and we found a noose in the garage. Was gonna top himself but chickened out. We'll put him before the magistrate later this morning.' Brad paused. 'Listen, mate, this must be a lot to take in right now. I know it doesn't take away the pain of losing Jayne, but we got him. We got the bastard!'

'I know, that's great news. Really. It'll just take a while to sink in. I need to talk to Pat and somehow find a way to explain it to the kids.'

'Yeah, I bet that'll be tough. Is there anything else I can do for you?'

'Yeah, there is now that you ask. Tidy up your desk. I'm coming back to work today.'

'Are you sure? Don't go making any rash decisions because of this news. Take as much time off as you need to, really Jarrod.'

'I've had enough time. I can't sit on my hands anymore. I had already decided, before your call. I need to focus on Kaleb Carmichael. He's still out there and I know I can help. I need to feel useful. Being back at the station is what I need right now. The kids are happy and safe here for now.'

'Well okay then, if you feel up to it.' Brad sounded unsure. 'I'll tell Ross Benfield. It'll be good to have you back.'

'But be warned,' said Jarrod. 'I've been a pain in the arse to live with lately, so don't get too excited.'

Brad chuckled. 'So, what's new?'

'I'll be seeing you real soon, my friend. And Brad, thanks for the call.'

'Don't mention it. I'll see you in a bit then, hey?'

'Yeah, mate. See you soon.'

Jarrod stared at his phone, processing the news. Willmott's confused demeanour gave him the cover he needed. For now, he'd avoided raising suspicion of his involvement. He had no blood on his hands, his conscience was clear. He only hoped he wouldn't later regret showing mercy. Maybe letting Willmott die would have been the kindest thing to do. It would have put an end to his torment. Jarrod hoped the courts would restore his confidence in the justice system.

His mind drifted back to Kaleb Carmichael. He still had the handwritten note from the funeral scrunched up in his wallet. He pulled out the tattered piece of paper and read the words over again. *Revenge is the only true justice*. Jarrod had set himself free, but not in the way Kaleb Carmichael had in mind.

Pat appeared in the lounge room in a dressing gown and sat on the couch beside him. 'I heard you talking on the phone.' Her words hung in the air. She just looked at him and waited for him to speak.

He looked into her eyes and took her hands in his. 'They got him, Pat. They got the bastard who killed Jayne.'

She put a hand to her mouth and gasped, as though she'd been holding her breath all this time. 'Oh, thank you, Lord.' She leaned her head against his shoulder.

Jarrod wrapped his arm around her, and she wept against his chest. They were tears of sadness and relief. The news did little to ease the pain of Jayne's senseless death, however it brought some closure.

Soon the farmhouse was buzzing with activity as Julie prepared breakfast for the three kids. Darren embraced his role as kids' activities director and excitedly explained the adventures he had planned for the day. Katie's and Matty's smiles beamed as they ate their cereal. The farm had become their haven, a distraction from the sadness of their previous lives where sorrow had become the norm. It lifted Jarrod's spirits to see them smiling. He decided to leave it until another time to tell them about the man who crashed his car into Mummy and Daddy. There was no point dragging them back into that state of sadness. He didn't want them reliving that again, not yet. He discussed it with Pat and she agreed. Best to let the kids be for now.

After breakfast, Jarrod got himself ready and explained to the kids that Daddy was returning to his job as a police detective. They didn't seem to mind and gave him a kiss and hug.

Matty smiled cheekily. 'Catch some bad guys,' he said as Jarrod headed for the door.

'I sure will, big man. I'm off to catch some bad guys.'

~

Jarrod swung by home to change into work clothes. When he arrived at the station, he received a warm welcome from the Traffic Branch and General Duties officers who all made a point of shaking his hand. He went upstairs and bypassed the CIB office. When he arrived at his office, he eased into his chair, looking around at the familiar surroundings of his desk. It was like coming home. Even the pile of unfinished reports and court briefs had a welcoming allure to them. It was the best remedy, and he knew the time was right for him to return to the fray. He discretely returned his Glock to the safe while Brad was still out of the office. All was back to normal, as much as it could be in the circumstances. But before he could focus his attention on Kaleb Carmichael, there was something he had to do.

'I need to see him,' he said when Brad returned to the office.

'Who do you need to see, Jarrod?' Brad said warily.

'Willmott.'

Brad sighed and looked concerned. 'Are you sure? You know you can't have any contact with him, don't you? We don't want to give those defense pricks any reason to fight the case. You know what those lawyers are like, Jarrod. You're too close to the case. We need to avoid any suggestion of intimidation or harassment.'

Too late for that, Jarrod thought. 'Yeah, I know. I won't interfere. You have my word. I just want to see him, you know, for closure.'

Brad stood with hands on hips, huffing through his nose. He pondered the proposal. 'Okay, but I'm coming with you. He's down in the watchhouse. Just take a look at him from the corridor. You can't go in the cell or talk to him, okay?'

Jarrod smirked. 'Last time I checked, I was still your superior officer. Don't get too used to giving me orders.'

Brad frowned. 'Yeah, well I need to look out for your interests. We got a deal?'

'Sure. Just a quick visit in the watchhouse. No interaction. Got it.'

They headed downstairs and followed the long, internal corridor to the first entrance to the watchhouse. Brad pressed the buzzer, and they looked up at the security camera with a wave.

'Come on in, boys,' crackled a voice over the intercom. The electric lock clicked, and they pushed open the heavy steel door. They passed through two more secure doors until they were at the charge counter.

'You know where to go,' said the sergeant. 'Your man is sitting quietly in his cell. He's had breakfast and a shower and seems to have gotten hold of himself. He's been crying like a baby for hours.'

The sergeant threw Brad a set of keys. He caught them with one hand, and they headed for the door leading to the main cell corridor. Brad turned the key and pushed the steel door open. On either side of the corridor were three individual cells. At the end was a larger bulk cell used for prisoner exercise and holding of temporary prisoners who were being processed for release.

As they entered, Brad turned to Jarrod and whispered, 'He's in the last cell on the right.'

Jarrod nodded and prepared himself for his second encounter with George Willmott. He stopped in front of the cell and peered in through the door's thick, shatterproof glass. Willmott sat on a mattress on the floor wearing brown watchhouse scrubs. His legs were crossed, and he rocked back and forth in a trance-like rhythm. Jarrod watched him and saw the same pitiful man he'd threatened to kill only the night before.

Alerted to their presence, Willmott stopped rocking and turned his head in their direction. He looked at Brad with recognition before his eyes moved to Jarrod. He stared with despair in his eyes, a broken man. Jarrod felt his cheeks burning and sweat beading on his top lip as Willmott's eyes locked onto his. He studied Jarrod with uncertainty.

Willmott considered Jarrod and slowly raised one hand, pointing his index finger at him. 'The Grim Reaper.'

Jarrod's stomach tightened and threatened to make him hurl all over again.

'Did the Grim Reaper send you?' Willmott said, his voice low. He stared at Jarrod, still pointing.

He wore a look of confusion that told Jarrod he hadn't recognised him. Jarrod remained silent to avoid him recognising his voice.

Brad looked at Jarrod with a deadpan expression. 'What did I tell you? He's lost the plot. Come on. Have you seen enough?'

Jarrod nodded.

They left George Willmott alone in that cell to contend with his demons. Jarrod sure as hell still had his own to deal with.

One of his demons had a name. Kaleb Carmichael.

TWENTY-ONE

IT didn't take long for the news of Willmott's arrest to go viral after the story was picked up by local journalists attending morning court. In a small town like Lockyer this was big news. The radio on Brad's desk was tuned into the local radio station, 4LK. *"In breaking news, a man has been arrested in connection with the death of a local detective's wife in a hit and run crash last month. George Willmott, a fifty-seven-year-old local man, appeared in the Lockyer Magistrates Court this morning and was remanded in custody to reappear next month for a committal hearing."*

Jarrod stared at the radio as the news bulletin continued onto the next breaking story. Jayne's death had been reduced to headline news. He was still riding the waves of grief and he was reminded again that he had to keep fighting to stay afloat.

Brad returned to the office with two steaming cups of instant coffee. As he placed Jarrod's on his desk he said, 'Are you okay?'

'Yeah, I'm okay. Willmott's court appearance just made the morning news bulletin on the radio.'

'I guess that was inevitable. They'll be calling in, wanting media interviews next. I'm sure Ross Benfield will take care of that. The last thing you need is to be dealing with the media.'

Jarrod nodded in agreement. He took a sip of coffee and vacantly gazed out the window as his mind wandered back to the events of the last few days. The words spoken by Kaleb Carmichael in his recent phone calls played over in his mind. He'd gotten inside Jarrod's head, urging him to seek his own retribution, to be just like him. Jarrod decided he wouldn't mention the calls or Carmichael's late-night visit to his house. It would only prompt an investigation into his relationship with Carmichael. He didn't need his movements over the last few days to be put under the microscope. Jarrod's colleagues already suspected Carmichael was in hiding somewhere in Lockyer. He had no new information that could help lead to his arrest. Some things were best left unsaid.

Brad's voice snapped Jarrod back to the present. 'What's on your mind, mate? Anything you want to talk about?'

'No, I'm fine. Thanks. Anyway, I suppose you should give me a briefing. Get me up to speed.'

Brad sipped his coffee and rubbed his chin as he gathered his thoughts. 'Well, most of our resources are tied up with the search for Kaleb Carmichael. The Corrective Services Investigation Unit has a team set up in the MIR. They're taking the lead since Carmichael was already in the prison system at the time of his escape. Detectives from the Major Crime Squad are also here, and we have every blue shirt available out doing door knocks. Everyone has been working around the clock on overtime. Cars are being searched at roadblocks on all the roads out of town and the CIB guys are following up on reported sightings. That's a needle in a haystack. So many nut jobs calling with bogus reports, but they all need following up. Ross Benfield is managing the media. We have a SERT team on standby, they're camped out the back of the station using our radio tech's workshop as their base of operations. The town is crawling with coppers.'

'And you? What's the boss had you doing?'

The corner of Brad's mouth twitched into his cheek as a fake smile formed. He scoffed through his nose. 'Me? I'm just a dog's body. Been bouncing around like a shit-kicker, helping out as needed.'

'What do I always say? We're all shit-kickers in this job.' Jarrod lightly punched Brad in the shoulder. 'I'm back now. You get to ride with me.'

Brad smiled. 'Lucky me.'

Jarrod scratched his head with his biro. 'How have you been handling routine jobs?'

'To be honest, we've got a backlog. Any youth crime jobs deemed routine are either on the back burner or have been detailed to the Tactical Crime Squad to follow up. The Department of Children's Services has brought in more staff from other areas to help with child protection jobs. I've been in contact with our Child Abuse Unit at Headquarters, and they have staff on standby to help with any urgent cases if needed. Thankfully, nothing has come in that can't wait. Everything's been about the search for Kaleb Carmichael.'

'Okay, well we can only do what we can do. Sounds like you've done the best you could.'

'God knows we've missed you around here.'

'On that note, I guess I better check in with the boss. Is Benfield back in his office?'

Brad craned his neck and peered through the gap between filing cabinets in front of the glass partition separating their office from the CIB office. 'Yeah, looks like he's in there.'

'Come on then,' said Jarrod.

They carried their coffees out to the hallway and into the CIB office next door. Liam Dawes frowned as his chubby fingers tapped away on a computer keyboard. He turned his head and his face lit up when he saw Jarrod. He jumped from his seat and lumbered over to him with his hand outstretched. 'So good to see you back, Jarrod.' They shook hands and Liam wrapped his other arm around Jarrod's back in a fond man hug.

'Good to see you too, Dawsey. How you been, old mate?'

'Arses hanging out of our pants as usual, over worked and under paid. You know how it is.'

Jarrod smiled. 'Yep, that's how we roll.'

Murray Long leaned back on his chair with his feet on his desk, arguing on the phone with someone. He looked up at Jarrod and gave him a wave mid-sentence. 'No, you listen here, dickhead, that's not what I said and you know it. Yet again you've taken what I said out of context.'

Liam shook his head, smiled. Mouthed the word 'journalist'.

Long wasn't one for subtlety when it came to journalists, or anyone else for that matter. Jarrod gave him a salute and then knocked on Ross Benfield's open door. The boss was sitting at his desk, flicking through a pile of reports.

'Hey, Boss,' said Jarrod.

Benfield peered over his bifocals and set the reports down on the desk. He rose to his feet. 'Come in, come in, fellas. O'Connor, I've been expecting you.' He looked at Brad. 'A little birdie told me you were coming back in today.' Jarrod and Brad stepped into his office, and he gave Jarrod a firm handshake. 'It's good to see you. You're looking well. How are the kids?'

'They're fine boss. Thanks for asking.'

'Good. Good to hear. Take a seat, both of you. No doubt you've heard we had a breakthrough with the arrest of the other driver involved in your crash?'

'Yes, Boss. Brad has given me a full briefing.' Jarrod glanced at Brad. They had agreed to not mention their earlier visit to the watchhouse.

Not one for small talk, Benfield got straight to the point. 'I guess I don't need to explain that you've walked back into a real shit storm. The media are driving me nuts with this Kaleb Carmichael business and the bosses in at Headquarters are on my back. The Police Commissioner wants a briefing every few hours. We're under enormous pressure to find this lunatic.'

'I understand,' said Jarrod.

'He seems to have taken a real liking to you, O'Connor. Have you had any more calls from him since he gave us the tipoff about the murder of Kevin De Vries?'

Jarrod felt his face blush as his heart rate increased. His hands went sweaty, and he shifted uncomfortably in the chair. 'No, boss. I haven't heard from him since,' he lied.

Benfield didn't seem to notice the deception. 'Well, make sure you report any further contact immediately.'

Brad gave Jarrod a sideways look. He wasn't so easily convinced. 'I will, Boss. So, what do you need me to do?' Jarrod said, changing tack.

'You and Harding head down to the MIR, take up with the Intel guys. I know they have a backlog of inquiry logs to go through. You can take your pick. There's a pile of leads and possible sightings of Carmichael we need to follow up. Off you go. I've got to prepare for another press conference in twenty minutes.'

Benfield shuffled his pile of reports and waved his hand as he dismissed them from his office.

Good chat, Ross, Jarrod thought with an inner smile. He didn't take it personally. He could see the pressure Benfield was under and he meant well.

'Is there something you're not telling me?' Brad said as they walked back into the CPU office.

'No. What do you mean?'

'You seemed pretty uncomfortable when Benfield asked if Carmichael had been in contact with you.'

'You'll be the first to know if I hear from him again, okay?'

'Don't hold out on me, Jarrod. You know you can trust me.'

'I know, mate. Honestly, I haven't heard from him.' Lying to Brad killed him but he'd already made his decision on this. No one could know, it was that simple.

Jarrod put his empty coffee cup down on his desk. 'Come on, let's head down to the MIR and see what jobs they need us to follow up on.'

They kitted up and headed down the corridor towards the major incident room. It had been set up in the large conference room and buzzed with detectives taking phone calls and writing updates on whiteboards. As Jarrod and Brad entered, stern looking faces glanced up at them with disinterest before returning their focus to computer screens. The MIR had been taken over by big city detectives who weren't particularly interested in getting to know the locals. They worked in teams with each allocated a specific role, whether it be surveillance, investigations, tactical, communications or intelligence. They headed over to one of the few faces Jarrod recognised. Sergeant Kev Leitch, the local intelligence officer, was embedded with the team from the Bureau of Criminal Intelligence and was busy collating tasking sheets.

'Hey, Kev. What have you got for us this morning?' said Brad.

'Ah, hey guys,' said Kev, obviously happy to see some familiar faces. He stood up and shook their hands. 'Good to see you back on deck, Jarrod.'

'Thanks Kev, good to be back. The Boss said you've got some follow up inquiries for us?'

'Take your pick.' Kev pointed to a pile of tasking sheets. 'We've triaged all the recent reports from members of the public who've called the dedicated hotline with information. These are the ones needing follow-up. The info from crackpots, prank callers and psychics is all in another pile. To be honest, there's nothing really reliable, most are reports of prowlers or clothes being stolen off lines. Although, there's a report about a suspicious campsite out of town that might be worth a look.'

Brad scanned through a handful of tasking sheets. 'Any recent sightings?'

'No, that's the thing. This guy is a ghost. We've had no firm sightings at all. We've had teams of detectives running out inquiries around the clock. We've worked through hundreds of tasking sheets but have come up with diddley-squat. I'm beginning to think this guy has taken off interstate.'

'No, he's still here,' Jarrod said, a little too confidently.

'And how do you know that, Jarrod?' asked Kev.

'Yes, Jarrod, how *do* you know that?' said Brad accusingly.

'When he contacted me to report Kevin De Vries' murder, he said something that really stuck in my head. "There are greater powers at play here." Those were his words. It's like he's working to a plan.'

Kev scrunched his face. 'What plan?'

'I don't know, but he has a strong connection to this town. Something's drawn him back here. He's methodical, so we can't count on him making mistakes. He covers his tracks too well.'

'So how do we find him?' said Brad.

'He'll show his face when he's good and ready.'

Kev turned his attention back to the pile of intelligence reports. 'Yeah, well in the meantime we've got to keep working through these. Which one will it be?'

Jarrod flicked through the pile of tasking sheets until one caught his attention. It was the report Kev had mentioned about the suspicious campsite. It related to an incident from the night before and read "*Informant was driving along Glenwood Road at 10:00pm and noticed the light from a campfire on a hill in bushland*". Jarrod looked at the specific location and recognised it straight away.

'We'll take this one,' he said. 'Good seeing you, Kev. Let's go Brad.'

TWENTY-TWO

AS they walked across the station car park, Brad read through the details of the tasking sheet. 'This reported campfire overlooks Vincent Miles' abandoned property. You do know that, don't you, Jarrod?'

'Yep, I realise that.'

As Jarrod opened the driver's door, he was hit by a wall of trapped hot air. Brad sat in the passenger's seat and closed the door. The car had been baking in the mid-morning sun. Jarrod slid into the driver's seat and perspired immediately. The steering wheel was hot as a branding iron.

Brad wound down his window. 'You also know that ever since all that shit went down at that place, there's been reports of ghost hunters and teenagers hanging around there at night?'

'Yeah, I've heard those rumours,' Jarrod said as he put the car in gear and cranked up the air conditioning. He negotiated the visiting police vehicles double parked in "no parking" zones almost blocking the tight driveway.

'The SERT guys have already searched the Miles property,' said Brad. 'It was one of the first places they looked. But there was nothing. We even had surveillance sitting off it, but they eventually got called away. Resources spread too thin, trying to chase up every lead and reported sighting.' He faced Jarrod with a worried look. 'We still haven't made the connection between Vincent Miles and Kaleb Carmichael. Does that worry you?'

Jarrod looked left and right as he turned out onto the street. 'Of course, it does. But we'll join the dots sooner or later. It might be the key to catching him.'

'Those times he spoke to you. What exactly did he say?'

Jarrod thought for a moment, recalling Carmichael's words the day Jarrod cornered him in that basement car park – before shooting him. He replayed in his mind the things Carmichael said on the phone. The words in his notes. 'He never said anything specific. He mentioned Miles a few times, saying he was following in his footsteps, finishing what he had started. Something along those lines. But he never told me how they knew each other.'

'Do you reckon there was any truth to it? He could have been talking shit, couldn't he?'

'Yeah, I've thought about it,' said Jarrod. 'By the time Carmichael came on the scene, Miles' name had been plastered all over the news. Carmichael could just be a copycat. Maybe he took it upon himself to adopt Miles' mantra, make himself feel important. You know, part of something bigger.'

Brad twisted his body in the seat and stared at Jarrod. 'But? I can feel a "but" coming.'

'*But,* my instincts tell me there's more to it. The way he spoke, the words he used. It sounded a lot like Miles. I can't help but feel there's a real connection between them, that he's telling the truth. It would explain the similarities in his motivations.'

Brad studied the tasking sheet. 'So, there is a chance Carmichael could be hiding out on the Miles property?'

Jarrod shrugged. 'Don't know. That's why we're going out there now.'

Brad's hands fidgeted with the sheet of paper. 'Well, I haven't been back to that place since Miles shot me. I can't say I'm too keen to go back there, that place makes me real uneasy.'

'Don't worry about it. It's probably just another red herring, but we gotta check it out. It's the best lead we've got.'

Brad stared out his window, deep in thought.

'Don't go getting too worked up about it, it's probably nothing,' Jarrod said. 'It could have been anyone up on that hill. Pig shooters, teenagers drinking, hikers, anyone. There's a phone number for the informant on the report. Try giving them a ring to get an exact location of where they saw the campfire.'

As they headed out of town, Brad got hold of the informant, a man named Angus Stevens, who saw the campfire the night before on his way to his graveyard shift at the abattoirs.

Brad hung up the phone. 'Stevens said he travels that road most nights and knows the area well. He saw the fire on a hill under a big tree, overlooking the Miles property. Says it was a full moon so he could see the tree against the night sky. Sounds like a rational kind of guy. He didn't want to waste our time but thought he should report it.'

They headed out of town and within twenty minutes were approaching the Miles property. A sense of dread fell over Jarrod. Every memory he had of that place was filled with bitterness and death.

As they turned onto a gravel road, Brad raised his hand. 'Slow down. Up there, look.'

Jarrod braked and scanned the landscape through the windscreen.

Brad tapped his window, pointing to something outside. 'There, that has to be the tree up on that hill.'

Jarrod pulled over to the shoulder and the car was engulfed in a passing cloud of dust. They peered out towards a clump of bushland up on top of a hill a few hundred metres away. At the summit, an ancient ghost gum towered high, limbs stretching out. It leaned, threatening to topple, its roots exposed from the dry soil. The weathered branches had long been stripped of their foliage. Huge, shattered limbs lay scattered on the earth below.

'Doesn't seem to be any easy way up there,' said Jarrod. 'We'll have to climb the fence and make our way up on foot.'

'Great, I only just bought these Windsor Smiths,' sighed Brad. 'I guess we'll lose the ties then?'

'I guess so.' Jarrod grabbed the radio handset and booked off. The coms operator took note of their location and time.

The sun beat down hard and after negotiating the barbed wire fence without ripping their trousers, they began the trek through knee-high dry grass towards the base of the hill. They trudged through the open field, negotiating loose rocks and dead tree stumps. They scaled the slope and entered a thicket of trees and dense lantana.

'Stay clear of the lantana, they sting like a bitch.'

'Yeah, I know,' grumbled Brad.

When they reached the top of the hill, they came upon a small clearing that couldn't be seen from their approach. Jarrod stopped to catch his breath and looked back down towards the path they had just walked. He spotted the car parked off to the side of the road. It looked small from up there. He turned on the spot, taking in the panoramic view of the entire Miles property. Off in the distance, he made out the ruins of the dilapidated farmhouse, old grain silos, rusting farm machinery and discarded car bodies. A breeze gave some respite from the heat, and he wiped the sweat from his brow with his shirt sleeve.

The old tree groaned as its dead branches threatened to snap off with each gust of wind. Brad didn't seem to care much for the view and kept walking towards another thicket of bush on the far side of the summit. As Jarrod gazed out over the property, bitter memories flooded back. He closed his eyes and images he'd tried to suppress flashed by in a jumbled blur. In his mind's eye he saw a dead woman holding her lifeless baby, a charred corpse and muzzle flashes of a gun.

'Jarrod, over here,' Brad called, his voice hushed.

Jarrod opened his eyes and hurried over. Brad pointed to something hidden within a clump of trees. As Jarrod's eyes adjusted, he made out the shape of a green, dome-shaped tent. A sturdy stick, wedged in a horizontal position in the forks of two small trees, served as the support beam of a lean-to frame. Vertically stacked branches with leafy foliage formed an effective camouflage for the tent. A wisp of white smoke rose from the embers of a nearby campfire.

Brad held his index finger to his lips. He drew his pistol and stepped closer to the tent. Jarrod drew his Glock and fanned out to the other side of the tent, covering Brad as he moved closer. Not knowing if anyone was hiding inside, they crept closer, guns pointed towards the tent. A dry stick made a loud crack under Jarrod's shoe. He froze and held his breath. Brad gave him a stern look. If anyone was inside, they would know by now they had company. Brad shook his head, knowing they'd lost the element of surprise.

'This is the police,' he called. 'If there is anyone in the tent, come out now.'

They trained their guns on anything that might appear from inside the tent. There was only the sound of chirping birds and the old tree creaking with the breeze. Brad gave Jarrod a nod and they moved to the tent. Jarrod stepped closer and covered Brad as he reached down with his free hand to take hold of the tent door zipper. He tugged the zip and the flap opened. Jarrod reached down and pulled it open so Brad could see inside.

'Clear,' he announced. 'There's no one here.'

They bent down and inspected the interior of the tent. A sleeping bag was unrolled on top of a foam pad. A rolled up black jacket served as a crude pillow.

A battery-operated lantern stood at the far end of the tent.

Jarrod looked around. They were alone, a long way from backup and easy targets for an ambush. Brad reached into the tent and searched the jacket and sleeping bag. 'Nothing,' he said. 'Wait. Hold on. I found this.'

'What is it?'

He handed Jarrod a small, tattered, spiral notepad. Slid inside the wire coil was a worn-down, red colouring-in pencil that had been sharpened with a blade. Throughout the notepad were erratic scribblings in red. Crudely drawn, grotesque images of demons with horns and disfigured faces with blood streaming from their eyes stared up from the pages. Jarrod made out the words *"retribution"* and *"revenge"* scribbled across many of the pages in clumsy handwriting. As he flicked through the pages, trying to make any sense of the scrawled ramblings, he came upon a symbol he knew all too well. It was the three-dimensional Metratron's Cube that had inspired Vincent Miles and fueled his delusions. Jarrod recognised the handwriting and the hairs on the back of his neck bristled. It was the same writing style and pencil colour as the notes Kaleb Carmichael had left on his car at the funeral and the one in his letterbox.

He was about to place the notepad in his pocket when a loose piece of paper fell out and floated to the ground. Reaching down, he retrieved it from the dirt and unfolded the torn-out page smudged with finger marks. There were two names written in the same red pencil. The first name was Kevin De Vries, the security guard murdered in Kings Cross by Carmichael. A line was crossed through the name, as though it had been struck from a checklist. Below it was written *"Detective Jarrod O'Connor"*. Jarrod held it up and showed Brad.

'Oh, shit,' said Brad.

'It's Kaleb Carmichael's for sure. Call it in.'

'You gotta be shittin me,' said Brad as he pulled out his mobile phone. 'Lucky. Strong phone signal up here.' He called the MIR direct line to pass on details of their find.

While Brad was on the phone, Jarrod looked around the immediate vicinity of the campfire and noticed boot prints in the dirt. A log had been used as a seat. Firewood was stacked nearby. A spade leaned against a tree. Empty cans of baked beans and stew had been tossed into a freshly dug hole. He'd been camping rough, probably looting supplies from wherever he could get his hands on them, stealing whatever he needed to survive; God help any poor soul who got in his way.

On the ground beside the log, Jarrod noticed a black, hard case coated in dry mud. He picked it up and wiped the lid. The word "Beretta" was embossed on it. He figured it had once been buried. Maybe part of a hidden cache. He prised off the lid, and the gun and magazines were missing. According to the compliance plate inside, it was the case for a Beretta 92 A1 semi-auto with a 10-shot mag. Jarrod noticed a cardboard ammunition box in some long grass. He picked it up, but it was empty. It once held fifty 9mm rounds. On the ground behind the log, he found a rifle case. He prodded it with his shoe, but the canvas case was empty. He wondered where Carmichael had gotten his hands on such weaponry. He scoured the tree line and felt the thump of his heart beating like crazy.

Jarrod whistled just loud enough to get Brad's attention. He put his hand over the phone and came straight over.

When Brad saw the ammo box and gun cases, his eyes widened. 'Shit,' he said under his breath. He spoke into the phone again. 'Request urgent backup. Suspect possibly armed.'

When he got off the phone, he stood beside Jarrod. 'They're on their way. I'm not liking this. Feels like we're sitting ducks up here. We're too exposed.'

'Agreed. We don't want to be here when he gets back. Let's get the hell out of here and wait for backup.'

'Good call,' said Brad.

Jarrod scanned the surrounding bushland. All was quiet and there was no sign of movement, however a person could easily be concealed in the scrub. For all they knew, Carmichael could be watching them. He grabbed the pistol case and ammunition box. Serial numbers might determine their origin. He placed the notebook in his back pocket.

They descended, walking much faster than the trip up, scanning and covering their rear. They made it to the base of the hill and hurried across the open plain towards the relative safety of the car. Brad held the barbed wires apart as Jarrod climbed through the fence. Jarrod did the same for him. They waited in the car with the air conditioning cranked on high.

Brad gazed out at the hill. 'We could have bumbled into an ambush.'

'I know.'

They sat in silence, waiting.

Brad put his window down and tilted his head, listening. 'You hear that?'

Jarrod listened. What first sounded like the buzzing of a bee, became the distinct tinny engine noise of a two-stroke trailbike. It grew louder, coming from the other side of the hill. It idled, revved, and then faded until it dissolved into the sounds of the bush.

A rumble of cars came from behind. Jarrod looked in the mirror to see a motorcade of police vehicles throwing up a cloud of dust as they skidded to a halt. Liam Dawes and Murray Long were first out, followed by uniforms.

Jarrod and Brad got out to meet them.

'Thanks for getting here so soon,' said Jarrod. He pointed to the hill. 'It's up there. There's a hidden campsite and we found empty gun cases. It's Carmichael and he's armed.'

'How do you know it's Carmichael?' asked Dawes.

Jarrod handed him the note. 'Looks like I'm next on his hit list.'

Long shielded his eyes from the harsh sun, scanning the surrounds of the abandoned Miles property. 'Righto, let's take a look.'

'Déjà vu,' Jarrod said. The manhunt for Vincent Miles and the bloodshed that followed were still fresh in his mind.

'Yeah, here we are again. Good times,' said Long, sarcastic as usual. 'No point setting up surveillance. I'm guessing we've blown the element of surprise.'

'Yep,' said Jarrod. 'There's not a lot up there. But there might be some forensic evidence in the sleeping bag and jacket inside the tent. Also, we heard a motorbike. Could just be a local property owner, but worth tracking down.'

'Did you see it?' said Long.

'Nah,' said Brad. 'Just heard it from behind the hill. It took off.'

'Okay, we'll send up the SERT guys to secure the campsite,' said Long. 'We'll start coordinating a land search once we can get more troops out here and some trailbikes. These uniform crews can do mobile patrols in the surrounding back roads.'

They all turned their heads towards the sound of another vehicle.

A black armoured BearCat rumbled up and a team of six SERT officers filed out. Dressed in their black combat gear and helmets, armed with assault rifles, they formed up while Long briefed their commanding officer. Within minutes they had fanned out on foot and were moving stealthily up the hill towards the campsite.

A police van pulled up and Sergeant Glenn Marcus jumped out with a spring in his step. Police dog Jed barked excitedly from the cage. After a quick briefing with Jarrod and Long, Marcus had the erratic German Shephard hooked up to the lead and following the SERT officers up the hill.

'What now, Jarrod?' asked Brad.

'Well, Murray has things under control here. If Carmichael was nearby, he'll be on the move. Let's go for a patrol around the back roads, we might get lucky.'

They gave Long a heads up. The car's air conditioning was a welcome respite. As they pulled away, Jarrod looked in the rearview mirror at the escalating police activity. It wouldn't be long before local property owners were alerted to the renewed police presence and the media tipped off. Carmichael would be revelling in all the excitement, the thrill of the manhunt stroking his ego.

Jarrod wondered what part he would play in Carmichael's master plan.

TWENTY-THREE

EVERY police unit available patrolled the dusty back roads. As he drove, Jarrod scanned the palette of browns and greens for anything out of place, a moving shadow or figure within the vast paddocks and rolling hills. He pulled the car over and buzzed open his electric window. He killed the engine.

'What's wrong?' said Brad.

Jarrod sat perfectly still, both hands grasping the steering wheel. As the rust-coloured dust cloud dissipated, warm air flowed in through his window. He looked out, taking in every detail. Wire fences lined both sides of the road, ironbark posts crooked and weathered. On one side, a mob of kangaroos hid from the midday sun, lazing in the shade of a stand of trees. On the other, galahs drank from muddy puddles, the last dregs of a dam. Grey wings contrasted against rose-pink faces and chests. The chorus of squawks and bickering, combined with the light whistle of the breeze and chirping crickets, formed an orchestra of country sounds.

'I'm just listening. Thinking.' Jarrod said. 'Why did Kaleb Carmichael come back to Lockyer?'

Brad looked out his window and shrugged. 'Dunno. Unfinished business? A score to settle. Who knows?'

'What brought him to Lockyer in the first place?'

'To kill his stepfather.'

'Right. But what do we really know about him? I mean, he was off the grid for years. Then out of nowhere he emerges and wreaks havoc. He was a ticking time bomb. What sent him over the edge?'

Brad pursed his lips and shrugged.

Jarrod continued, thinking out loud. 'We know he had an abusive childhood. I get that. He suffered more than any child should suffer, but his transformation into a killer? I dunno, I just don't get it. Did he go mad or was he somehow programmed to kill?'

'Who knows, Jarrod? How many crazy arseholes have we dealt with over the years who went against the natural order of things? Sometimes we just have to accept it's a fucked-up world with some really fucked-up people.'

Jarrod started the ignition. 'I guess you're right. I'm done trying to make sense of it.'

He drove off, the galahs screeching and launching into flight as the wheels spun in the gravel. They cruised more back roads, occasionally passing other police cars with a wave.

Radio broadcasts gave sit-reps of the activities around the hilltop campsite. A foot search was underway, the terrain too rugged for vehicles. There would be a delay in getting police trailbike riders out. Glenn Marcus reported that Jed had picked up a scent leading from the campsite, but it had gone cold at a set of trailbike tracks. Jarrod's hunch was correct. Carmichael was on the move.

Jarrod circled past the police activity at the hill and found himself driving down an all-too familiar dirt road. A gap in the fence line marked the entrance to a long driveway. Jarrod pulled up and leaned forward with his forearms on the steering wheel. He sighed. 'Best we check it out.'

Brad nodded with reluctance. 'Guess so.'

Jarrod steered into the driveway and drove slowly, long grass scraping the underside of the car. The old Miles farmhouse came into view, a festered sore on the landscape. He pulled up at the entrance to the front yard where the gates lay consumed by weeds. They had fallen under their own weight, the hinges rusted and brittle. The house had succumbed to the elements, shrunken from the world. The log stilts upon which the weatherboard cottage stood now leaned as if the earth had shifted beneath it.

'I can't believe it's still standing,' said Brad. 'I thought the council was going to bulldoze this place.'

'I heard the Public Trustee was caught up in red tape trying to find any living descendants who might have a claim to it. There's still mystery around the disappearance of Vincent Miles' parents years ago. If no one comes forward to make a claim, then I guess they'll sort it out in court.'

'Yeah, well at least the council filled in the bunker.' Brad's lips curved into a wry smile. 'I had hoped local shitheads would have set the place ablaze by now. Imagine if a wildfire were to sweep through, eradicate the whole place. I reckon it would allow the town to heal.'

'No arguments from me.' Jarrod vacantly stared at the house. His thoughts drifted back to Kaleb Carmichael. 'What brought you here?' he said under his breath.

Brad gave Jarrod a long look. 'What's going through that head of yours?'

'What's the connection between Vincent Miles and Kaleb Carmichael? What are we missing?'

'Well, let's consider what we do know. They both had ties to this town. Vincent Miles grew up here as a kid. He went off the rails after his parents went missing and then came back here after serving time. Carmichael, on the other hand, only came here more recently after he tracked down his stepfather. As far as we know, he never spent time in prison, so he wouldn't have met Miles there. Maybe they crossed paths after Carmichael arrived in town.' A Cheshire grin spread across Brad's face. 'You know how shit usually attracts more shit, flies to a turd and all that.'

'Well let's assume they did know each other. What sort of influence would Miles have been on Carmichael? I mean, we saw how Miles manipulated Clare Kingston and Edward Ryan, he got in their heads like a cult leader. Can you imagine the likes of Carmichael, a young man with so much hatred for the world, coming under the influence of a lunatic like Vincent Miles? Something set Carmichael off. Overnight he became a murderous vigilante and we never found out why. We figured he just finally snapped. What if there's more to it?'

'Like what? You think Miles had something to do with Carmichael killing all those people?'

'I don't know what to think anymore.'

They sat in silence, staring at the old farmhouse. Tattered curtains hung limp inside glassless windows. Jagged glass in window frames tapered to points like shark teeth.

Jarrod tilted his head trying to make out a red graffiti tag spray painted over the front wall. *Freak*. Fair enough, he thought. Below was a crudely painted stick figure hanging from a noose.

Jarrod's chaotic thoughts worked overtime until they formed an idea. 'Think about that campsite up on that hill. Carmichael chose that spot as it gave him an ideal vantage point and escape routes. He must have thought it was safer than camping out here at the farmhouse where he could be cornered. But if he came back here for a reason then he must be looking for something. Something has drawn him back to this place. Why else would he risk getting caught when he could have disappeared to some remote corner of the country?' He paused to allow his thoughts to fall into a more logical pattern.

'Like those gun cases,' said Brad. 'He must have known where to find them.'

Jarrod followed the thought process. 'And we know Miles stashed caches of weapons all over this place. We searched but who knows what we might have missed, particularly if it was buried. Miles might have told him where to find the guns.'

Brad frowned. 'So, is it just about the guns? Is that why Carmichael has come back?'

'No, I think the guns are a means to an end. He needs them for something bigger. Something else is driving him.'

A flicker of movement caught Jarrod's attention, a fleeting shadow inside one of the windows.

He leaned forward and squinted through the dust-coated windscreen.

Brad followed his line of sight. 'What is it?'

'I don't know, I thought I saw…'

Boom! The windscreen exploded, showering them with glass.

Jarrod's brain stuttered, a high-pitched ringing in his ears. His eyes took in too much light, blinding him. Every part of him paused while his thoughts caught up. A muffled groan, like someone yelling underwater. He shook his head and blinked away the fog. A gurgling sound, now much clearer. He turned and looked at Brad, head slumped against his window, blood gushing from a gaping wound to his throat.

Jarrod ducked beneath the dashboard just as another gunshot rang out, a projectile whizzing past his right ear. His headrest burst into shredded foam. He looked up at Brad, a gurgling sound escaping his mouth as he choked on his own blood. Jarrod reached across and grabbed Brad's collar, pulling him downwards so that his body slumped against him. He yanked the door handle. Pushing the door open with his foot, he slid out of the car, his knees landing in gravel. Sharp stones tore at his skin. He heaved Brad's upper body so that he lay on his side across the centre console. Blood spurted from the wound and Jarrod pressed his hand on it to stem the flow. It was sticky and warm, and oozed between his fingers and up his arm. He applied more pressure. Brad's eyes were open, pleading with Jarrod as he gasped like a fish out of water. His face was pale.

'Hold on, mate. Stay with me.' Jarrod pulled out his folded handkerchief and pressed it like a pad, but Brad was bleeding out. Suffocating. It was hopeless.

Another sharp crack of a gun and a burst of sunlight pierced through a hole in Jarrod's door. He made himself small, pressing against the pillar. Another gunshot and a loud ping against the front of the car, a hiss from the radiator.

The choking and gasping stopped, followed by a shallow hiss of exhaled breath. Everything went quiet. Brad's body went still.

Jarrod shook his shoulders. 'Brad, no! Wake up! Come on mate, stay with me.' He took his hand away and Brad's head lolled to one side. In that horrible moment, Jarrod knew his best friend's life was over.

'Aarrgghh!' he yelled, slamming the heel of his palm against his own forehead. He wiped his bloody hand against his shirt and pulled his Glock from his holster. He needed to focus, find where the shots were coming from.

He moved into a crouching position and peeked through the gap between the pillar and the door frame. There was movement inside a window and a muzzle flash. A gunshot cracked, and his door window shattered.

He ducked, shaking glass fragments from his hair. *Fuck this*, he thought. He inhaled through his nose, and in one motion he rose to his feet, aimed towards the house window and fired a string of four shots. They boomed in his ears and echoed in the distance. He dropped behind the cover of the car. He waited and listened, his head throbbing. Nothing but silence.

He reached into the car and grabbed the radio handset. 'VKR, 501 urgent! Urgent! Shots fired. Officer down. Miles farmhouse. Need back up. Taking fire!' His voice sounded like someone else's.

The radio crackled to life with units responding. Nearby crews scrambled. Backup would be there soon. Jarrod was pinned but he just needed to hold out a bit longer.

A shrill voice yelled from inside the derelict farmhouse. 'This doesn't end here, O'Connor. I told you your day of retribution was coming. Everything's now in motion, you can't stop it.'

Jarrod recognised the voice. He couldn't pinpoint where Carmichael was. Thuds on the floorboards moved about the house.

'Cat got your tongue, Jarrod?' A deranged laugh echoed in one of the empty rooms.

Jarrod clutched his Glock, the handle slippery from the blood on his hands. 'I'm coming for you, arsehole,' he yelled from behind the car door.

'Good for you, Jarrod. That's the spirit. Glad you finally grew a set of balls. But that won't be happening today. My search isn't over. It won't end until I say it ends.'

Boots shuffled inside the house towards the back door. Jarrod peered over the car door towards the shady area beneath the house. Beyond the wooden stilts, he saw movement, boots striding down the back stairs. The imposing figure of Kaleb Carmichael appeared around the front corner post, rifle raised. Tufts of auburn hair fell from under a hood and dangled over his eyes.

Jarrod dropped and waddled in a crouched position towards the rear of the car. A shot rang out and the projectile clanged against the car door. He face-planted into the dirt and crawled around to the other side of the car. Senses sharpened with adrenaline, he peered up and saw Carmichael reloading a bolt-action rifle. It was a tiny window of opportunity, so Jarrod took his chance. He popped up into a shooting stance, aimed and fired. The first round hit the post, sending shards of splintered wood flying. Carmichael threw himself behind the post, the rifle falling from his clutches. It clattered on the ground and lay in the open, out of his reach. Jarrod fired again. The gun shook in his grip and sweat stung his eyes. He wiped his face with his shirt sleeve and waited. Carmichael retreated towards the back of the house. Jarrod fired twice more as Carmichael dashed between house posts.

From the road, sirens grew louder. Jarrod ran from the cover of the vehicle in pursuit of Carmichael. As he made it to the first corner post, he heard the kickstart of a motorcycle and an engine revving. Carmichael emerged straddling a trailbike, smoke spewing from the exhaust pipe. The back wheel spun and fishtailed as the tyre gained traction in the dirt. The engine growled as he roared away from the house towards a paddock dotted with trees. Jarrod raised his gun and fired until the slide locked to the rear, out of ammo. He ejected the mag and reloaded.

Carmichael zig-zagged and swerved, negotiating logs and rusted tractor carcasses as he fought to keep the motorcycle upright. Sirens screamed in Jarrod's ears. Car tyres crunched on gravel and doors slammed. Kaleb Carmichael accelerated away and disappeared into a thick veil of bushland. The whining of the motorcycle engine faded behind the rolling hills.

TWENTY-FOUR

HARRY McNelly was out repairing the fence separating his farm from the neighbouring property. Bloody wild pigs had torn right through the chain wire. They'd come from the paddocks beyond the fence line, overgrown eyesores they were. Harry peered over the fence. Ever since the farmhouse was abandoned, its ghostly whispers floated in the breeze and meandered across fields of spinifex and wiregrass and over the rise through swaying branches. Harry could hear them from his porch in the night's stillness. They gave him the chills. His wife, Alice, was now petrified to be left alone in the house. Every day he reassured her, tried to make her feel safe.

The eeriness had always been there, ever since the disappearance of Margie and Gerry Miles. Such a nice couple, always putting themselves out to help others. Harry didn't buy into their happy-clapper, born-again evangelism, but they were decent Christian people, nonetheless. As for their boy, Vincent, conniving little bastard he was, Harry often wondered how two kind-hearted people could spawn such a horrible child. He always knew the demented prick would eventually self-destruct. He wasn't surprised when he heard he'd blown his own head off. Good riddance. Things had settled down after all that sorry business when the police and media had swarmed, helicopters flying over, looky-loos everywhere. But the whispers in the trees lingered.

Harry thought back to when Vincent was a boy. The kid wasn't right in the head, a few roos loose in the top paddock. Harry always feared what he might be capable of. He often wondered if Vincent had something to do with the mysterious disappearance of that little boy, Tom Baker, all those years ago. Then there was the tragic death of

Vincent's cousin who suffocated in a grain silo. When Margie and Gerry went missing out of the blue, Harry feared the worst. He gave a statement to the police, but they didn't dig deep enough. Didn't ask the right questions. It was all too convenient to write off their disappearance as a missing persons case. Vincent had hoodwinked them all. According to the cops, the couple probably skipped town to start afresh, or maybe they owed money. Such bullshit. Harry didn't buy that for a second. They were honest people who loved working the land that had been in their family for generations. They had no reason to just up and leave.

As far as Harry was concerned, the whole thing smelled of foul play and Vincent was smack-bang in the middle of it. What stunk the most was that the Teflon coated arsehole remained living there, bold as brass and was never held to account for his parents' disappearance. Then he brought that poor young woman to live with him. And that innocent little baby. Hearing what happened broke Alice's heart. Such a tragic waste.

Harry was snapped back into the present when he heard the first gunshot. He stopped working on the fence and listened. The shot came from the direction of the Miles farmhouse over the ridge. At first, he thought maybe it was larrikins shooting rabbits with a .22 but the loud crack of the next few shots definitely came from a higher calibre weapon. Something was wrong. Seriously wrong. Harry waited and listened. Nothing but silence at first. Then all hell broke loose. More shots rang out, a gun fight. Harry's old chestnut mare, Nelly, pulled against the reigns tethered to the fence. She neighed crankily, stomping her hooves.

'Steady, old girl. Shhhhh, settle down now.' Harry stroked the white blaze running down the length of her nose. She settled but grew irritated as the *blat blat* of a revving engine grew louder. He recognised the high-pitched whine of a trailbike. Someone was riding his way fast. He couldn't see it at first through the thick bush forming a natural buffer between his land and the Miles property. A speeding motorcycle flashed in and out of view through the dense tree line.

Then Harry heard the police sirens, and his heart sank. *For Christ's sake, what now?* Nelly reared up onto her hind legs and pulled the reins free from the fence. She whinnied and galloped off, bucking and kicking out her back hooves. She was spooked out of her mind. Harry knew there would be no catching her. He watched and listened as the motorcycle came in and out of view, circling past him. Changing direction, it headed down the fence line towards the gate into Harry's property.

Harry hobbled his beefy frame. His knees had given out years ago from a lifetime of climbing up and down off tractors. He gasped. 'Alice!' She was alone in the house. It would be a slow walk in his decrepit state. Sharp pain shot through his knees and thighs with each step as he trudged down the slope towards the house. His boots crunched on dry grass and twigs as he stomped his way through the scrub. The toe of his boot caught the edge of a hidden rock and his ankle rolled at an awkward angle. He heard the *crack*. The immense pain dropped him like a sack of spuds. He tumbled down the slope, crashing hard against a charred tree stump. He cried out in agony and clutched his ankle. His thoughts returned to Alice. He needed to get to her. She could be in danger.

The revving of the motorcycle engine faded to an idle. Harry heard the clank of a chain and the familiar creak of the gate hinges. The motorcycle revved again and rocketed towards the house. The engine died and all went quiet. Harry rolled onto his haunches, sharp stones and sticks cutting into his hands and knees. He had to do everything in his power to get to his wife. His best friend; his soulmate. The thought of some arsehole getting to her made Harry seethe. He knew she wouldn't cope. She was frail. She would be terrified.

He struggled to his feet, yelping as a sharp pain tore through his ankle. He breathed through it, determined to get to Alice. A blood-curdling sound stopped him dead in his tracks. Alice's screams echoed through the valley. Harry hobbled faster, negotiating the uneven terrain with each agonising step. Her screams came again. Harry felt lightheaded, and he feared he would collapse. He lost his footing and crashed to the ground, faceplanting in the dirt. Hissing. He froze. A pair of soulless eyes staring, mouth gaping, fangs prominent. A forked tongue flickered. The snake reared its head, neck flattened, leathery underbelly golden. Its striped body coiled like a spring. A tiger snake. In his state of panic and hyperventilation, one bite could mean death.

He panted into the dirt, puffs of dust irritating his eyes. Another scream, a panicked shrill that made the hair stand up on the back of his neck. *Fuck the snake.* With a grimace of determination, he rolled away from the snake. The gravity of the slope yanked him. He tumbled out of control, flailing his hands and legs to gain purchase on anything that would slow his descent. He clawed at the earth, grabbing handfuls of dead leaves and dirt. The world spun out of control until he finally came to rest at the bottom of the hill, his landing softened by a patch of cool grass. He couldn't move, his body ached, and he didn't know up from down. His head spun and he was nauseous. He suspected he had broken a few ribs. As he fought to control his senses, he lay there and listened. All he could hear was the familiar melancholy of the bush, the chirping of crickets and the warbling of a magpie.

A dry stick snapped, and heavy footsteps approached. Someone or something was creeping towards him. He was helpless, a sitting duck. He lifted his head and blinked to clear the fog from his eyes. Through blurred vision, the outline of a shape materialised. A shadow fell over his prone body, and he made out the features of muscular legs and chest. Nelly whinnied and shook her head, her hairy lips pressing against his cheek. The old horse had come back for him. She sniffed his face and lay down beside him.

'How's my girl?' he said, his voice raspy.

Nelly nudged Harry's shoulder with her nose. He gripped the bridle with one hand and grabbed her mane with the other. He made a clicking noise with his tongue. 'Up, girl. Up.' Nelly rolled into a kneeling position and Harry slung his bad leg over the saddle. As she rose to stand, Harry pushed himself off the ground with his good foot and managed to stay on. Her front legs strained as she lifted his heavy frame. He slid his boots into the stirrups for balance and took hold of the reins. He made another clicking noise and prodded Nelly with his heels. 'Come on girl, take me home. Go home, Nelly.'

The old horse turned for home. A wave of dizziness threatened to knock Harry right out of the saddle. He hugged Nelly's neck for dear life. His reliable old steed crossed the gully and headed for the clearing that opened to a grassy pasture. Nelly quickened her pace as she came upon the familiar gravel road separating the house and stables. Harry spotted it straight away. The garage door was open, and their car was missing. A battered old dirt bike leaned against the garage wall, a Suzuki JR80 with a torn seat, yellow mud guards and black engine casing. He'd seen it before. It had been in the Miles family for years. He studied the front of the house for any movement. The hinges of the flyscreen door creaked with the breeze.

Nelly instinctively veered towards her safe refuge in the stables. Harry let go of her neck and steered her with the reins. He clicked his tongue and Nelly walked through an open gate into the house yard, her shoes clip-clopping on the concrete pathway to the veranda stairs. A wind chime tinkled.

'Alice!' Harry called. 'Alice? Are you okay? It's me. You can come out now, it's safe.' He hoped the lunatic on the motorbike had just stolen the car and left Alice alone. He prayed she was inside hiding.

'Alice!' he called, more urgent this time. As each second went by without a response, Harry's fear rose. He rode Nelly up to the base of the staircase and prepared for the painful dismount. As he swung his injured foot over the saddle, a pain cut through his ribcage as though pierced with a dagger. He eased himself out of the saddle, sucking in breaths with each stabbing pain. Harry tried to put weight on his injured foot in the stirrup, but his leg buckled with pain. He let himself fall, landing heavily on the grass beside the concrete path. Small mercies. Nelly trotted off and disappeared into the stables.

Harry groaned as he pulled himself up using the staircase handrail for support. One agonising step at a time, he limped up the staircase.

'Alice! Where are you?' Harry's anxiety peaked. Only the wind chime broke the silence.

He hobbled to the front door. As he stepped inside, he called out to Alice again. Country music played from the radio in the kitchen. When he last saw her, Alice had been making an apple pie. He had kissed her on the cheek and wiped flour from her nose. For the first time in ages, she had smiled up at him, a sparkle in her eye. 'Don't be long,' she had said, kneading dough and humming along with Dolly Parton.

Harry now entered the kitchen. It was in disarray. A stainless-steel bowl had been sent flying and flour was all over the floor. Utensils and baking trays were strewn on the bench and a broken egg was splattered on the floor. The phone had been pulled from the wall and lay in pieces. The car keys were missing from the fruit bowl. Harry and Alice didn't have mobile phones, they never saw the need. What would he do? How would he call for help?

He couldn't bear to think how terrified she must have been. Where was she? What had that mongrel done to her? He had failed to protect her. Harry wasn't a spiritual man, but he prayed she would come home to him. He begged God for forgiveness. He hadn't been there when she needed him.

He leaned against the wall and slid to the floor, lying in a mess of flour, his eyes welling with tears. Lowering his face into his hands, he sobbed.

'Where are you, Alice?'

TWENTY-FIVE

ALICE drove in silence, her hands gripping the steering wheel so tight her knuckles were white. She mustered the courage to glance into the mirror. Her eyes met his. The ghastly looking man in the back seat pointed a handgun at her head. He glared at her, his eyes lifeless and cold, his face disfigured. He had spoken to her with such disrespect, spitting orders like she was a dog, threatening to blow her brains out. He had barged into her home and dragged her out to the car. He now hunkered low and out of sight.

'Keep driving towards town until I tell you to turn,' he snarled. 'Try anything cute and the last thing you ever see will be your brains splattering on the windscreen.'

Alice's eyes snapped to the front. Her thoughts shifted to Harry. He would be worried sick. She whimpered and gasped, unable to get enough air. She felt lightheaded, her chest tight.

From behind, the man grabbed a fistful of her hair and yanked her head back. She yelped. 'Shut up and just drive. Stupid, old bitch.'

He let her go. She released one hand from the wheel and wiped her eyes. Flashing blue and red lights up ahead caught her attention. A flurry of people and cars came into view as the Miles property drew nearer. There were police cars everywhere. She slowed behind a line of cars. Up ahead, police were waving at drivers to pull over. A surge of hope evaporated when Alice remembered the gun aimed at the back of her head. She glanced into the mirror.

The horrible man in the back seat slid down to the floor and pulled a picnic blanket over himself. 'Don't even think about doing anything stupid.'

Alice shot her eyes straight ahead.

'When you get to the front of the line you act all nice like, and don't draw any attention. If they get suspicious, you floor it and you drive and don't stop. You hear me?'

Alice nodded. Cars were being waved through one at a time. The white car ahead of her was a hotted-up thing with blue racing stripes running along the roof and down the middle of the boot. Its double mufflers rattled and spluttered. Alice could see the police officer talking to the driver. From his expression in the side mirror reflection, the young man didn't look happy. He pointed his finger at the police.

'Remember what I told you,' the man in the back whispered.

Alice nodded and kept her eyes straight ahead. She took a breath and wound down her window. She could hear the driver of the hotrod yelling obscenities at the police officer who was now also raising his voice. From what Alice could hear, the driver was arguing about being pulled over. The police officer opened the car door and ordered the driver out. The man jumped out, waving his arms about. He poked the officer in the chest. A scuffle broke out and the police officer wrestled the man to the ground. Another officer, who had been stopping cars from the other direction, ran over to help.

Alice put her hand over her mouth. 'Oh, my.'

'What is it?' the man with the gun said. 'What's happening?'

Alice watched on as the arrested man was hauled to his feet and bent over the bonnet of his car and handcuffed.

'The police are arresting a man.'

'Just stay calm and wait.'

Alice waited while the police frog-marched the man to a police car and tossed him into the back seat, still yelling. Another officer hopped into the car with the racing stripes and drove it off to the side of the road. The officer climbed out and headed for Alice's car.

Alice's heart thumped inside her chest.

'Sorry about that ma'am,' the officer said, panting to catch his breath. He leaned down to eye level with Alice. 'Bloody clown reckoned we were wasting his time. Got himself locked up for his troubles. Idiot.'

Alice forced a smile, biting her trembling lip. 'What's all this about, officer?'

'Oh, the roadblock? There's been a serious shooting incident. Have you seen a man on a motorcycle wearing no helmet?'

Alice held the officer's gaze, unblinking. She willed him to read her mind, to understand the danger just arm's length away, to pull her to safety and arrest the man in the back seat. She remembered the gun and the threats and shook her head. 'No, I haven't. What has this man done?'

'Sorry, I can't go into specifics. Do you live locally?'

'Yes, my property is just down the road.'

'Where are you heading?'

'Just into town for some groceries.'

'Do you have friends or family in town you could stay with? It might not be safe out here until we catch this guy.'

Alice thought about Harry out there somewhere, alone. 'Um, not really. My husband is home. He's just out fixing fences.'

The officer stood upright and glanced around her car, squinting against the sun's reflection in the back window. He leaned closer to it, shielding his eyes from the glare. A loud thumping and a man's yelling caught his attention. From inside the rear compartment of the police car, the hotrod driver kicked at the window.

'Hell!' said the officer under his breath. 'Drive through ma'am. Take care and please call triple zero if you see anyone acting suspicious. Don't approach anyone you don't know, keep your doors locked and please report any sightings of a motorcycle or a man on foot.'

'Oh, okay. I will officer,' said Alice, her voice feeble.

The officer turned towards the ruckus.

Alice wiped her sweaty palms down her dress and put the car into gear. She drove slowly past the police cars and line up of traffic on the other side.

As she accelerated away, her passenger kicked off the blanket. 'Well done. You didn't give me a reason to kill you, yet.'

The man waited until they were further down the road before climbing up into the seat, his head low, eyes darting.

Alice looked in the mirror. The man gave her a humourless smile and a wink.

'Take me to the cemetery,' he said.

'Why?'

Alice's eyes returned to the road. He didn't answer right away. Her eyes were drawn to the mirror. She studied his face. The skin on one side sagged as though melting from his face. The eyelid drooped over a bloodshot eyeball, the pupil as black as the depths of hell. Tufts of auburn hair fell from the hood covering his head. In that moment she saw him for what he was, a desperate young man.

'Why?' he said, curious.

'Yes, why?' Alice almost choked with fear as she muttered those words. Her eyes drifted back to the road. She could no longer bear the sight of that horrid face. She focused on the task of driving, controlling the steering wheel, her arms jelly. It felt as though an unseen force was controlling her movements. She was just a spectator, looking down from outside her body. She concentrated on keeping the car on the road as she drove towards town.

'What's your name?' the man asked with an odd tenderness in his voice.

'Alice.'

'My name is Kaleb, Alice. I'm a disciple of the angel of death.'

Her eyes returned to the mirror. 'What?'

'You heard me.'

'What have you done?' Alice's voice quivered. 'Why are the police looking for you?'

'I kill people, Alice.' He paused, waiting for the impact of his words to sink in.

Alice's body went rigid as she fought the urge to cry out for help.

She calmed herself and focused on her breathing. They drove in silence.

'Do you think that makes you special, hurting people?' Alice finally said.

He leaned forward so that his face was beside hers. She could feel the warmth of his breath on her cheek.

'Oh, I *am* special, Alice. *Real* special. But I only kill when I need to. Revenge or…' He ran the muzzle of the gun through her curls. Her scalp tingled and her body shuddered. '… or to tie off loose ends.'

'Am I a loose end?'

'I haven't decided yet, Alice. Depends on whether you are a good girl.'

'What did you mean before, when you said you are a disciple of the angel of death?'

'What I'm doing is all part of a bigger plan. There's a greater power at play, something bigger than you or me. I've been promised salvation.'

'Who have you killed?' Alice said.

She glanced into the mirror. His face contorted into a strange smile. He held her gaze. She tore her eyes away and returned her focus to the road ahead.

'There's no beating around the bush with you, is there, Alice? I like that. No bullshit. Do you really want to know who I've killed, Alice?'

She didn't answer, deciding she didn't want to know and regretted asking the question. She feared she was next.

He leaned back into his seat, making himself comfortable. 'Well, for starters, I killed the man responsible for these scars. I burned him alive,' he chuckled. 'That one was the most satisfying. Have you ever smelt burning human flesh, Alice?'

She didn't answer.

'I'm not sure what's worse, the smell of your own flesh melting off your face or the smell of another person in flames. The fat under his skin sizzled like pork crackling. He screamed like a wild boar. The same noise those filthy animals make when you flip 'em and stab them in the heart, when they know they're about to die. That was the best moment of my life, if you really want to know, Alice.'

He seemed to enjoy recounting his stories. 'I've killed others who deserved it, people who wronged me. The judge who set that man free, the solicitor who defended him in court, I even killed my own father. Did you know that, Alice?'

She shook her head. As her thoughts cleared, things made sense. She recalled hearing about a man the police were hunting after he escaped custody. There were radio news broadcasts about the manhunt for a killer. She had avoided watching the television reports or reading newspapers, not wanting to know about the horrible goings on in the world. She just wanted to be left in peace on the farm.

Alice lifted a hand to her mouth and gasped. 'Oh God, you're him! Those poor girls, and that old lady.'

He leaned forward and placed his mouth close to her ear. 'Yes Alice, I killed those two little sluts. They had it coming, they got what they deserved. The old lady, well, that was just unfortunate. I liked her.'

Alice's eyes welled and she fought back tears. She felt cold and hollow inside, her lips trembling. 'You're a monster.'

He leaned back and chuckled. 'A monster? I've been called that before. Maybe it's true. You see, Alice, they turned me into a monster. I suffered because of them and now the world will pay.'

Alice wiped her tears with the back of her hand. 'What do you want from me? Why won't you just let me go? Take the car. Leave me on the side of the road. I won't say anything to the police. I promise.'

'I can't Alice, it's not that simple. You're now part of this, you're part of my story. You have to share my journey now. I'm so close to finding the book of knowledge. Soon I will discover the key to my salvation. His writings contain all the answers.'

'Whose writings?'

'The Angel of Death, of course,' he said, as though the answer was obvious.

She heard him fidgeting. He leaned forward and held a knife out in front of her, its handle black in his grip, the blade sharp and menacing. He held the edge of the blade against her throat and stroked her hair with his free hand.

'Listen to me carefully, Alice,' he whispered.

She held her breath, her body rigid under his touch.

'Drive me to the cemetery and you'll have all the answers you need.'

'Will you let me go?' she pleaded.

'I will set you free, I promise.'

She slowly nodded, hanging onto hope that if she just did what he asked he might let her live.

They were passed by more police cars hurtling in the opposite direction with their lights and sirens wailing. He took the knife away and sunk back into the seat. He peered out through his window and cackled. 'Fucking pigs, they have no idea.'

Alice knew where the Remembrance Gardens Cemetery was. Her own parents were buried there. It sprawled over rolling hills, shaded by ancient maples and bunya pines. Towering cypress hedgerows bordered the cemetery as a natural screen, separating the world of the living from the dead. The man, who called himself Kaleb, ordered her to take the backroads. Soon the cemetery entrance came into view. There was a woman selling flowers. Kaleb seemed to know where he was going and instructed Alice to drive past it and around to the other side. He directed her up a service track until she lost sight of the main road in the mirror. He told her to park and turn off the engine. She cranked the handbrake lever, and they sat in silence for what seemed like an eternity.

He stroked the side of her face with his fingertips and spoke tenderly. 'You remind me of my mother, Alice. She was younger than you, but you have her spirit.'

Alice sat frozen, not daring to move a muscle.

'My mother suffered through life until she was set free through death. I was with her when she died. It was so peaceful in the end. She looked relieved when it was finally over. I knew she'd gone to a better place. Once my destiny is fulfilled, I'll join my mother in paradise.'

He leaned between the front seats and gently kissed Alice on her left cheek. 'I'll set you free too, Alice.'

TWENTY-SIX

JARROD sat zombie-like in the driver's seat of the shot-up car. He had repositioned Brad's lifeless body so that he was sitting upright, more dignified. His partner's hollow eyes gazed out through partially closed eyelids towards the frenzied police activity outside. A dog unit had set off on foot in the direction Carmichael was last seen heading. Two police trailbikes buzzed past, their revving engines fading to a dull hum as they cut across the paddock and disappeared over a distant hill. Murray Long barked orders as backup units arrived. The SERT team had cleared the abandoned farmhouse.

Tyres crunched on gravel as a patrol car took off again, fishtailing in the driveway towards the road. Police sirens wailed. The stony face of Long peered through Jarrod's open door. He placed a firm hand on Jarrod's shoulder. 'You're okay now, mate. We'll get that bastard.'

Jarrod's eyes fell to his shaking hands, sticky with blood. He looked up and met Long's gaze. He couldn't utter a single word, his body numb. He exhaled and looked back at Brad, the gaping wound, the congealed blood. The magnitude of his partner's death bore down on him, a weight crushing his chest.

Long squeezed Jarrod's shoulder and sighed. 'I'm so sorry. Harding was a good copper.'

Jarrod nodded and swallowed hard against a lump wedged in his throat.

Long looked over towards the farmhouse and scanned the surrounding bushland. 'We're gonna get this arsehole.' He nodded, convincing himself. He turned and let Jarrod be.

Time slid by in fast forward. Police scurried about like ants. Ross Benfield huddled under a portable marquee, briefing high-ranking officers Jarrod didn't recognise. They shared the same solemn expression. Jarrod was ushered to the back of an ambulance to be checked over while scientific officers worked the scene, taking measurements and snapping photographs from every angle. His attention was drawn to Long shouting, an excited edge to his voice. Jarrod climbed out of the ambulance to see what was going on.

Long leaned against the open door of an unmarked CIB car with one leg inside the footwell. The coiled cord of a radio handset stretched as he yelled into it. He tossed it back into the car, not bothering to secure it to its dash mounting.

'Hey boss!' he yelled.

Benfield looked over.

'One of the crew was just waved down by an old guy on a horse down the road. Carmichael dumped the trailbike and took the man's wife hostage. They're in a black Honda SUV. He's on the move.'

Benfield peeled away from the brass. 'Put out a BOLO.'

'On it!' shouted Long.

Benfield rejoined the other bosses where animated conversations followed. They seemed to agree on a plan. More police cars were soon on the move, throwing up a fresh cloud of dust as they thundered out onto the road, accelerating away in both directions.

Jarrod watched on in a daze, a spectator. He was startled by a vibration in his trouser pocket. He slid out his phone and checked the screen for the caller ID. "Caller Unknown". He was tempted to ignore it but as it vibrated insistently, something told him he should answer it. He swiped and lifted the phone to his ear. 'O'Connor here,' he said, his words gravelly.

'Come and get me, *Jarrod*.' Carmichael's voice, playful.

Jarrod seethed. 'Then show yourself, you gutless coward.'

Carmichael laughed without speaking.

'Tell me where you are, arsehole. I'll be there in a heartbeat. Let's finish this!'

'What's the rush, Jarrod? You seem to be in a hurry to die.'

'You'll pay for what you've done.'

'Maybe, maybe not. Destiny will decide.'

'Tell me where you are and we'll see how things play out.' Jarrod fought to stay in control. He knew he was being baited.

'Vincent Miles,' whispered Carmichael.

Jarrod's stomach lurched at the sound of that name. 'What?'

'You heard me. Vincent Miles. Your old friend.'

'What's he got to do with this? Tell me! No more riddles.'

'He's got *everything* to do with this!' Carmichael fired back. He sniggered, taunting. 'Cat got your tongue?'

'I don't understand?'

'Of course, you don't. But you will.'

'How?'

'It's time you and I fulfill our destiny together. Today is your day of retribution.'

'My retribution?'

'You had your chance for salvation, to take your revenge against the man who killed your wife. But no, you were weak. You didn't have the stomach for it. You're pathetic. I waited but you failed the test. I'm your only chance to save your soul.'

'There'll be no saving my soul,' said Jarrod. 'Not after what I do to you.'

Carmichael chuckled. 'At last. There it is, finally. The darkness. Use it! Let it fuel your rage. Feel its power.'

'What do you want from me?' Jarrod kept his voice low. He checked himself and looked around. In the chaos no one seemed to notice him, except for Murray Long. He stared at Jarrod, suspicious. Jarrod moved behind the ambulance out of earshot. He pressed the phone to his ear.

'I could have killed you whenever I wanted,' Carmichael went on. 'But it was only right to give you a chance to find your salvation before I came for you. You had earned that chance, so I watched and waited. But it wasn't to be, so you've forced my hand. I have to finish what

Vincent started.'

'Yeah? And what's that exactly?'

'I was gutted when I heard he died, but I realised it was my time to take his place. It's what he would have wanted.'

'How did you know Vincent Miles?'

'He took me in and became my friend and mentor. He saved me in more ways than you can imagine. He still gives me strength. Why do you think you couldn't kill me? Why was I able to escape? Even now he's guiding me. His spirit has steered me down the path of redemption.'

'What redemption?' said Jarrod, cynical.

'Revenge for Vincent's death,' said Carmichael. 'You tricked him. He died believing the Kingston children were dead. But they weren't, were they? His soul is restless. He won't be at peace with his beloved Clare until I avenge his death by killing you. Then I will finish his mission and kill the Kingston children once and for all. I'll send their souls to their mother. She's still waiting for them.'

'You're as deluded as them.'

'That's where you're wrong. You'll see.'

'You should have killed me when you had the chance!'

Carmichael chuckled. 'You're a hard one to kill, I'll give you that. You're like a cockroach or a cane toad. A pest, but resilient. Shame about your partner, though. I got him easy enough.'

'Fuck you. You'll pay, I promise.'

'It's your fault I had to blow a hole in him. All you had to do was stay away, leave me alone to find what I was looking for. But no, you had to stick your nose in.'

'What were you looking for?'

'All in good time, Jarrod. If there's one thing I've learned, it's that you have to be patient. It is a virtue, after all.' He giggled.

'Let's get this over with.'

'Are you willing to risk it all? Risk the lives of Matty and Katie?'

The mention of Jarrod's kids jarred him. 'Leave them out of this!'

Jarrod spat through gritted teeth. 'This is between you and me.'

'Hit a soft spot, did I?'

'No more games,' said Jarrod. 'Where are you? I'll come.'

'Remember the place where Vincent's blood stained the ground? I'm sure you do. Meet me there in thirty minutes. Come alone, you know the drill. If I see any sign of your friends then I'll disappear, but when I return it will be to slit the throat of your little brats. I'll make you watch as I slice them up. When I've killed you, I'll come for the Kingston children.'

Jarrod ignored the taunts. 'Where's the woman you took hostage?'

'I set her free. Don't be late.' The line went dead.

Jarrod swallowed the panic rising from his gut. He had to hold his nerve.

Long appeared. 'What's going on, O'Connor? That was him, wasn't it?'

Jarrod's eyes met his gaze. 'I need your car keys.'

TWENTY-SEVEN

THE setting sun was poised to breach the horizon. A smearing of clouds blended with a reddening sky, casting an orange hue over the cemetery. Steel gates hung open from sandstone pillars. Jarrod pulled the car over beside a flower stand. He recognised the wily old woman. She was packing up, loading buckets of fresh flowers into her van.

He lowered the window. 'Excuse me, ma'am.'

She looked up, curious eyes locking onto his. Wiping her hands on her apron she shuffled over, wary. She studied him, frowning at his ballistic vest and the blood stains on his shirtsleeve.

He held up his badge. 'Police.'

She moved closer. 'Yes? What's wrong?'

Despite his rising anxiety, Jarrod kept his voice even, routine-like. 'I'm looking for someone. Has anyone come through here recently?'

She considered the question and stared at him. Green eyes penetrated from behind wrinkled eyelids, like emerald stones in desert sand. 'You've been here before.' Not a question.

'Yes. I bought flowers from you.'

'Did you find the answers you were looking for?'

Jarrod held her gaze. 'No, not yet.'

She smiled. 'You will, love.'

He didn't have time for riddles. 'Please, it's important. Has anyone come through here?'

She side-glanced at the gates and shook her head. 'Not this way.' The corners of her eyes crinkled as a sad smile formed. 'It's been quiet today. It seems the living don't have time for the dead these days. Their lives are all so busy.'

'Are there any groundsmen about?'

She squinted at the sun as though considering the time. 'Nope. They'd have knocked off by now. Who are you looking for?'

'A young man. Scarred face. Possibly with an older woman.'

'There was this one car. Black. Drove past, slowed but kept going down the road.' She pointed a gnarled finger. 'Headed down towards the bottom corner of the cemetery, then disappeared.'

'Who was in the car?' Jarrod urged.

'A woman was driving. I didn't see her face.' She gave it more thought, tapping her chin with her index finger. 'Odd.'

'What was odd?' said Jarrod, unable to quell his impatience.

'Someone was sitting low in the back seat, a hood over their head. I didn't get a good look.'

'How long ago?'

'Maybe an hour.'

'Thank you. Listen, you better leave, it's not safe. A dangerous man is on the run.'

Strangely, Jarrod thought, her expression didn't falter. She leaned closer to his window and reached for his forearm resting on the sill. She took hold of his wrist, her touch warm and gentle. Her gaze hardened. 'Be strong, dear. Be brave. Walk into the fire.' She patted his armed tenderly and a smile broke her grim façade. 'Have no fear.'

She turned and headed back to her van.

Jarrod shrugged off the strange woman's words. He drove through the gates, his heart racing. He slowed at the section of lawn graves where Jayne was buried. The hill loomed in the background, the lone tree sprouting from its crest. He remembered the day of Jayne's funeral and the hooded figure standing in the tree's shade, watching him. Jarrod now knew Carmichael had been taunting him back then, his plans already set in motion, spying from the shadows.

He drove deeper into the cemetery. Elongated shadows crept across a sprawling checkerboard of statues and headstones. Carmichael's instructions over the phone played over in Jarrod's mind. *Remember the place where Vincent's blood stained the ground?* He did know it, all too well. What game was Carmichael playing now? Was he really luring Jarrod into a confrontation, a battle to the death where fate decided the victor? Was this Carmichael's crescendo, his grand finale? No, it couldn't be. He'd said it himself. He was determined to finish what Miles had started, to take his place. Either way, Jarrod couldn't care less. The delusional ramblings meant nothing to him. The white-hot rage of Brad's murder drove him. Revenge was all that mattered.

Jarrod pulled over and got out. He checked his Glock and ammo and proceeded on foot. He knew he was walking straight into a trap, but Carmichael wasn't the only one working to a plan. Jarrod wouldn't make the same mistake again. He was counting on Carmichael emerging from the shadows, buoyed by bravado. The sadist wanted an audience, a face-to-face confrontation to test Jarrod's resolve and to spruik his prophetic garbage. Carmichael was desperate for validation. Jarrod was determined to not give it to him but for now he had to play his game. He followed a row of graves, sliding in and out behind statues and headstones for cover, just in case.

He drew closer, knowing exactly where he was. He spotted the white marble cross. The grave of baby Jazmin Miles was just a few rows over. He stopped and listened. Nothing but an eerie silence. Even the cicadas and crickets held their breath. Up ahead, two angel statues rose high, gazing to the heavens, arms outstretched. He sensed Carmichael's presence, watching him. Jarrod swivelled, scanning his surrounds. No movement. He pressed on until he came to it, a tiny grave and headstone. He crouched and swept his hand across the engraving, brushing away a coating of dust. Rust coloured stains clung to the grooves of the letters. Dried blood. Vincent Miles' blood. Jarrod read the inscription. *'Baby Jazmin Miles. In god's loving care.'*

He sensed movement behind him, the shuffle of boots on gravel moving closer. He slowly rose to his feet, releasing the holster hammer strap with his thumb. He gripped the Glock's handle, ready to draw. He turned.

Out in the open, two rows away, stood Kaleb Carmichael.

TWENTY-EIGHT

A hunting knife was sheathed on Carmichael's belt. He held a Beretta pistol down by his side. He no longer hid beneath the hood. His auburn hair had grown scraggly, crudely tied back into a ponytail. His eyes were vacant and cruel, scars menacing. Jarrod noticed the blood on Carmichael's hands and his heart wrenched. *Whose blood?* He remembered the woman taken hostage. Was she the latest victim of Carmichael's cold indifference? Reacting to Jarrod's look of horror, Carmichael smirked and wiped his free hand across his chest, leaving bloody finger smears across the front of his grotty pullover. He stood rigid and resolute. Their eyes locked, neither willing to blink, to concede weakness. He tilted his head and studied Jarrod.

Jarrod waited for Carmichael to speak first.

'I wasn't sure if you'd come, *friend.*'

'Why do you say that?' said Jarrod.

'Because you're a coward. You didn't have the guts to take revenge against the piece of shit that killed your wife. It was your chance for salvation. I was tempted to go after him myself, but he wasn't my kill. He was yours!'

'Why do you care?' Jarrod clenched his teeth, a shooting pain stabbing his jaw.

Carmichael clawed at his scars, scratching. 'I wanted you to know what it feels like to purge, to give in to your rage. Revenge is primal, powerful. It cleanses your soul. You and I are connected. Don't you feel it? It was my gift to you, this chance for redemption, before I killed you.'

'Sorry to disappoint.'

Carmichael smiled. 'You don't mean that. Not that it matters now.'

'So, how does this play out?'

'I've seen it in my dreams, visions. You'll die soon, right here. Vincent will rest in peace, and I'll keep searching until I find what I'm looking for. I'll finish what Vincent started.'

'What are you searching for?'

'That's not your concern.'

'So why here? Why now?'

'I'm tired of running. You brought the fight to me, so I figure today is as good a day as any to settle the score.'

Jarrod caressed the handle of his gun. 'What makes you so sure you'll be the one walking out of here alive?'

'I trust in fate. I always have.'

'Fate,' Jarrod scoffed. 'We make our own fate.'

A sinister smile emerged. 'True. I'm a testament to that. I'm still here, aren't I?'

'I'll tell you something, *friend*. I've also had a vision.'

'Oh really.' Carmichael laughed. 'Do tell.'

'You might think you're on some holy pilgrimage like that lunatic Vincent Miles. You think your atrocities are somehow justified, that you're serving some noble cause. But that's all bullshit. You're just another sick fuck who needs to be put down like a rabid dog. I'll tell you what *my* vision is. You're gonna rot in hell, you disfigured freak!'

Rage boiled in Carmichael's eyes. His face twitched as he raised the pistol. 'Now you die.'

The gunshot rang out, deafening. Birds screeched and fluttered from their treetop perches. Carmichael spun as though he'd been clipped by an invisible passing vehicle. Jarrod dived to his right, crouching behind a headstone with his gun drawn. Two more shots, *boom boom*! One leg was taken out from under Carmichael's weight, and he dropped to one knee. Blood spurted from a hole in his cargo trousers below his thigh. He screamed, clutching his shoulder, blood seeping between his fingers. He raised the gun and fired wildly in all directions, his face contorting into a grimace.

Murray Long darted out from the shadows, firing again as he moved for cover behind a headstone. His shots zipped over Carmichael's head.

Carmichael aimed and fired two shots at Jarrod, chunks of headstone exploding above his head as he ducked. Sensing movement, Carmichael rolled onto his back and fired two shots towards Long who was pinned behind a headstone.

The words of the old flower lady echoed in Jarrod's mind. *'Be strong, dear. Be brave. Walk into the fire. Have no fear.'*

Jarrod rose and moved forward, gun raised. Carmichael rolled and fired at Jarrod. Shock waves reverberated against Jarrod's vest chest plate with the force of a sledgehammer. He stumbled backwards, reeling from the impact. He gasped, the air punched from his lungs. He pushed through the pain, driving one foot in front of the other. Just ahead, Carmichael writhed on the ground, squealing like a wounded, wild pig. In one last desperate attempt, Carmichael raised his gun, grip shaky. As he fired, Jarrod swerved and dived. The shot whizzed past his ear. He face-planted and the Glock fell from his grip, clattering in the dirt out of reach.

Jarrod forced himself to his feet, sucking in air. He fought the crippling pain in his ribs and ran straight at Carmichael, hurling himself forward, guided by tunnel vision. Their eyes met, and in that split second, Jarrod saw it – fear.

He thrust his boot at Carmichael's head, his laces connecting the man's face with a sickening crunch of broken cartilage. His upper body flung backwards like a ragdoll. Jarrod followed up with a second kick to his sternum. He stomped on Carmichael's hand until the pistol fell free and he kicked it away. Jarrod's knees buckled, his lungs starved of air. Carmichael still had fight left in him and kicked out, his boot striking Jarrod in the stomach. Jarrod fell on his side, wheezing. A glint of steel caught his eye and he rolled away from Carmichael who clawed at the dirt with one hand, knife menacing in the other. Jarrod drove the heels of his shoes into the dirt, pushing himself away as Carmichael inched closer.

Feet stomped, coming closer. 'Drop it, arsehole!' yelled Long, standing over Carmichael with his gun pointed at him.

Carmichael froze and dropped the knife. He slumped face down in the dirt. Long kicked the knife away. Jarrod gripped the top edge of a headstone and heaved himself up, gasping. He retrieved his gun and stood alongside Long. Applying pressure on the trigger, he aimed at Carmichael's head, ready to execute him where he lay.

Sirens grew louder. Tyres crunched and skidded. Doors slammed. Urgent voices yelled.

'Do it,' Long whispered. 'Before they get here. Put this mutt down. Do it for Brad.'

Jarrod aimed, feeling the subtle click of the first trigger pressure point.

'Wait!' Carmichael cried, spitting blood out of his mouth. He rolled onto his back, palms out. 'Don't do it.'

Jarrod stood firm, his aim steady and true.

Carmichael pleaded. 'There's a book of secrets. Vincent's secrets.' His words were laboured. 'It's… it's what I'm… searching for. Kill me… and the secrets will die with me.'

'What secrets?' said Jarrod.

'It's all in his book. Who he killed. Where they're buried. He hid it, somewhere on his property. It's why I came back. I needed to read his words, to find my own salvation. He told me it has the answers I'm looking for.' He was desperate now. 'I *have* to find that book!'

The voices grew louder, approaching from all directions.

Jarrod glanced over his shoulder and returned his gaze to Carmichael. 'Why should I care about that? If I kill you, it's all over and those secrets die with you. Once and for all.'

'Can you live with that?' Carmichael's voice was low. He panted, his face pale and sickly. He was bleeding out. 'It will eat you up inside… not knowing the truth.'

'Why should we believe you?' said Long.

Carmichael ignored him, his eyes locked on Jarrod. 'Have I ever lied to you?'

Jarrod stepped closer and pressed the gun against his forehead. Carmichael closed his eyes and waited for his end to come. He didn't see Jarrod raise his gun and strike the butt against the back of his head. He slumped and Jarrod kneeled on his back, applying handcuffs.

Kaleb Carmichael was right. Jarrod could never live with himself. If there were grieving families out there, they needed answers. It was his duty to help them find closure.

The so-called book of secrets had saved Kaleb Carmichael's life. For now.

TWENTY-NINE

BENFIELD strode towards Jarrod and Long, his nostrils flaring. 'What the hell were you two cowboys doing? When you called it in, I gave you a direct order to stand down until the backup crews could set up a perimeter. The SERT team was on its way.'

'It was my call, boss,' said Jarrod. 'There was no time. I had to play his game. First sign of the cavalry and he would have disappeared for good. He threatened to come after my kids. It was personal.'

Benfield turned to Long, glaring. 'And you went along with this?'

'Yes, boss. O'Connor let me out down the road and I approached on foot to get the drop on Carmichael before the backup crews spooked him. O'Connor was the decoy.' Long glanced at Carmichael, lying prone next to Jazmin Miles' grave. He was conscious again, mumbling gibberish under his breath. Uniform officers were already rendering first aid. 'We got him, didn't we?' Long said with a sassy tone that raised Benfield's hackles even more.

Benfield's eyes fell to Jarrod's chest and bulged when they registered the neat hole piercing his vest. He eyed Carmichael, blood gushing from his broken nose, gunshot wounds to his shoulder and leg. 'Only just, by the look of things.' He looked at Jarrod and the tightness in his eyes eased. 'You got hit. How bad is it?'

Jarrod flinched as an invisible knife stabbed his ribs from the inside. 'Hurts like a bitch but I'll live.' He looked at Carmichael. 'He's the one who needs urgent medical treatment. He knows things. We can't lose him.'

'What things?' said Benfield, eyes narrowing.

'Details of more victims.'

Benfield's shoulders sagged as he sighed. Something caught his eye. 'Oi! Over here!' he called, waving at two paramedics who cut their way through a huddle of police officers. 'Man down, gunshot wounds.'

The paramedics lugged over their medical kits and a stretcher and received a handover from the officers who'd packed gauze bandaging over Carmichael's wounds. The paramedics took over and worked to stem the bleeding.

'His vitals are low and he's going into shock,' said one paramedic. 'We need to get him to hospital ASAP.'

'Those cuffs are staying on. This man's a killer,' said Long. 'He's bloody dangerous.'

The paramedic hesitated, his eyes widening. 'No arguments here.' He turned his attention back to his patient. 'We'll do what we can but it's not looking good.'

'Murray, you right to ride along in the ambulance?' said Benfield.

Long nodded. 'Yeah, I'm good.'

'Take a uniform with you and I'll get another crew to follow the ambulance to the hospital. Take no chances and do *not* let Carmichael out of your sight, conscious or not. Talk to no one. Ethical Standards will want to interview you both about what went down here.'

'Got it,' said Long, resolute.

'This guy will need surgery,' one paramedic piped up as he applied more bandaging to Carmichael's leg. 'If he survives the drive to the hospital, that is.'

'Stay with them, Murray,' said Benfield. He put his arm around Jarrod's shoulders, an awkward but sincere gesture. 'Walk with me.'

He led Jarrod to a seat intended for cemetery visitors. They sat. Jarrod groaned, his ribs biting.

'We'll get that looked at, son. I'll get a crew to take you to hospital,' said Benfield. 'Just take a breath.'

Jarrod hunched forward, crippled by chest pain. His breathing was laboured, his hands shaking.

'What happened, Jarrod? Why the lone renegade bullshit?'

'He wanted a confrontation, so that's what I gave him.'

'Stupid,' said Benfield. 'Brave, but monumentally stupid. But, after what you've been through, I can make allowances for your poor judgement. I just wish you had waited for backup, so we could lock this place down and send in the SERT boys.'

'To be honest, boss. I think I wanted it just as much as he did. I had to confront him. Alone.'

'He really did a number on you, didn't he? Got under your skin.'

'You don't know the half of it.'

'And I'm guessing I don't want to know.'

'You might be right.'

'Yeah, well, I guess I'll have to be creative when I write up my report. It's over, Jarrod. We have him. He can't hurt anyone else now.'

At that moment the dam of pent-up emotions burst, and Jarrod sobbed, his shoulders heaving. His head fell into his hands. The loss of Jayne, the love of his life. Brad's murder. His own guilt. It was all too much. He shook his head and closed his eyes, willing it all away, wishing it was just a nightmare and he'd wake up in Jayne's arms. His ribs jolted with each sob. His trembling fingers smeared tears from his face. He felt Benfield's hand on his back, comforting him. He lost track of time, all the while Benfield sat with him, not saying a word.

Jarrod rubbed his eyes and turned to Benfield. 'That woman, the old lady from the farm. Any sightings?'

'Not yet. Crews are out searching for the car.'

'What's her name?' said Jarrod.

'Alice. Alice McNelly. Her poor old husband's a mess. We'll find her.'

'I think she's dead. Carmichael had blood on his hands, and a knife. She wasn't any more use to him.'

Benfield sighed. 'Fucking psychopath.'

'I looked into his eyes. I mean, *really* looked into them. There was no humanity. They were soulless, empty.'

'I've seen that look before, a long time ago. Terrifying, I know. But it's done. Come on, the ambos are about to haul him off.'

They stood and watched as Carmichael was taken away unconscious, an oxygen mask over his mouth and nose. He was strapped to a stretcher, his hands now handcuffed at his front. Jarrod and Benfield followed. Carmichael was carried down an aisle between graves to the awaiting ambulance vehicle, flanked by Murray Long and several uniforms. They loaded Carmichael into the back and the doors were secured behind Long and another officer. Under a halo of blue and red lights, the motorcade of ambulance and police vehicles sped away.

The scene of the shooting was encircled with crime scene tape. Portable spotlights were being erected and Benfield busied himself, barking instructions. Crews were out searching but there was still no news on the missing woman.

Jarrod edged away and found a quiet spot in the shadows. He pulled out his phone and called Pat.

She answered after two rings. 'Jarrod! What's happening? There's been media reports. A police shooting and manhunt. Are you okay?'

'I'm fine,' he reassured. His words felt hollow.

'Thank God!' She paused. 'The shooting? They're saying an officer was killed.'

Jarrod's composure faulted, the lump in his throat choking. He forced the words through his tears. 'Brad. It was Brad. I was with him.'

'Oh, love. I'm so sorry.' She didn't press for details. 'Where are you? Can you come home?'

'I'm at the cemetery. It's where we got him.'

'Who, Jarrod? Tell me it's him. Please tell me you got that monster.'

'We got him. Carmichael's in custody. We can go home, Pat. We can take the kids home. Start afresh.'

Pat sounded lost for words. She just cried. So did Jarrod.

'Do you want to speak to the kids? They're getting ready for a bath.'

'No, it's…' Jarrod clipped his words as pain stabbed his ribs.

'You're hurt, aren't you? I can tell. What aren't you telling me?'

'It's just my ribs. But I'm okay.' Jarrod spared Pat the details. She knew when to not ask, just like Jayne did. Besides, she'd only worry herself to death. No, he'd wait until he could tell her in person. 'I won't be home for a while. Just need to get checked out. I'll talk to the kids later. Leave them be.' In truth, Jarrod longed to hear Katie and Matty's voices, but he feared he didn't have the strength, that he'd break down over the phone and upset them.

'Okay, Jarrod. Come home soon. We miss you.'

He knew she'd understand.

After the call, Jarrod's attention was drawn to Benfield having an animated phone conversation. He went over to see what it was about.

When Benfield hung up, his stooped posture said it all. 'One of the crews just found the woman's car up a cemetery service road, hidden in trees. Her body was inside. Stabbed. Poor woman didn't stand a chance.'

Jarrod's heart sank as his worst fears were realised. He felt faint and his knees buckled. It was all too much. He lowered himself to the grass and shivered as a chill ran through him.

'Come on,' said Benfield, offering Jarrod a hand. 'You're going to the hospital. No arguments.' He helped Jarrod to his feet.

'Who's going to tell Mr McNelly about his wife? I feel responsible. I'd like to talk to him.'

'That's gallant of you, Jarrod, but it's not your responsibility. None of this was your fault. You can't carry all this on your shoulders. I'll send a crew to go see him.'

Within minutes he was in the back seat of a patrol car on the way to hospital. By the time he arrived, he could hardly walk, the pain in his ribcage debilitating. The accident and emergency staff were attentive. He'd met some of them before – Jayne's colleagues. He knew he was in good hands.

After his X-ray he was made comfortable in a private room. Two cracked ribs. No surprises. It could have been far worse. When he'd taken off his vest, the plate was shattered. Thankfully, it and the Kevlar had absorbed the impact. One whole side of his chest was already purplish black with deep tissue bruising.

Long popped his head in. 'I see you're getting all the special treatment. Take a slug to the chest and everyone panders to you.' He gave a wry smile.

Jarrod shifted in his bed with a grimace. Pillows were stacked behind to prop him into a half sitting position. He groaned as another pain shot through his ribs, the morphine hardly taking the edge off. 'Yeah, well I wouldn't recommend it.' His words were slurred in his own ears. It had all caught up with him. The stress, the exhaustion, the pain killers. 'Any word on Carmichael?'

'He's in surgery. Last I heard, he was stable. Armed SERT officers are on guard. Media circus is downstairs.' Long slid a chair closer to Jarrod's bed and lowered his voice. 'Toe-cutters just interviewed me. It's all sweet. They reckon it was a clean shoot. Tell 'em exactly what happened and don't leave anything out. We're all good. They'll interview you when you're up to it.'

Jarrod gave a woozy thumbs up, his eyelids heavy. 'Can you call Pat for me? Tell her I'm staying in overnight. Tell my kids I love them, and I'll be home tomorrow.'

'I will mate. You rest up.'

Jarrod's last conscious thought was of Kaleb Carmichael bleeding out, handcuffed and squirming in the dirt.

THIRTY

BRAD'S funeral was seven days later. In contrast to the day's solemn mood, the sun shone bright and cheerful. Saint Paul's cathedral was crowded beyond capacity. Standing mourners were crammed ten deep on all sides of the jam-packed pews. The congregation spilled out onto the lawns. People peered through stained glass windows to catch a glimpse of proceedings. A gallery of news reporters and camera crews assembled outside. The service had all the traditional protocols and trimmings of a police funeral. Farewelling a fallen comrade was something the police department had always done well and with an abundance of pride. The Police Commissioner read out Brad's service history and gave a moving speech about the thankless sacrifices made by frontline police officers to keep the community safe.

Jarrod sat in the front row, inconsolable. He flinched when he followed the priest's cues to stand to recite prayers or to sing hymns. The pain in his ribs nagged as a constant reminder of his own brush with death at the hands of Kaleb Carmichael. He welcomed the pain, embraced it. He wished he could suffer more, as penance. He wished it was him in that casket and not Brad. It should have been him. His physical injuries paled into insignificance compared to the crushing pain of grief. His suffering was personal and despite the lifelines thrown to him by colleagues, he was drowning in guilt and regret. He'd dragged Brad into a dangerous situation, been careless and near-sighted. The weight of responsibility magnified gravity; his body heavy as though sinking in wet cement.

As the service ended, the national and police flags were folded and draped over the coffin's polished mahogany. Brad's police cap sat proudly on top beside a framed photo of him receiving a service medal. A brilliant bouquet lay at the head of the coffin. As it was wheeled down the aisle, Jarrod followed the solemn procession towards the grand cathedral entrance. He joined Brad's older brother Karl, two mates from his academy squad and two old school friends, as pallbearers. The weight of Brad's body felt heavy in Jarrod's grip, triggering a flashback of Jayne's funeral. They lifted the coffin from the trolley and carried it down the front steps towards the awaiting hearse. The police pipes and drums band led the way, playing a provocative rendition of *Going Home*. They slid the coffin along the rollers until it came to rest inside the rear of the hearse.

The Police Commissioner headed up the guard of honour and saluted as Brad's final journey began. The long winding driveway of the cathedral was lined with uniformed and plainclothes police of all ranks, saluting in tribute. The funeral procession was escorted by horses from the mounted unit. Only the echo of their hooves clip-clopping on bitumen broke the respectful silence. A formation of motorcycle officers followed behind, ahead of two police dogs and their handlers, all in full ceremonial uniform. Jarrod was equally proud and heartbroken as he watched them turn out onto the street. Traffic officers stopped motorists who got out of their cars and joined pedestrians in spontaneous applause. Hundreds of officers in the honour guard did an about turn and broke away. In the sea of people, Jarrod spotted Brad's parents and younger sister. His jacket was soaked with their tears as they embraced in mutual grief.

The burial was a private ceremony, the finality of it heartbreaking. It forced Jarrod to relive the anguish of Jayne's service and the trauma of the shootout with Carmichael. All the pent-up emotion and turmoil in Jarrod's heart erupted in that one moment. As Brad's coffin settled deep in the red earth, Jarrod sprinkled rose petals into the grave.

'See ya, mate,' he whispered, and he walked away. He couldn't look back. Leaving Brad in the ground, alone in a dark box, felt so wrong. He got in his car and drove home where he spent the afternoon with Katie and Matty. Their smiles and chatter a welcome distraction.

The following day, the town said goodbye to Alice McNelly. Her funeral was held in a stone chapel on the edge of town, too small to hold the hundreds of townsfolk who turned out. Jarrod sat outside under a marquee, listening to the service through loudspeakers. In his welcoming address, the priest told the congregation it was the same chapel where Alice and Harry had been married thirty-five years earlier. They'd built a long and happy life together.

Her murder had shaken the town to its core. Her innocence and vulnerability added to the tragedy of her death. In life, she chose solitude on the farm, but in death, she was lovingly embraced as one of their own by townsfolk she had never met. Although he hadn't known Alice, Jarrod felt a strong connection to her. In the eulogy, read by her nephew, the absence left by Alice's death was described as a gaping hole that could never be filled. The world was a better place for having had Alice in it, he said, and her goodness would linger forever. It was said that a part of Harry also died when his soulmate was taken from him. When the service was over, Jarrod's heart sank as the poor, old bloke was pushed out in a wheelchair flanked by family. He looked broken, crushed by the weight of his grief. According to the leaflet, Alice's body was to be cremated and her ashes spread over her beloved rose garden on the farm.

That afternoon, Jarrod sat at his desk and stared at the jacket still hanging on the back of Brad's chair. He couldn't bring himself to put it away. Brad's presence felt as real as his coffee mug, case files and notepad left untouched on his desk. Jarrod expected to see him padding in the office any minute, huffing and puffing, sweaty from riding his bike to work, quick with a smart-arse comment. He ignored the impatient blinking of the red message bank light on his desk phone. In the background, the police radio scanner chatter crackled from the speakers and the routine hum of station activity echoed in the hallways. Officers hurried up and down the stairs, going about their business of day-to-day police work. The tragic events of the week soon made way for the drudgery of responding to the never-ending calls for service. The community still needed its police, and it was important to show a unified front. There was an expectation of resilience and an unwavering commitment to doing their jobs even in the face of losing one of their own. They had to dust themselves off and get on with it.

~

Over the next few weeks, the investigation into the Carmichael killings had been handed over and the media frenzy simmered. The Homicide Squad had taken over the case; a move welcomed by the local detectives. They'd been spread too thin, and the outside assistance was a godsend. Carmichael had survived. A bedside court hearing had been held to formally charge him with fresh murder indictments and a string of offences since his escape. According to the surgeon, he would recover from his gunshot wounds. He'd been moved into secure isolation in the medical wing of the correctional complex in the city. As each day passed, Jarrod tried to push Carmichael out of his thoughts, busying himself with the daily grind of new investigations. Brad's replacement was yet to be selected, which suited Jarrod just fine. He preferred to work alone. It was too soon for a new partner; he wasn't ready. In the meantime, the CIB helped with his caseload.

Weeks blurred into months and Jarrod fell back into a steady routine, however a nagging feeling of unfinished business gnawed away at him. His better judgement told him to get on with his life, to distance himself from Kaleb Carmichael; to let time heal as he faded away into oblivion, rotting in a prison cell. However, something Carmichael had said that afternoon at the cemetery stuck with Jarrod, like dogshit on his shoe. It was the reason Jarrod didn't pull the trigger. He couldn't get Carmichael's ramblings out of his mind. The idea of a so-called "book of secrets" had clawed into his skin.

'There's a book of secrets. Vincent's secrets,' Carmichael had said in desperation as Jarrod threatened to blow his brains out. 'It's what I'm searching for. Kill me and the secrets will die with me.'

The words played over in Jarrod's head. It was Carmichael's

reason for returning to Lockyer. He was searching for something so important, he risked getting caught. Toying with Jarrod in the process was just for his amusement, his way of creating a sense of theatre. His real goal was finding this book. Perhaps there were unsolved murders, more bodies to be found. Or maybe the whole story was just another charade.

Jarrod fought the urge to buy into Carmichael's games, that is, until the phone rang one morning.

THIRTY-ONE

THE man on the other end of the phone spoke with the gravelly voice of someone who smoked a pack a day. He introduced himself as Chief Warden Jeff Oldfield. 'Is this Detective Sergeant Jarrod O'Connor?'

'Yes, it is. How can I help you?'

'Call me Jeff, mate,' he said, his tone lighter. 'Your *friend* Kaleb Carmichael is currently a guest at our fine establishment. It's my responsibility to keep him alive until he stands trial.'

Jarrod's stomach fluttered as though he'd fallen from a great height. 'What's this about, Jeff?'

'He's asked to see you. Refuses to speak to anyone else.'

'What's he want with me?'

'As I said, mate, the prick won't talk to no one. He's segregated from the general population of inmates and refuses to come out of his cell for his daily exercise. Just sits on the floor meditating. He told the guards he has something important to tell you. Something about *the book* and clearing up unsolved murders? He said you'd understand.'

Jarrod gripped the phone until his knuckles went white and closed his eyes. He knew this day would come.

'You still there?' said Oldfield.

'Yeah, I'm still here. Did he say anything else?'

'Nope.'

Jarrod hesitated, his mind suddenly numb.

'Listen,' said Oldfield. 'I wouldn't normally bother the coppers with the shit these prisoners can spin but given his history I thought it worth the call. Makes no difference to me, but I figured you might be interested in what he has to say. Just say the word if you don't want to speak to him and that'll be the end of it.'

'No, thanks Jeff. I appreciate your call. I'll come. I'll have to get it approved by my bosses. When's a good time?'

'He's not allowed visitors except for his legal counsel, and they rarely see him. Don't blame 'em. He has a free calendar, so you name a time and we'll have him ready for you.'

'Can you do me a favour, Jeff?'

'Yeah sure, mate. What is it?'

'Tell him I said I'll come when I'm good and ready. I don't want him to think I'll come running. I'm not pandering to this arsehole.'

Oldfield chuckled and wheezed a phlegmy smoker's cough into the phone. 'Understood. Let the prick sweat it out a little longer.'

'Tell him I've got some personal business to take care of. The man who killed my wife in a car crash is fronting court tomorrow. I need to be there for that.'

'Oh shit, mate. That'll be tough. Of course, you do what you have to do.'

'How is he, I mean physically after his…' Jarrod paused. 'His injuries?'

'You mean the holes you blokes riddled him with?' He chuckled. 'Well done on that, by the way. But, hey, couldn't you have aimed a little to your left and saved us all this trouble? Keeping this shit stain alive is a waste of taxpayers' money.'

'He's a hard bastard to kill.' Jarrod allowed himself a small chuckle of his own.

'Not from a lack of trying, from what I hear.'

'You heard right. One last thing. How's his mental state?'

'His mental state? Well, for a murderous psychopath, I guess he seems quite stable. Although he's adamant about talking to you about this book. It's the only thing that gets him riled up.'

'Good.'

'That's the spirit,' Oldfield said with another hearty chuckle. 'The piece of shit ain't goin' nowhere. He can marinate in his cell until you're ready to see him. You look after yourself and your family, mate.'

They arranged for Jarrod to travel down to the prison in three days' time. He needed to psych himself up in preparation for George Willmott's sentencing hearing the next day. In a statement delivered by his defense solicitor at the committal hearing, Willmott expressed to the court his overwhelming shame and a desire to spare the family the torment of a drawn-out trial. Jarrod wasn't in court that day. It had been two weeks since Brad's funeral and he just didn't have the strength of mind or body. The truth of it was he didn't trust himself. He had no idea how he would react when he saw that man again. He didn't know if he'd break down in a blubbering mess or if he'd leap from his seat and scale over the prisoner dock to beat him to death with his bare fists. Rage, grief and compassion waged a war inside Jarrod, and he didn't know which emotion would win.

Willmott's early plea of guilty was one small saving grace. He had remained in custody ever since the day he handed himself in. Jarrod was still conflicted. Had he made a mistake by letting him live? Was Kaleb Carmichael right when he accused him of being a coward for not dispensing his own swift justice? Jarrod's need for vengeance still gnawed at him. He hoped the judge would see fit to deliver an appropriate sentence, however, his faith in the courts was on shaky ground.

He'd written his victim impact statement which would be tendered to the court. It was an outpouring of grief he'd written late one night alone in his study after the kids had gone to bed. Finding the right words to express the never-ending sadness that had plagued him since the awful night of the car crash was nearly impossible. His words felt hollow as he penned a clumsy attempt to articulate his loss, and that of his two small children who missed their mummy terribly. Pat had also written her impact statement. It was brief and, as usual, she didn't mince her words.

'Mr Willmott. You have robbed our family of a shining light,' she wrote. 'We've suffered in darkness ever since that night you took to the wheel of your car drunk. Nothing you can do or say will ever change what you did or bring back what you've taken from us. God will judge you. May your soul find peace. I pray that one day I can forgive you, but today is not that day.'

The statement typified the strong woman of faith Pat was. Her statement was brutally honest and pointed. Jarrod was ashamed to admit he didn't have her strength. He was consumed with hatred. He was weak.

Nothing would stop him from sitting in that court room and staring his wife's killer in the eyes, one last time. Carmichael could wait until he was ready to see him on his own terms. Carmichael wouldn't rob him of his time in court or stand in the way of his journey of closure and healing. He wanted Carmichael to sit in his cell and stew. Making him wait would take away his control, to establish that he no longer dictated terms. Jarrod was desperate to hear what Carmichael had to say but he had to contain his eagerness. A few more days wouldn't hurt.

Tomorrow was not about Kaleb Carmichael and his twisted narcissism. It would be Jayne's day. In Jarrod's heart, he knew she would be watching.

THIRTY-TWO

PAT and Jarrod agreed, for the sake of Katie and Matty, they would stick to the normal morning routine. They had decided not to tell them about the sentencing hearing. The kids had only settled back into school and life at home without their mummy. Jarrod had resolved to telling them the outcome of the sentencing that night. It was only a matter of time before they asked what happened to 'the man who crashed into Mummy'. The last thing he wanted was for them to hear about it from some kid at school who overheard their parents talking about it. Small town gossip. Kids could be blunt and cruel, even when they didn't mean to.

Barefoot, with messy bed hair, Matty wandered out of his room when he heard the commotion in the kitchen. He clapped his hands with glee when he saw the stack of butter pancakes drenched in maple syrup that Jarrod had cooked in the electric frying pan. Pat poured Matty a glass of milk and he happily climbed onto his new big-boy chair at the table to his favourite breakfast. Katie, not as impressed with her father's exploits in the kitchen, sat beside her little brother and prodded a fork at her pancakes.

'Thanks, Dad,' she said, a little forlorn. *Dad*. Not *Daddy* anymore.

When did that change happen? He hadn't even noticed. 'What's the matter, sweetheart? Don't you feel like pancakes today?'

'Yeah, it's just that,' she pursed her lips and frowned, 'Mummy used to make the pancakes. It just reminds me of her. It makes me sad.'

'I know I can't make them as good as Mummy did, but I'm doing my best. How about you have a taste and tell me what you think? She'll be proud of me for trying, don't you think?'

She gave an uncertain nod and broke off a mouthful of pancake with her fork, dipping it into the melted butter and maple syrup. After placing it in her mouth, she chewed. Despite herself, a smile emerged.

'Good?' said Jarrod with a hopeful smile.

'Yeah. It's pretty good.' She tucked in.

Pat helped get the kids dressed into their school uniforms while Jarrod made their lunch. Cheese and crackers, fruit sticks, vegemite sandwiches, apple juice poppers and a banana. He drove them to school and by the time they arrived at the drop off point at the front gates, the kids were in good spirits and ready for the adventures that lay ahead. They took turns in giving Jarrod hugs and kisses and off they ran, hand in hand, towards a frenzy of kids running around like lunatics in the playground. They turned and gave Jarrod a wave before disappearing into the fray. He drove home where Pat had tidied up and gotten herself dressed for court.

By 10:00am, Pat and Jarrod were sitting in the front row of the courtroom, her shoulder pressed against his, clasping his hand in hers. He'd been in there many times, either giving evidence in trials or assisting the police prosecutor during bail hearings. This was the first time he was there as a family member of a victim. While they waited for the proceedings to start, he swivelled his head and took in all the detail of the heritage charm he'd never really taken the time to admire. It was as though he was there for the first time, looking through fresh eyes. He gazed out the casement windows at the sprawling lawns and gardens of the surrounding parklands. The hypnotic whir of sprinklers outside helped to ease the nerves swirling inside his gut. He stared up at the high ceiling and busied himself studying the patterns of the pressed metal fretwork. The courtroom felt hollow. The slightest sounds were amplified and echoed off the walls. As he shifted his body restlessly, the wooden bench seat creaked. The ceiling fans spun with a constant hum.

He sensed someone sitting two rows behind and glanced over his shoulder. A young man in a clumsily knotted tie tapped away on a laptop, biting his bottom lip. Jarrod turned his body for a closer look. A red lanyard dangled from the young man's neck, displaying the word "media" embroidered into the fabric in white lettering. A laminated media accreditation card hung from the lanyard. Jarrod recognised the logo for the *Lockyer Chronicle*, the local rag. The journo continued typing, unaware Jarrod was eyeing him. His face radiated youthful energy and enthusiasm. He looked up and gave Jarrod a polite smile. Jarrod nodded and the young journo resumed his frantic typing. Jarrod guessed he was one of the fresh interns straight out of university, doing his time at the bottom of the food chain as the court reporter. To Jarrod's relief, he seemed to have no idea who he was. Their case was the first of a long list of sentencing hearings in the District Court that day. The journalist had a long day of court reporting ahead.

Onlookers filled the courtroom, streaming in through the back door. People whispered as they discussed where they should sit, taking up positions in the back rows. Jarrod glanced around at the faces and recognised a contingent of police officers, some on duty and others on their days off, all there to show support. Many of Jayne's work colleagues and old friends arrived and shared warm smiles and waves with Jarrod as they made eye contact. He mouthed 'thank you' and nodded his appreciation for them being there for Jayne. He estimated around fifty people were now sitting patiently in the courtroom waiting for the sentencing hearing to get underway. It reminded him of the congregation at Jayne's funeral. There were other faces he didn't recognise. Her death had impacted on so many people in town, including patients she had treated in the emergency ward. So many townsfolk had been touched by her gentle care. It was heartwarming to see these friends and strangers alike, all showing solidarity in Jayne's memory. He was comforted knowing he was not alone in his grief.

The Legal Aid Service appointed defense barrister entered the room from the side door wearing his black robe, fumbling with his curled wig in one hand and a briefcase in the other. Jarrod assumed he had just come from the court cells where he had received final instructions from his client. The Crown Prosecutor entered from the opposite side door, exhaling a lungful of cigarette smoke as he stepped from the balcony into the courtroom. He hurried over to his place at the bench and sat down behind a stack of law books and case files, putting on his wig. The defense barrister, now wigged, took his seat at the other end of the bench and rifled through a folder, pulling out a copy of the brief of evidence.

The side door leading to the court cells swung open and a burly young constable entered the room leading George Willmott by the elbow. Whispers grew louder around the courtroom as he was led into the dock wearing no restraints. The constable closed the wooden gate, locking Willmott in like an animal in a pen. Jarrod was immediately taken by how frail and thin Willmott now looked. The skin on his face was gaunt and saggy. He sat and rested his hands on his knees and stared blankly towards the windows on the far side of the room. He was a mere shadow of his former self, a man accepting of his fate.

The door from the judge's chambers swung open and a tall man with a pot belly called the room to attention. 'Silence. All stand,' announced the bailiff, his voice cracking like a whip.

The crowd fell silent, and everyone rose to their feet. Judge Morrison, a rotund man, waddled in and waved for everyone to be seated as he sat and clanked his gavel to bring the court to order.

The proceedings went as expected, the whole time Willmott's stare fixated on the floor. He seemed not to have the courage to make eye contact with anyone in the room, or maybe it was just shame. The facts of the case were read out by the prosecutor detailing Willmott's movements before he drunkenly crashed into Jarrod and Jayne's car and fled the scene. The defense read out his client's antecedents and gave a grim account of Willmott's hopelessness after the passing of his wife to cancer. Excuses weren't being made; the defense knew that wouldn't wash with the judge. His strategy was to mitigate any suggestion of intentional criminal conduct of his client. He conveyed to the court his client's depression and excess drinking that led to the awful and tragic "accident".

Jarrod braced himself as the prosecutor read out the victim impact statements one by one. Hearing them being read out loud in the court gave them new significance, heartbreaking and powerful. Women sobbed at the back of the courtroom and there was a long silence as Judge Morrison turned to Willmott to ask if he would like to make any final comment before sentencing. Willmott, deep in thought, turned his head and scanned the room for the first time. His eyes met Jarrod's in recognition, an intense gaze. The regret in his eyes said more than any words could convey. His eyes moved to Pat and she held his gaze, resolute despite the tears streaming down her cheeks.

After an agonising pause, he broke away from Pat's gaze and looked at his lawyer for permission to speak. The lawyer gave assurance with a nod and Willmott looked up at the judge.

'Your Honour.' His voice was weak. A hush fell over the court, every set of eyes glued to the diminutive figure hunched in the dock. He coughed into a fist to clear his throat and started again. 'Your Honour. There is nothing I can say to take away the pain I have caused. To the lady's family, to Jayne's family, I am so sorry.' He turned and stared into Jarrod's eyes. 'I dare not ask for your forgiveness as I know I don't deserve that. If I could swap my life for your wife's, I would do it gladly, in a heartbeat. I was a good man, please believe that.'

Jarrod stared back into his eyes, and they remained entangled in each other's gaze until Judge Morrison interrupted.

'Thank you, Mr Willmott. I have heard all the evidence and victim impact statements. Your early guilty plea has saved the family the added stress of a trial and will also be taken into account, along with your clean record. However, the tragedy that unfolded as a result of your reckless actions warrants an appropriate sentence.'

Jarrod held his breath and turned to Pat who sat rigid as a statue with her eyes closed. They had been waiting to hear these next few words for months. The time of reckoning had arrived, the sentence about to be handed down.

'For the charges of dangerous driving causing death, drink driving and failing to remain at the scene of a traffic incident…,' the Judge began, 'I sentence you to twelve years imprisonment with a possibility for parole after serving a period no less than eight years.'

The silence was broken by gasps and whispers. It was difficult to gauge the level of acceptance of this sentence by the crowd, however Pat and Jarrod had been given a good indication of what to expect. The prosecutor had suggested anywhere from eight to twelve years. Jarrod was neither shocked nor outraged. He accepted the sentence, but mostly, he was numb. Perhaps it was a combination of relief and closure. They could now get on with rebuilding their lives. It was finally over.

'Anything further, gentlemen?' said Judge Morrison.

Both lawyers replied in unison, 'No, Your Honour.'

'Constable, take the prisoner away. He shall remain in the custody of the Department of Corrections to serve out his sentence. Thank you, ladies and gentlemen. Court is adjourned.' The Judge slammed his gavel with a clank, the echo bouncing off the walls.

'Silence. All stand,' called the bailiff. The judge lumbered from the court room towards his chambers.

Willmott's eyes met Jarrod's and their gazes locked, despite the hive of activity going on around them. The courtroom came alive with the chatter of loud voices and banging doors as people exited into the morning sunshine. Willmott pursed his lips and nodded with a look of remorse. His eyes, glazed with tears, projected raw sadness and regret. Jarrod lifted his chin and inhaled slowly, looking down over the bridge of his nose. He returned a nod in silent recognition of the man's gesture. For the briefest of moments, they shared a private connection, unseen by those around them.

The man responsible for Jayne's death was handcuffed behind his back and led away.

THIRTY-THREE

THE day of Jarrod's visit arrived. He'd hardly slept since receiving Jeff Oldfield's first phone call. The anticipation of again coming face to face with Carmichael consumed his thoughts as he pushed through the routine of each day. He was distracted, endless possibilities of the secrets Carmichael might reveal floating in and out of his subconscious. He marked time. The nights were worst of all. In bed, he stared at the ceiling, his mind bustling, the darkness stretching on. He'd climbed out of bed each morning exhausted, denied yet another good night's sleep. Maybe his deliberate delay tactics had done more damage to him than to Carmichael. Or was Carmichael suffering, frustrated by the urge to toy with Jarrod again?

Jarrod left around midday for the two-hour drive to Sydney's Western suburbs. The industrial sprawl concealed the prison in its camouflage of grey, featureless buildings and factories. The dated facility was a nod to the nineteen-fifties. Its outer perimeter was bordered by a high-tension, steel mesh fence with coiled razor wire woven along the top. A second barrier ran parallel to the outer perimeter, creating a ten-metre grassy "no man's land". Watchtowers with tinted windows stood high and accusatory at each corner of the sprawling prison complex. Each was manned with a guard armed with a sniper rifle, pacing up and down. Just inside the inner fence stood the red brick walls of the high security wing. Jarrod counted four brick chimneys towering above the roofline. He guessed these pre-dated the modern electric heating systems that had been installed and now served only to maintain the prison's heritage charm, standing as a reminder of its infamous and grim past.

Jarrod veered into the main entrance and drove along the narrow bitumen driveway until he was waved to a halt by the stern-faced security guard stationed at the boom gate booth. He peered in through Jarrod's window and thoroughly inspected his identification. He looked up and studied Jarrod's face before re-examining his police badge photo. Satisfied, the guard checked the visitor schedule.

'Detective O'Connor. You're on the list. Please proceed past the public car park and drive right up to the steel doors where you will receive further instructions.' The guard spoke into his radio and keyed in the code to open the electric boom gate.

With an expressionless nod he motioned for Jarrod to proceed through. The steel mesh perimeter fence loomed ahead. He followed the road towards two massive steel doors, large enough for a semi-trailer to drive through with room to spare. The car was engulfed in the shadows of the colossal barrier designed to separate inmates from the outside world. He felt a stark eeriness, as though he were approaching the gates of a medieval castle. A regular sized steel door, immediately adjacent to the huge gates, swung open and a burly prison guard appeared. He approached Jarrod's window and repeated the routine of checking his identification.

'Thanks, Detective. Are you carrying any firearms today?'

'No, mate. I'm not armed.'

'Okay then. So, when the gates open, please drive inside and park your vehicle off to the left for mandatory screening. Please then walk over to the reception desk where you will be given further instructions.'

'Understood. Thanks, mate.'

The guard stepped back inside the door and slammed it closed behind him. With a loud electric buzz, the main steel doors creaked and inwardly crept open, giving Jarrod his first view inside the prison beyond the outer perimeter. Old memories flooded back. He hadn't been inside for years, not since he was a junior constable working the compulsory rotation in the City Watchhouse. Transporting inmates to and from the prison for their court appearances in the city had been a daily task.

Now sitting in his car, he watched as the steel doors fully opened with a loud clunk, the hydraulics exhaling with a hiss. Just inside, he recognised the transition bay used for screening delivery vehicles. The guard waved him forward and he drove into the bay, his eyes adjusting to the dreary artificial light of florescent bulbs. The guard approached his door and held it open for Jarrod as he climbed out.

'Follow me, sir.'

'No need to call me sir. I work for a living.'

The guard didn't seem to catch onto his joke and led Jarrod to the reception desk. Two metres in front, a bold yellow line and a pair of yellow footprints were painted on the concrete floor. "Do NOT step past the yellow line" a sign read.

The guard saw Jarrod hesitate when he reached the yellow line. 'That's a no-go zone for prisoners. Please step up to the desk and sign the attendance register.'

Behind the desk, a gruff looking guard with sweat patches in the armpits of his shirt slid a clipboard over the counter. A pen dangled from a chain. Jarrod filled out a form with his details and reason for visit.

'Interview with inmate Kaleb Carmichael,' he wrote.

As Jarrod slid the clipboard back across the counter, the guard behind the desk looked over his bifocal spectacles. 'All visitors must undergo a pat down search, even coppers.'

'No problem.'

Jarrod held out his arms as the other guard applied gloves and patted him down, pinching and shaking his clothing from top to bottom, left to right.

'Thank you, sir.' He nodded at his colleague. 'All clear, Frank.'

'Wait here,' grumbled the guard behind the counter. 'Chief Warden Oldfield is on his way.' He spun around on his chair and went back to his newspaper.

A few minutes later, a staff only door inside the reception office swung open and a barrel-shaped man, no more than five and a half feet tall with a salt and pepper flat top, stepped into the room. Frank abruptly folded his newspaper and pretended to shuffle some official paperwork.

'Checking out the form guide, hey Frank?' said the keg on legs. 'Any hot tips for this Saturday?' The man gave Frank a hefty pat on his shoulder with a knowing grin.

'No, boss,' said Frank, like a kid caught with his hand in the lolly jar.

The man opened the door leading to the transition bay and stepped out. He extended a hand to Jarrod, tattoos on his forearm visible under the folded cuffs of his long shirt sleeve. *Military*, Jarrod thought. He adjusted a simple brown tie loosely hanging around his thick neck. 'Detective O'Connor I assume?' he said with a friendly smile as Jarrod took his beefy hand into his. The bones in Jarrod's hand crunched as the man clamped his grip. 'Jeff Oldfield. Hope my boys here have been looking after you?'

'Good to meet you, Jeff. Call me Jarrod.' He shot Frank a look. 'And yes, your staff have been very professional.'

'Glad to hear it.' He opened his hands. 'Welcome to our humble establishment.' His grin was contagious. Jarrod couldn't help but like him. 'You good to go?'

'Sure.'

'Follow me. Let's go see your friend.'

'Lead the way.'

Jarrod followed Jeff through the reception office and out the rear door that opened to a long hallway. A blast of cool air hit his face. The cavity brick walls were painted a sickly pale green and the spotless concrete floor shone with a varnish-like glaze. Their footfalls echoed off the walls as they walked down the narrow, windowless hallway.

'We've told Carmichael you're coming to see him,' said Oldfield, striding his stumpy legs at a purposeful pace.

'Oh, yeah? How did he react to that?' Jarrod quickened his steps to keep up.

'He said nothin' as usual. I gave him the news in person, but he wouldn't acknowledge me. He's just been lying in his cell staring at the ceiling.'

They came to an elevator door at the end of the hallway which triggered an old childhood memory of Jarrod's favourite TV show, *Get Smart*. Jeff extended his security pass that was attached to his belt on a retractable cord and swiped a console. It beeped and he pressed the elevator up button. They waited as a high-pitched howl of wind whistled from somewhere deep below in the bowels of the elevator shaft. A clunk was followed by a whoosh of air as the elevator doors slid open.

Jeff held his hand against the edge of one of the doors to keep it open. 'After you,' he said, waving Jarrod in like a bell boy.

They stepped inside the stainless-steel box and Oldfield pressed the down button. Their reflections were elongated on the shiny walls. The doors closed, encasing them in the tight space as the elevator descended into the depths of the old prison.

'The high security wing is down in basement two,' said Jeff. He seemed to sense Jarrod's growing anxiety.

Jarrod nodded and wiped his sweaty palms on his trouser legs.

The elevator shuddered and came to a halt. The doors slid open, and they stepped out into another ghastly green hallway. Just off to the right was a reception counter where a young corrections officer stood behind a thick pane of glass. He spoke through a mesh circle in the glass. 'Hey, Boss. The prisoner is waiting in the holding cell. Visitor booth number two is ready.'

'Thanks Nathan.' Oldfield's voice echoed off the concrete floor and walls in the waiting area. Another yellow line was painted on the floor two metres from the reception counter. Muffled voices of prisoners yelling out in their cells bounced off the walls further down the corridor making them seem a lot closer than they were.

'Okay, Jarrod. So, here's the drill. I'll take you down to the visitor side of the booth. Carmichael will be brought into the other side of the booth behind a grill which you'll be able to talk to him through. There's a camera on your side which our guys will monitor from the control booth just here. Any issues just press the intercom button and sing out. The boys will come running.'

Jarrod nodded and inhaled through his nose, slowly exhaling out his mouth to control his heart rate that had suddenly kicked into a higher gear. He followed the warden down the hallway and came to an open door. He peered into the tiny white room. Inside, a stainless-steel chair was bolted to the floor. On the other side of a steel mesh panel was another room, a mirror image. Below the mesh divider was a stainless-steel ledge used by defense solicitors to take notes while interviewing their clients. The prisoner's side had a similar bench and a stool bolted to the floor. Jarrod scanned the room on his side of the divider. An intercom box was secured to the wall and a camera with a blinking red LED light was mounted up in the corner behind a protective Perspex case.

Jarrod stepped inside and sat on the chair. Jeff grabbed the door handle. 'He'll be in soon. You ready?'

Jarrod cleared his throat. 'Ready as I'll ever be.'

'Good luck. I hope he gives you the answers you need.' Jeff closed the door and Jarrod remained in the tiny room alone, his ears ringing from the silence.

Jarrod fidgeted as he waited, his heart thumping inside his chest. He pushed down on his knees to stop his legs bouncing.

The sounds of movement and voices came from the other side. A guard opened the door in the opposite room, his head turned as he talked to someone in the hallway. 'In here,' he instructed and waited impatiently with the door open.

Jarrod heard the rattling and clinking of leg irons and the shuffle of shoes on the concrete floor. Kaleb Carmichael appeared in the doorway, dressed in a brown T-shirt and khaki green smock pants. His clothes hung loose from his now thin frame. He wore white Velcro joggers and shuffled with small steps, his movements restricted by the leg restraints. His hands were secured in handcuffs attached to a chain around his waist. His head was shaved and auburn facial hair sprouted in patches between smears of scarred skin. He had a distinct limp and favoured his left shoulder.

His eyes, sunken with dark shadows, locked onto Jarrod's as he came into the room. Instead of sitting on the stool, he stepped up to the divider and pressed the scarred flesh of his forehead against the steel mesh. He closed his eyes and inhaled through his nose, sniffing Jarrod's scent like a wild animal.

'Behave or you'll be back in the hole,' the guard bellowed from the doorway.

Carmichael sat on the stool, not once breaking eye contact with Jarrod. As the steel door on Carmichael's side was latched closed behind him, Jarrod gritted his teeth, determined not to show any fear.

Jarrod clenched his jaw and spoke first. 'So, Kaleb. I hear you wanted to see me?'

Carmichael's eyes narrowed at the corners and his lips formed a grotesque grin.

'Good to see you, *Jarrod*.'

THIRTY-FOUR

KALEB Carmichael's soulless eyes drilled into Jarrod's through the transparent steel mesh. An unsettling coldness emanated from his gaze. He wore a contrived smile, twisted and unnatural. Confined in that tight space, sharing the same air, a sour taste rose from Jarrod's gut. His mouth was dry, and his chest contracted with a tightness that restricted his breathing.

Jarrod leaned forward and lifted his chin so he could see Carmichael's hands resting on the ledge with interlocking fingers. The handcuffs and waist chain limited his range of movement.

'So, you're still alive then?' Jarrod said dryly.

His ugly smile widened. 'So it seems. But you know what they say, *Jarrod*. What doesn't kill you makes you stronger.'

'Is that a fact?'

Carmichael pursed his lips and gave an assured nod. 'That's a fact. My resolve grows stronger every day.'

'Your resolve to do what?'

'To right the wrongs of this world. That day will come sooner than you think.'

'Oh, yeah?' Jarrod raised his eyebrows, skeptical. 'How so?'

Carmichael leaned closer, matching Jarrod's forward posture. 'Don't you worry, you'll be the first to know.' He winked a deformed eyelid as though they were sharing a personal joke.

Jarrod sat upright, folding his arms and clenching his fists under his elbows. He changed tack. 'No more bullshit. You wanted to speak to me. I'm here.'

'Are you really here? You hear my words, but you never listen. You need to clear your mind and really, really listen to the universe.

Then you'll finally understand what I have to say.'

'And exactly how do I clear my mind with so much noise in the world?' Jarrod held his steely gaze.

'Is your mind still clouded by the need for revenge? Do you regret your decision to let your wife's killer live?'

'I've made my peace with that. He'll serve his punishment and I'll move on and live my life. I have no regrets.'

Carmichael leaned his elbows on the stainless-steel bench and maneouvered his handcuffed wrists so that he could rest his chin in his hands. He studied Jarrod intently.

'If that's what you want to believe, then you're only deceiving yourself. You can't fool the universe. It knows the truth.'

'I can live with my choices. Can you live with yours?'

'I've never known guilt. I've only ever felt pain and hatred. Vincent taught me to turn my fears and need for revenge into a power you'll never understand.'

'You're right. I don't understand. I've seen some really crazy shit in this world, but I will never understand the likes of you and Vincent Miles.'

Carmichael flinched as though he'd been stabbed in the shoulder. He cradled an elbow with his other hand and sat upright with closed eyes, controlling his breathing. He rested his hands in his lap. 'Shooting pains. They come and go. Your bullets smashed my bones, but not my spirit.'

'Do you want my sympathy?'

Carmichael chuckled. 'There's so much I want from you.'

Jarrod leaned forward, his nose nearly touching the mesh. He could smell Carmichael's body odour. 'No more games. What is it you need to get off your chest? I'm listening but my patience is wearing thin. Tell me about the other victims.'

'What do I get in return?'

'Nothing. There are no deals to be had. Don't waste my time.'

Carmichael leaned forward, their faces only centimetres apart. He stared back, his eyeballs darting left and right between Jarrod's eyes. The seconds drew on as he seemed to fight an inner battle to decide to talk or not, to reveal his dark secrets. Jarrod wondered if he was listening to deranged voices in his head.

Carmichael closed his eyes and drew in a long breath. He exhaled and opened his eyes. 'The book of secrets, that's where you'll find the answers.'

'The answers to what?'

'How you can find salvation,' he said as though it was obvious.

Jarrod clenched his jaw so that his back teeth grinded. 'What else?' He fought the urge to scream at him to cut the bullshit.

'Unsolved murders.'

Jarrod felt a tripwire in his gut twang. Carmichael's words hung in the air. He felt his eyes crawling over his face. Crisp silence lingered in the cramped space between them. Carmichael's nostrils flared in anticipation, staring at Jarrod unblinking. As if having heard its own starter's pistol, Jarrod's heart thudded in his chest.

He rubbed the bristles on his chin with his thumb and forefinger. 'That's what you told me that afternoon in the cemetery. I couldn't decide then if you were just bluffing to buy time or if you were in fact telling the truth. I'm still not sure. Which is it?'

'You spared my life, didn't you? Something stopped you from putting a bullet in my head right there and then. You were going to execute me, weren't you?' he said with the hint of a grin. 'I saw it in your crazy eyes. You were mad like a wild animal. Madder than me. See, Jarrod, you *are* just like me.'

'Don't make me regret not killing you. Tell me about the book and these murders.'

'Well, the thing is, I only saw it once. It was one night, not long before Vincent died. He had just performed a cleansing ritual with Clare and Edward out by the bonfire on his family property. The book was tied with leather strips and wrapped in a tattered piece of cloth. He was writing in it. I only saw the book in the light of the flames.

Bound in a red leather cover, it was. He let no one near it, guarded it with his life. He said he would slit the throat of anyone who tried to read it while he was still alive. He kept it hidden somewhere out there on that property. That night he confided in me. I'm not sure why.' He looked away, his thoughts drifting.

'What did he tell you?'

Carmichael's gaze lazily returned to Jarrod, as though he was waking from a dream. 'What?'

'I said, what did he tell you? When he confided in you?'

'He told me it contained all his secrets, that it held the key to solving some murders.'

'What murders?'

'Old ones. Vincent's murders.'

'Where is it now?'

'I don't know.'

'You don't know? You lead me along all this time and you don't fucking know?' Jarrod stood, turning for the door. 'I don't have time for this bullshit. I'm done.'

'He gave me a clue.'

'What?' said Jarrod over his shoulder as he reached for the intercom buzzer.

'He gave me a clue, like a riddle. Solve it and it will lead you straight to the book.'

'A riddle? You gotta be shitting me.' Jarrod sat back down, against his own better judgement. 'So why didn't you solve this riddle for yourself?'

'I almost did. I was so close. I just needed more time to search his property. Vincent was clever. He didn't make it easy to find.' Carmichael gave another of his smirks. 'A real trickster, he was.' His smirk evaporated. 'But you and your mate turned up and… well, we know how that all turned out.'

Jarrod swallowed against the rising anxiety, the memory of Brad's body. All that blood. He gritted his teeth. 'So, what is it? This riddle?'

'All in good time. Before I tell you what he said, there's something I want in return.'

'I told you, no deals.'

'Don't be hasty. Just hear me out. I don't want much. I'll tell you about the clue Vincent left as to where he hid the book…' his voice trailed off to nothing.

'If?'

'If you bring the book to me when you find it. Once you're done with it of course.'

Jarrod considered and folded his arms. 'Why is this book so important to you?'

'He promised his spirit would lead me to it, that the book would give me salvation. Only after he was gone could I read it. He told me it would reveal my destiny, that it contained further instructions for me to follow. I *need* to read that book. Don't you see? My body might be locked up here but the words in that book will set me free.'

'And this riddle? What makes you think I'll solve it?'

'You're a smart man, *Jarrod.* I have faith in you. Come on, you're intrigued. I know it. Vincent Miles got in your head, just like he got in mine. I know you'll find it. Don't you want to see what it says? Those unsolved murders?'

'What's the riddle?'

'Do you swear you'll bring the book to me when you find it?'

Jarrod hesitated. 'Yes. Now tell me the riddle.'

'I'll meet you halfway. I'll tell you what he told me about the murders. You can go off and play detective. If what I tell you rings true, if you discover there are in fact unsolved cases, then you'll know I'm telling the truth. Do your research, find out what you can about these cases and then come back here and tell me about them. I need to know the details. It will help me understand.'

'Understand what?'

'To understand what inspired Vincent. To learn more about his past.'

He was really starting to piss Jarrod off. He wasn't going to reveal all his cards at once. His knowledge of the riddle was the only thing he had left to leverage. He was still playing games, but Jarrod had no choice but to play along.

'Okay, you have my word. If what you tell me links up with unsolved cases, then I'll come back and discuss the details with you.' Jarrod knew he was making a deal with the devil. 'Do I have your word you'll then tell me the riddle to help find this book?'

'Have I ever lied to you?' He smiled, satisfied with the arrangement. 'For what it's worth, yes, you have my word.'

What was his word worth?

'Tell me about these cases. What did he tell you?'

'He told me he got the taste for killing when he was a teenager. He said his first sacrifice to his demons was a young boy, Tommy Baker.'

That name was familiar. Jarrod remembered hearing about the case when he was first transferred to Lockyer. Brian Rogers, a retired detective from the local CIB, told him about it one night at a Christmas party at the station. Jarrod remembered him saying the little boy's unsolved disappearance took its toll on him and the team of detectives who worked the case. Tears welled in the old detective's eyes when he recounted the story. The boy simply vanished without a trace from his family farm, right under the nose of his mother who was home at the time. Brian said the hardest thing he ever had to do was tell the boy's parents they had run out of leads and that they had to close the investigation until new information came to hand. For Brian, it was unfinished business, an open wound. It was the case he could never solve. Brian died a year later of cancer. He went to the grave not knowing the fate of that little boy. It would have to be over thirty years since he went missing.

'What did he tell you about the boy?'

'Not much, except that he was the only one who knew where his body is.'

Jarrod had his notebook out, scribbling key words. 'What other cases did he tell you about?'

'Well, he said he killed his cousin. Pushed him into a grain silo and the kid suffocated to death. Vincent seemed especially proud of that one.'

Carmichael was enjoying telling these yarns, like a schoolboy sharing a secret he'd sworn to keep.

Jarrod looked up from his notepad. 'Where? When?'

'I don't know, that's for you to figure out. That's all he told me.'

'There must be more. That can't be it.'

Carmichael gave a Cheshire grin.

'Tell me. What else?'

He held his index finger to his lips and whispered. 'His parents.' He paused, stringing out the suspense. 'He told me he killed them.'

Jarrod knew there had always been a shroud of mystery around the disappearance of Vincent Miles' parents. He was always a suspect, but nothing could ever be proven.

'Go on.'

'He said killing his parents was the moment of greatest enlightenment. He said he hated them, that killing them gave him the freedom to discover his true purpose in life.'

'Which was?'

'You already know all this.'

'What else did he tell you about his parents?'

'Only that his parents were still with him. I never understood what he meant by that. Maybe he made a wallet out of their ears.' Another humourless chuckle.

'Did he give you any more details? Think. Anything?'

'No,' Carmichael said. 'No more questions. I've told you all I know. Go find out what you can, and you'll see I'm telling the truth. Learn what you can about Vincent, and then maybe you'll solve the riddle. I'll be here waiting for you. I have all the time in the world.'

He rose from his stool and shuffled towards the door on his side of the partition.

Jarrod jumped to his feet. 'Wait!' He pressed his hands against the steel mesh. 'There's something I need to know. How did you know Vincent Miles?'

Carmichael stopped, tilted his head and looked up at the ceiling. He slowly turned around and shuffled back past the stool to the mesh divider. He leaned forward and pressed his scarred lips against the cold steel, his whisper barely audible. Jarrod turned his head so that Carmichael spoke into his ear.

'Vincent Miles was the greatest man who ever lived,' he began. 'He was the Angel of Death. He gave me the strength to seek my revenge against those who deserved to die. He simply appeared in my life one day, like an angel. I was just walking along the road from my grandfather's house. I was thinking about killing myself. Ever since this,' he touched his face, 'all I ever wanted to do was just die.'

Jarrod remembered the day Carmichael tried to burn him and Brad alive inside his grandfather's old farmhouse where he was hiding out.

'I was alone with no family. My life was a living nightmare. I had nothing, except for the memories of my mother and grandfather and hatred towards the men who had taken everything from me. Out of the blue, this four-wheel-drive pulls up beside me and Vincent winds down his window. Do you know what his first words were to me?'

Jarrod turned his head to face Carmichael. He could feel the man's warm breath through the mesh. Jarrod shook his head.

'"Are you lost, Brother? Come with me and let me help you find what you're looking for," he said. I don't know why but I just got in, no questions, and drove off with him. I never looked back. He didn't care about my scars. He saw past them, deep into my soul. We drove for hours, and he just listened. He was the only person I'd ever been able to talk to. When we arrived in Lockyer, I stayed with him at his farmhouse. There were others who followed his teachings and that's where I met Clare and Edward. He taught me to embrace my hatred and to follow my destiny. He showed me that revenge would be my salvation. After his death, I stayed in hiding in Lockyer and waited for the right time to come after the man who did this to me.' He stroked his disfigured face with his fingertips.

'I remember what you did to Frankie Arnold.' An image flashed into Jarrod's mind's eye of the macabre scene of Carmichael's stepfather's skin melting away as his body was consumed by flames.

'It was no more than he deserved,' said Carmichael, as though he was reading Jarrod's thoughts.

'And all those other people you killed? Did they deserve to die as well?'

'Like you, Jarrod, I have no regrets. So now you know my story.' He leaned away from the barrier, turned his back on Jarrod and headed for the door. He twisted his head over his shoulder. 'Don't forget our deal.'

'Guard!' he yelled, thumping the door with his fist.

The door swung open, and the guard appeared in the doorway.

'I'm done here.' Carmichael didn't bother to look back at Jarrod as he shuffled from the room, his chains clinking in the corridor as he disappeared.

Jarrod sat alone in that room listening to the distant hum of prison life, cell doors banging and prisoners heckling guards. He stood and pressed the buzzer to the intercom. He had to get out, he couldn't breathe.

THIRTY-FIVE

AS Jarrod drove out of the prison gates, the sky that had been clear that morning was now a palette of greys. The heavens grumbled and opened up, rain pelting on the roof of the car as he navigated his way out of the city. The rhythmic swoosh of the windshield wipers was hypnotic. Tyre spray from cars ahead misted the glass. As he drove along the highway, his mind consumed by a million thoughts, the glum sky darkened as night descended.

He called home on hands-free. Pat answered and her voice was loud in stereo through the car's speakers. After a quick chat, she handed the phone to the kids who took turns telling him about their day at school. He listened with a rejuvenated smile as Matty babbled on about his kangaroo paintings and Katie explained how she'd learned about the dancing rituals of the Indigenous people. He told them he'd be home late and reminded them to brush their teeth after dinner.

'Yes, Daddy, we know,' they sang in unison.

After they said goodbyes, Jarrod hung up and drove in silence. He was reassured knowing that Pat and the kids were home safe. The process of rebuilding their lives together was underway. Day by day, bit by bit.

His thoughts drifted back to his conversation with Kaleb Carmichael and the unsolved murder cases. His light mood blew away in an instant, as if stolen like smoke by the wind. He decided he wouldn't waste any time in getting a start on working the old case files. He'd get stuck in that night as soon as he got back into town. He swung by the BP service station on the outskirts of Lockyer and grabbed a coffee and meat pie from Carol. As usual, she greeted him with, 'How you doin' tonight, darl?' and a warm smile. He ate the pie on the drive into town while the coffee cooled in the centre console cup holder, ignoring the crumbs flaking into his lap.

As he pulled into the Lockyer Police Station car park, the rain fell heavier, as if welcoming him home. He grabbed the coffee and climbed from the car, covering his head with his briefcase, soaked by the relenting downpour. He dashed to the back door and placed the briefcase at his feet, hunting around in his trouser pockets for his badge. He pressed his badge ID card against the swipe panel and the orange light flashed green. After the door beeped and clicked, he stepped inside, soggy as a drowned rat.

'God damn it!' he said to no one as he wiped his drenched shoes on the doormat. He stepped into the kitchenette just off to the left of the back door and grabbed a handful of paper towels to dry off his briefcase. He gave the radio operators a wave as he slinked past the communications room doorway. When he reached the base of the staircase, he used the wooden handrail to haul himself up the steps. Upstairs, he walked past the empty CIB office and flicked on the lights to his office. He walked past Brad's empty chair and dumped his briefcase on the floor beside his desk.

He fired up the computer and sipped his coffee as the operating system chimed. The hard drive buzzed as the old machine came to life. He had already decided in what order he would research the three cold cases; the cousin who died in the grain silo and the disappearances of Tom Baker and Vincent Miles' parents. Over the last few years, the Information Bureau had started scanning and uploading old hard copy case files into the new online crime reporting system, so he was hopeful he'd find some records. The grain silo death was going to be tricky as he had little information to go on. He searched old online media reports to establish a date and location. An incident like that would have been big news in a small town.

His hunch was correct. It didn't take long to find archived news articles about the death of twelve-year-old Dillan McAllister, twenty-nine years earlier. '*BODY OF BOY FOUND IN SILO,*' read the front-page headline of the *Lockyer Chronicle*. A grainy black-and-white photograph showed a man and woman hugging, overcome with grief. The caption read '*Dillan McAllister's parents console each other after the discovery of their son's body.*' In the photo's background stood another man and woman and with them was a boy, maybe early-teens. Their faces were out of focus, giving them a ghostly, smudged appearance. Jarrod tried zooming in on the photo, but it only pixelated and distorted even more.

He clicked open the police crime reporting system and entered the dates and name. To his surprise, an index number with "sudden death" crime class appeared in the search results. The missing persons report and coroner's findings had been uploaded. According to the report, Dillan and his parents had been visiting his cousin's family. Miles was their surname. Fourteen-year-old Vincent Miles was listed as a witness. According to his version, Dillan disappeared while they were playing hide and seek on the farm. He was never considered a suspect and when Dillan's body was found the report concluded with "death by misadventure" and was closed by the coroner as an accidental death.

Jarrod's gut told him there was more to the story and he was convinced Vincent Miles had a hand in Dillan's death. He wondered if Dillan's parents were still around. He'd be keen to re-interview them. He ran a search of their names and his heart sank when he came across a fatal traffic crash report. Ten years after Dillan's death, Frank and Betty McAllister were killed in a head-on traffic crash while holidaying on the Great Ocean Road. They died never knowing what really happened to their son. The only people who were there the day Dillan died were dead or missing. Jarrod figured it was futile spending any more time on this case. Nothing would ever be proven. Whatever really happened to Dillan on top of that grain silo would remain a mystery forever. He had no doubt Vincent had taken yet another dark secret to his grave.

It was getting late and a nagging headache had nested in the dark eaves of his skull. He gave in to the onset of exhaustion and decided to call it a night. He fired Ross Benfield a quick email to report on his interview with Kaleb Carmichael, expecting he would want to be briefed. He pulled the pin and headed home. The rest could wait until the next day.

The following morning, he would start unravelling the mystery of the Tom Baker disappearance.

THIRTY-SIX

JARROD'S mind floated inside a strange realm where reality and nightmares became one. The sensation of something squirming inside his skull tormented him. He gasped for air, his lungs filling with gluggy mud that oozed from his mouth and nose. He stood in an empty room before a mirror, frosted glass smeared with dust and cobwebs. As he reached to wipe away the grime, his hand continued beyond the glass as though he had dipped his fingers in water. A hand grabbed his and yanked hard. He fought with all his strength to avoid being pulled inside. A face appeared, horrid with mangled flesh. It mimicked Jarrod's every move, a grotesque reflection smiling back at him with menace in its eyes. Fat, eyeless worms slithered from the goblin-like creature's ears and nostrils. Jarrod was being pulled with more ferocity towards the dark world inside the mirror. Behind the creature stood the blurred image of a small boy. Jarrod couldn't make out his features, distorted behind a hazy veil of mist. The boy stared at him, red eyes glistening with tears. He reached out a hand to Jarrod, beckoning for help.

Jarrod's bare feet slid on the cold floor as he was pulled closer to the terrifying creature. He tried to scream but his throat choked with foul tasting mud. The face leaned out through the mirror and opened its mouth wide, like the hinged jaws of a snake. Bright white terror filled Jarrod. As the gaping mouth threatened to swallow him, he woke with a jolt, sitting upright in bed, clammy with sweat. He pressed a hand on his sternum, his heart hamming inside his ribcage. His lungs were pistons at full speed. Blinking in the darkness, his eyes were drawn to the red digits of his alarm clock. 2:05am.

He chugged water from a bottle on his bedside table and dragged himself out of bed to check on the kids. Both slept soundly in the glow of their nightlights. He returned to bed and reached across to the vacant spot once occupied by Jayne. He yearned to smell the fragrance of her shampooed hair, but all traces of her scent were long gone. The remainder of the night was spent tossing and turning, his mind racing. He felt exhausted, but sleep was an ocean away. The night crept by at glacial speed. Dawn emerged and light seeped in through the edges of the windows. He sat up and threw his legs out of the bed and rubbed his eyes. He leaned over, his back stiff, and pulled the cord to open the blinds. Outside, a slate grey sky loomed. The remnants of overnight fog clung to the treetops like white fairy floss.

He shuffled to the ensuite and leaned against the basin, staring at himself in the mirror. Dark bags hung under his eyes, and he hardly recognised the ragged face looking back at him. There was something hollow about his eyes, vacant, like the creature in his nightmare. He stepped into the shower, reinvigorated by the hot water tingling the skin on the back of his neck as he leaned his head against the wall tiles. He inhaled the steam, dissolving the haunting images of the creature that had terrorised his dreams. When he got out, he toweled off and wiped a porthole in the condensation on the mirror. After applying shaving cream, he ran a razor across the bristles of his jawline. His mind drifted back to the nightmare which he tried to rationalise away as his subconscious brain processing the emotional impact of everything that had happened. Whatever was causing them, wherever they came from, the nightmares were a constant companion. Rather than fighting them, he resolved to make sense of them, even to be guided by them. Hidden within their horror, maybe he would find the answers he was looking for.

He dressed and went into the kitchen and concocted a brew of coffee. Out on the front porch, he sat on the top step and blew steam from the rim of his mug, listening to the early morning symphony of sparrows and crested pigeons. They didn't seem bothered by the gloomy weather. Pat, a habitual early riser, came out nursing in both hands a cup of green tea. She joined him on the top step. For a while they just sat in silence, sipping their hot drinks, listening to the birds.

'You got home late,' she said, staring out towards the street.

'Yeah, sorry. I lost track of time when I got back into the office. Kaleb Carmichael kinda got into my head yesterday at the prison. I was going through a historical case connected with Vincent Miles.'

Pat glanced at him with a disapproving frown, her eyes drawn in tight. 'Don't you think it's time to let all this go, to put this case behind you? Behind us?'

'I can't. That's the thing, I just can't let it go. I had another nightmare last night. I can't shake them. I feel like this unresolved – *thing* will keep nagging at me until I solve these cases.'

'Maybe you need to see a sleep therapist?'

'I don't need some hippy therapist and their herbal remedies. I need to solve these old cases.'

'Is it your burden to bear, Jarrod? Why do you have to be the one to solve these cases? You've done enough, surely?'

Jarrod stared into Pat's troubled eyes. 'I feel like it chose me. I have no say in it. All this time, something has been pulling me closer and closer to…'

'To what, Jarrod?' Pat interrupted. 'What is it you're chasing? Do you think you'll ever find peace chasing these ghosts?'

Jarod's eyes lowered to his coffee as though the murky brown liquid would reveal the answers. He shook his head to banish those thoughts and raised the mug to his lips. No clarity came as he swallowed. 'I dunno, Pat.' He dwelt on her question some more. 'It sounds crazy, but it feels as though something is inside me, some spirit or presence that wants me to set them free – to find them peace.'

Pat sipped her tea and looked up at the grey skyline. 'Well, if that's true, I pray you find what you're looking for. For your sake and the kids'.'

She finished her tea and tipped the dregs over the railing into the garden. She leaned on Jarrod's shoulder as she stood with creaking knees. 'I'm here for you, Jarrod. You know that don't you?'

'That's one of the last things she ever said to me. Did you know that?'

'What do you mean?'

'That's exactly what Jayne said to me just before the crash. She said she was here for me. You two are so alike.' Jarrod gave her a hint of a smile.

Pat smiled back, her eyes sad. 'I guess we were. Anyway, the kids will be awake soon, so I'll start making pancakes.' She headed back inside and left Jarrod alone with his thoughts. That was typical of Pat, bouncing back with a stiff upper lip whenever a sad thought got her down. She refused to dwell on those moments and focused on the here and now, on what had to be done today. Maybe it was her way of distracting her mind from those sad thoughts, by keeping busy and tending to the needs of the kids. He decided to take her lead and followed her inside where the business of a new day was about to begin. The kids were soon up and about, and breakfast bustled. It was a welcome distraction, as were the pancakes.

~

Jarrod arrived at the station by 8:00am and as he reached the top of the stairs, Ross Benfield called out from his office. 'O'Connor! You got a minute?'

'Yeah, Boss,' Jarrod replied and took a detour through the CIB day room to Benfield's office. 'What's up?' he said as he poked his head inside the door.

'Come in, son. Sit down,' Benfield said from behind his enormous desk. He gestured with a nod for him to take a seat in one of two chairs positioned opposite.

Jarrod sat and waited for Benfield to speak but the man was in no rush to break the awkward silence. He leaned back in his reclining executive chair and folded his arms, considering Jarrod over his glasses. 'How are ya travelling, Jarrod? How's Pat and the kids?'

'They're good, Boss. All things considered.'

'Of course. Glad to hear it. How are you holding up?'

'Not getting a lot of sleep, but I'm okay.'

'I'm not surprised. Give it time.'

'So, um, do you need to speak to me?'

Benfield leaned forward, elbows on his desk. His eyes bounced to the computer screen and back to Jarrod. 'I read the occurrence sheet you submitted last night.'

'And?'

'Tell me what's *not* in the report.'

'Like what?'

'Come on, Jarrod. I can read between the lines. There's a lot more to it. What did Carmichael have to say for himself?'

Jarrod assembled his thoughts. 'He's still playing games.'

'Yeah, well, what did you expect? What's he up to now?'

'He said that Vincent Miles told him about some unsolved murders, mostly historical. Miles wrote the details in some kind of book, location of the bodies, that kind of thing. The book is hidden somewhere on the Miles property.'

'A book? Did he tell you where it is?'

'Not quite.'

Benfield shot Jarrod a skeptical look, one eyebrow raised.

Jarrod thought about the riddle Carmichael had mentioned. 'He said he had, um, information about where the book is hidden.'

'And let me guess, he'll give you that information in return for something?'

Jarrod nodded, now aware of how all this sounded.

'How do you know he's not just playing you, trying to get inside your head? More of his power games.'

'I don't know, not for sure. But my gut tells me there's some truth in it.'

Benfield removed his glasses and polished the lenses with his tie, more out of habit than of need. 'Tell me then. What does he want in return?'

'He said if I verify what he told me about these historical cases, to prove he's telling the truth, then he'll give me the information to find the book. But not before.'

'And what else does he want?'

Jarrod hesitated. 'He wants the book.'

'What? Come on, Jarrod, you can't be serious? If this book even exists, and contains information about unsolved cases, then it's evidence. We can't hand that to him. Please tell me you didn't promise him that?'

Jarrod broke eye contact and looked down at his hands. 'I didn't promise him anything.'

Benfield put his glasses back on and sighed, clearly not convinced. 'Go on then, tell me about these cases.'

'The first one was the death of a boy named Dillan McAllister, Miles' cousin. The case goes back nearly thirty years. It was written off as an accident. Kid suffocated in a grain silo on the Miles property.'

'It probably was an accident,' said Benfield.

'Apparently Miles was behind it. But anyway, it's a dead end. I looked into it. We'll never know for sure. All the key witnesses are dead or missing. Not worth dedicating any more time and resources to it.'

'Well, that's good news then. No point flogging a dead horse.' A drawn-out pause. 'What are the other cases?'

'Another missing boy, Tommy Baker. Around the same time.'

'Tommy Baker. I've heard about that case. That goes back a while. It was even before my time, if you can believe that. Kid just vanished. The case was never solved.'

'And then there was the disappearance of Vincent Miles' parents.'

'Yeah, I know about that case. Apparently, they just took off, abandoned their son and the farm.'

'And you swallow that story? It's a bit convenient, don't you think?'

'I have to agree with you. The case was written off by the

investigating coppers back then. I always wondered how seriously they looked into it. Too quick to write it off, if you ask me. Even the homicide cold case squad showed no interest, too many cases on their backlog, apparently.'

'I want to look into both cases. Vincent Miles is the missing piece of the puzzle. Carmichael might be stringing us along, but how could he have known about these cases on his own? He wasn't even born when they happened.'

'So, you want to re-open these cases? You know we don't have the resources to take staff offline right now. Our arses are hanging out of our pants just keeping up with jobs coming in.'

'Let me look into them, see what I can dig up.'

'Why? So you can report back to Carmichael so he can get his jollies?'

'It could be a means to an end. If it gets him talking about where this book might be hidden, who knows what other cold cases we might uncover.'

'I dunno, Jarrod. We're already pushed to the brink as it is, keeping up with the current caseload. Our pending jobs list is growing every day. We're still waiting on HR to find a temporary replacement for Brad, but none of the stations in the city or neighbouring regions can spare any staff, or so they tell me. I'm sorry, son, but the world is getting on with its business whether we like it or not. I know it's been tough on you lately, but we have to focus our resources on current crime. The District Officer tore me a new arsehole just this morning about the drop in clear-up rates lately.'

'I know, Boss. Can you spare one of your guys, maybe Dawsey, to take on my case load for one more week? That's all I need.'

Benfield pinched the bridge of his nose with his thumb and forefinger. He looked as though he'd been sleeping rougher than Jarrod had. He sighed. 'One week. I'll give you seven days to do what you have to do and then I need you back on deck focusing on our current crime. Is that clear?'

'Yes, Boss. Thank you.'

'Well, get to it then.' Benfield swivelled his chair towards his computer screen. Conversation over, Jarrod's cue to exit.

Jarrod lifted his weary carcass off the chair and headed to his own office. The first order of business was making himself another potent brew of instant coffee. He then settled in front of his computer. As the hard drive whirred and clunked, Jarrod sat hypnotised by the flashing cursor in the centre of the screen while the central crime recording system loaded. Being forced to rely on outdated police computers meant they were always two steps behind the crooks. Even the local grubs had better computers than the department. The police logo and login window finally appeared on screen.

The system accepted his security credentials and he was in. He rested his fingers on the keyboard and hesitated, his eyes fixed on the blank fields enticing him to enter the search criteria. Which case should he explore first? The missing Baker boy or the disappearance of Vincent Miles' parents? His mind drifted back to the hazy image of the boy in his nightmare. The kid seemed so alone, trapped in a hellish world guarded by a vile creature. He had reached out to Jarrod, helpless and innocent. Jarrod knew right then which case to examine first and typed in the words "Thomas-Baker-Missing". He scrolled through the long list of search hits until he came across an index number referring to an archived hard file of a thirty-one-year-old missing persons case. The reference details read *"BAKER, Thomas-5463459/CR/MP-LOCKYER-EVIDENCE-ARCHIVE"*.

That was the only digital trace of the file which pre-dated the electronic transfer of old case notes, witness statements and reports into the new computerised system introduced in the late-nineties. Jarrod gave a long, frustrated sigh as the realisation hit him that his next port of call would be rummaging through dust covered boxes in the evidence archive room in the station basement. He tried his luck with the Miles missing persons case and searched "Miles-Missing" and an even longer list appeared on screen – one of twenty. Running his eyes down the long list of case files, he clicked through page after page until an entry on page twelve jumped out at him. *"MILES, Margaret/Gerald-3792462/CR/MP-LOCKYER-EVIDENCE-ARCHIVE"*. From the dates, the cases were five years apart. Jarrod opened the bottom drawer of his desk and retrieved a tattered stack of manila folders bound by a purple hand-tied ribbon. The name on the top folder read *"MILES, Vincent"*. He found Vincent Miles' date of birth and calculated that he would have been thirteen-years-old when little Tom Baker went missing, and eighteen when his parents disappeared.

Armed with a printout of the two case reference numbers, Jarrod headed downstairs passed the meal room and down the long internal corridor towards the station cells. Off to the left, immediately before the watchhouse main entry, was an obscure door to the exhibit room. He peered through the square, porthole-sized window and saw the top of Des "Rocky" Turner's balding head leaning back against the headrest of a reclining office chair. He wore a tan knitted sleeveless cardigan over a crumpled short sleeve business shirt. The white collar was stained yellow from years of sweat and skin grime. His grey hair was slicked back with a comb he dipped in hair oil. His feet were propped up on his desk as he held up a newspaper and turned the pages in the form guide section. He was sporting a pair of flat-sole, vinyl shoes with Velcro straps straight out of a K-Mart discount basket. Forty years ago, Des was a banter weight amateur boxer, as evidenced by his flattened nose that kinked to the left. Ironically, that wasn't how he got the nickname.

The name "Rocky" had stuck after a send-off in the "beer garden" at the back of the station. Souped to the eyeballs, Des became feisty as he usually did when he'd had a skin full. Fists raised, he started shadow boxing up in the grill of one of the new young constables. Poor kid didn't know how to react. Des KOed himself with one of his wild air swings and ended up on his arse in the garden. He was taken home to his long-suffering wife in a blue light taxi. By the next day someone had stuck up a sign reading "Rocky's Crib" on the exhibit office door and it remained there to this day. Des wore the nickname like a badge of honour.

The trick with Des was to lodge exhibits in the morning while he was sober. It was common knowledge he was next to useless after lunch. He'd slip down to the Imperial Hotel and come back half pickled. He was just months off retirement and spent his days doing as little as possible. The bosses kept off his case, making allowances for the forty years he had served as a station administration officer. They figured as long as no exhibits went missing, they would let him bow out graciously, or in Rocky's case, ungraciously.

Jarrod tapped on the window with his knuckles and waited as Rocky cocked his head and peered over his bifocals, not bothering to take his feet down or lower the newspaper. Jarrod envied Rocky's don't-give-a-shit attitude. In a well-practised motion, he reached over without looking and pressed the button to the electronic door lock which buzzed and then clicked. Jarrod pushed open the door and was hit by a wall of arctic air-conditioned air carrying out with it an aroma, a subtle blend of Old Spice and moth balls.

'Morning Des. Got any hot tips for this Saturday?'

Des tapped his nose with his forefinger. 'A seasoned punter never gives away his tips. But if he does, he's giving you a bum steer. That's a fact.'

'Thanks for the advice. I'll take that on board.'

'I didn't know you had a flutter on the ponies, Jarrod.'

'Nah, I don't, Des. I can't tell a horse's arse from its face.'

Des gave a hearty chortle followed by a phlegmy coughing fit. He swung his feet off the desk and leaned forward, coughing into a handkerchief. Jarrod thumped Rocky's back between his shoulder blades with an open palm until Rocky hacked into his hanky.

'Thanks. I needed to clear that.'

'Gotta give up those nasty rollies,' said Jarrod.

'You my wife?'

'No.'

'Then don't you start.' Rocky wiped his mouth and slid the hanky into his trouser pocket. 'So, how can I help you, lad?'

Jarrod handed him the printout. 'I need to find these old files.'

Rocky held the sheet of paper with an outstretched arm and squinted as he studied the information. The wrinkles around his eyes stretched as his brow became a concerned frown. He peered up at Jarrod over his specs. 'I know both cases. I handled the exhibits. I'll never forget them. Why do you want to go dragging up the past? There's nothing in those old boxes but dead ends. You sure you want to dig up those buried skeletons?'

'Yes Des, I need those boxes. Will you help me or not?'

Rocky stared at him and sighed. He reached over and grabbed a huge bunch of keys labelled with coloured tags all hanging from a silver ring. 'Follow me,' he said with a groan as he lifted his stout frame from the chair.

He shuffled towards the roller cage door to the exhibit storage area behind his desk. His stumpy fingers found the right key and he unlocked the cage. He bent down and heaved it open with a loud, metallic shudder. He pushed the cage door all the way up and disappeared inside the darkened storage room. Florescent bulbs flickered and the room illuminated with a dull glow. The room was the size of a double car garage and was filled with rows of metal shelves and racks crammed with brown paper exhibit bags, boxes and plastic bags with tags. In the furthest, darkest corner of the room were two large boxes each occupying their own lower shelf. They were in isolation, separated from other exhibits as though contaminated with toxic materials.

Jarrod followed Des down the aisle until they came to the boxes. Both were non-descript cardboard storage cartons with lids fastened with masking tape. In black Nikko pen the name MILES was scrawled across the lid of one box and BAKER on the other.

'Everything that's left of both cases is in those boxes. Some records were misplaced over the years but most of the original witness statements and investigator logs should all be in there.' Des shook his head and then looked up at Jarrod. 'These haven't seen the light of day for years. Dozens of detectives have worked these cases over the years. No one has come close to solving either of them. I don't know what you expect to find that no one else has, but I hope you find what you're looking for.'

'So do I, Des. So do I.'

'I'll leave you with these, then. Knock yourself out.' Rocky shuffled away towards his awaiting form guide. 'Turn the lights out and close the gate when you're finished,' he said with disinterest.

Jarrod stood alone in that dark corner of the exhibit room, staring at two boxes whose mysteries had eluded a generation of detectives long before he came along. He raised a hand to his mouth and chewed his thumbnail, considering his plan of attack. He had to look at these cases with fresh eyes, approach them from a new perspective. Challenge all assumptions.

After locking up and killing the lights, Jarrod lugged both boxes out to Rocky's front office and stacked them on the floor.

Rocky put his newspaper down, sighing at the inconvenience, and thumbed through the pages of a huge logbook on the front counter. He peered over his bifocals. 'Keep the boxes for as long as you need. The dead have all the time in the world.'

Jarrod nudged the Miles box with the toe of his shoe. 'So, you reckon they're dead, Mr and Mrs Miles? It was written off as a missing persons case, wasn't it?'

'Blind Freddie could tell you that's a crock.' Rocky threw his hands in the air. 'But hey, I'm not a copper. What would I know?'

'And the little Baker boy? What was your gut feeling about that?'

'I reckon his body is still out there, not far from his home.'

'But wasn't the entire area searched?'

'Yep, but big search area. Bottomless quarry dam that was never properly dredged. The possibilities are endless. But he's out there, mark my words.'

'You reckon the two cases are connected?'

'Of course, they have to be.'

'How hard was Vincent Miles looked at as a suspect?'

'Not hard enough, if you ask me.'

Jarrod looked down at the boxes. 'Right then, time to take a fresh look.'

'Good luck, you'll need it.'

Jarrod made two trips, carrying one box at a time out along the corridor and up the stairs to his office. He cleared space in one corner and used a pair of scissors to slice open the seal to both boxes. Years of dust coated his fingers. As he opened the lids to each box, he was hit by the musty smell of old paper.

He had no idea what he was looking for. As he unloaded bundles of reports and old witness statements, he assembled them in chronological order. Disturbing the contents of these old files felt as though he was waking the ghosts of the dead. As he spread the old case notes across the carpet, he hoped he had the resolve to see it through to the end, no matter which dark road he found himself following.

Tom Baker and Vincent Miles' parents had been long forgotten. They deserved more. He needed to make things right, for both their sakes and his own.

THIRTY-SEVEN

JARROD spent the next two days sifting through old documents, looking for anomalies, similarities or anything that might have been overlooked. He sorted police reports and witness statements into chronological order, firstly focusing his attention on the Baker case. On a bright Saturday morning, Tommy vanished from the front yard of his farmhouse while his mother was attending to the washing. '*I went inside just for a few minutes to collect a new basket of washing. He had been playing on his swing set. When I came out and checked on him only minutes later, he and his bike were gone,*' explained Helen Baker in her witness statement. From that moment on, there were no sightings or the slightest trace of where he had disappeared to. Her husband wasn't home, his movements in town verified by other witnesses.

From all accounts, the abduction of Tommy Baker was devastating for the residents of Lockyer and loomed as a dark cloud over the entire town. It had stripped away the façade that Lockyer was a safe place to live. Once immune from the scourges of the city, the quaint rural town had lost its innocence. The boy had vanished without a trace from the front yard of his farmhouse. The community was shrouded in suspicion and rumour. The disappearance received national attention, however the case remained unsolved. As the agonising years slipped by, the investigation ground to a halt and found its way onto the Missing Persons Unit cold case pile.

An A4 size writing pad with a coiled wire binder and cardboard covers had been used to store pages of thirty-year-old newspaper clippings. Each had been cut out with precision and glued to the pages. The clippings were crinkled at the edges and faded with a tinge of yellow the colour of nicotine stains. The scrapbook proved to be a simple but effective method of preserving this snapshot in time. The clippings towards the front were bold headlines covering the first few weeks of the investigation. 'BOY MISSING', 'POLICE BAFFLED BY BOY'S DISAPPEARANCE', 'SEARCH WIDENS FOR MISSING BOY' and 'TOMMY BAKER MYSTERY - WHERE IS HE?'

The articles included grainy, black and white photographs of police and locals shoulder to shoulder searching bushland and a close-up shot of the boy's parents. Helen Baker was a pretty woman with dark hair styled into a wavy bob. She wore a simple white blouse and her eyes, glassy with tears, stared down the camera lens with a look of helplessness. Jarrod's heart sank at the sight of this poor woman who would never learn the fate of her precious little boy. Her husband, Jack Baker, had one arm around her shoulders in solidarity. He wasn't looking at the camera. Instead, his face was turned towards his wife, rigid in stony anguish. He was about the same age as his wife, early thirties and he boasted mutton chop sideburns above a strong jawline. He wore a wide-brimmed hat and a long sleeve work shirt rolled up high to his biceps. He had strong looking hands and the bronzed skin of a man who worked the land.

Jarrod flicked through the scrapbook and came across another headline. 'IS A CHILD ABDUCTOR AMONG US?' The article included quotes from locals who feared their sleepy community was harbouring a child killer. *How well do we really know our neighbours? Children should be safe in their own front yards. I'm scared there's a wolf hiding in sheep's clothing. Everyone is a suspect,'* one lady said. The article included quotes from Detective Sergeant Brian Rogers who appealed to the public for any information that could help solve the case. *'Behind the polite greetings and niceties exchanged by townsfolk as they pass in the street, mistrust and fear lingers,'* the author of the article speculated.

Jarrod turned the pages of the scrapbook and it became apparent that as time had slipped by, the clippings were no longer headlines. As the case grew cold so too did the media's interest and the story disappeared into obscurity with only the occasional and brief follow up story to report '*Police have run out of leads as the investigation into missing eight-year-old Tommy Baker continues to hit dead ends.*' On the first anniversary of the little boy's disappearance a special edition cover of the *Lockyer Chronicle* ran the '*Where is Tommy Baker?*' campaign and included a montage of photos capturing the different phases of Tommy's short life. There were photos of a toddler in his father's gumboots, riding a pony as a five-year-old and the most recent photo of him sitting proudly on his brand-new little BMX bicycle. The freckles on his fair skin, sprinkled across the bridge of his nose, were prominent in the photo. The image of the boy's face burned into Jarrod's mind.

Photos of a candlelit vigil on the lawns of the Town Hall completed the timeline of images. Jarrod studied the photos of Tommy Baker hoping for a glimpse of recognition however the boy's smiling face bore no resemblance to the blurred images of the small figure that haunted his nightmares. *What did he really expect?*

Jarrod located an old map of the area showing the Baker farmhouse, marked with a red cross, and surrounding search areas drawn in pencil in rectangular quadrants. The search area extended to nearby farms and the pine forest bordered by the old quarry. A knot tightened in Jarrod's stomach as he was jolted with a flashback of the lifeless bodies of those two boys being hauled out of the quarry lake in the stolen Mustang. He remembered the strange sensation that had taken hold of him the last time he had visited the quarry. A spirit-like presence had willed him to return, a force drawing him back towards a ghost-like image clouding his thoughts. He had hoped he would never have to return to that place.

Without any indication of Tommy's last known direction, the search area expanded to a radius of ten kilometres from the Baker farmhouse. To the west, the Baker and Miles properties met, divided by a five-hundred-metre-long wire fence. Every shed, vehicle, stable and farmhouse was searched. Volunteers with tracker hounds were brought in, however no reliable scent could be detected. According to the police reports, searches on horseback and trailbikes through the forest and vicinity of the quarry lake found no clues. The lake, littered with car bodies and debris, and water with poor visibility and high levels of toxicity, was simply too treacherous to send divers into. It was like throwing a dart at a map to choose where to deploy resources.

As Jarrod read through the investigation documents, he came across witness statements by the Bakers' neighbours. Margaret and Gerald Miles and their thirteen-year-old son, Vincent, were interviewed but had no information to assist the investigation. In Vincent's statement he said he knew Tommy from catching the same school bus into town, but he had not seen him the day he went missing. Vincent said he hadn't left their property all day, however his parents couldn't vouch for his movements in the morning when they left him alone when they attended a church service. In Margaret's statement she stated Vincent outright refused to come with them.

As Jarrod held Vincent's single page type-written statement up to the light of his computer screen, he moved his thumb over the boy's signature. At the bottom right of the document, scribed in inked cursive letters, read *"Vincent M"*. Oddly, the tiny shape of a hexagonal prism was drawn beside his name. The image reminded Jarrod of the strange Metatron's Cube that would later become the symbol behind Vincent Miles' delusions of divine power. It was the first real sign that his fixations may have manifested when he was just a boy. Jarrod guessed no one would ever know what triggered Vincent Miles' deranged mind. However, it seemed he was never flagged as a potential suspect and there was no record of him being re-interviewed by police.

After reading the last of the documents in the Tommy Baker file, Jarrod assembled them in order and stacked them back into the storage box. He remembered what Kaleb Carmichael had told him about Vincent Miles' admissions of being involved in Tommy's disappearance. He was determined more than ever to find the truth.

Jarrod turned his attention to the second box marked *MILES*. It was lighter and contained only a small bundle of documents and photographs. It was apparent that the disappearance of Margaret and Gerald Miles received very little attention compared to the Tom Baker case. He read through the missing persons report and attached witness statements. According to the report, forty-eight-year-old Gerald and forty-six-year-old Margaret were last seen by their son, Vincent, after an argument about him not going out to find work. In his statement, he gave a detailed account of how they packed their belongings into their orange Range Rover and left him there at the farmhouse. He said they had decided to start their lives afresh without him.

He produced a bundle of short letters written in the same handwriting, allegedly penned by his father. The letters wrote of how they had found a nice place to settle down and for him not to worry. They would send him money and when the time was right, they would come home to visit him. Eventually the letters stopped and according to Vincent he never heard from them again. Police were only alerted to their disappearance a week after their last sighting after members of their church community raised the alarm. Margie and Gerry stopped coming to prayer meetings and services which was totally out of character for them. They were so embedded with their community, no one could believe they would just pack up and leave without saying goodbye. The whole story sounded absurd.

Police obtained handwriting samples from Vincent, but they didn't match. Vincent was unable to produce the envelopes, stating he had thrown them away. There was no evidence of where the letters had been posted from and he said he didn't think to check. It just didn't add up and Vincent Miles remained a suspect. The case, although officially still listed as "unsolved", hit a standstill when no evidence could be found of foul play, despite there being no proof of life. They had simply vanished. Police searched the property and not even the slightest trace of evidence could be found. Margaret and Gerald Miles' bedroom had been cleared out of most of their personal effects and the car was never located. Had they skipped town and left their troublesome eighteen-year-old son to fend for himself? Or had they been the victims of a perfect murder? Without modern technology the investigation ground to a halt and eventually found its way into the station archives.

According to subsequent reports, Vincent Miles disappeared for over a decade but later came to the attention of police as his anti-social behavior escalated. He would be arrested in some outback town and disappear after his release, only to resurface in another part of the country causing more trouble. At some point he returned to his family home in Lockyer but regular stints in prison meant he rarely spent any long periods of time there. It was around this time that he met Roxy and the trajectory of his out-of-control life had hurtled towards Jarrod and his family.

A faded colour polaroid photo of the Miles family in happier times was attached to the inside cover of the main file with a paper clip. A tall and handsome young Vincent, maybe sixteen-years-old, stood between his parents as they posed for the photograph at the base of the stairs to their farmhouse. Vincent wore an unsettling frown, and he had one arm around his mother's waist and the other arm around his father's shoulders. His father was an impressive, athletic looking man and stood slightly taller than his son. He wore a crisp white, long-sleeved business shirt and black tie and trousers. Jarrod made out the shape of a cross on the front of a bible clutched in his hands. Margaret Miles was a stately looking woman with pale skin and brown hair in a short, wavy perm. She wore a sleeveless white blouse and cotton gloves, knee-length floral skirt and white high heel shoes. A white handbag hung from her forearm. There was no date on the photo, but Jarrod guessed it was taken some time in the late nineteen-eighties. He wondered who took the photo. Perhaps a friend from their congregation? In the background of the photo, the Range Rover was parked in the driveway.

Jarrod studied the photo, hoping it would reveal some answers.

He looked at the body language of Margaret and Gerald Miles. Both clenched their hands to the front, and if Jarrod wasn't mistaken, they appeared to lean away from their son's outstretched embrace. Their smiles were strained, uncomfortable. He sensed their son's touch made them uncomfortable. A young Vincent Miles stared into Jarrod's eyes with a look of foreboding, as though at that moment he already knew his fate.

Jarrod packed the photograph and file back into the box and slid it into the corner of his office alongside the Baker box. He hadn't uncovered the truth to these mysteries. It was naïve to think the answers would jump out at him. He needed to dig deeper. Kaleb Carmichael was the key. He needed to pay him another visit.

<h1 style="text-align:center">THIRTY-EIGHT</h1>

JARROD stared at his watch, mesmerised by the minute hand ticking in slow motion. Each second laboured against an invisible force pulling against time itself. The universe conspired against all who had the ill fortune of being trapped behind the walls of the high security prison. Slowness of time ground away at their sanity. Inmates endured a parallel dimension where the days, months and years of their real-world sentence blurred into an infinite cycle of endless days and tortured nights. Jarrod was free to leave at his choosing, yet he felt the air grow tight around him as each second passed.

As his watch ticked over to 12:01pm, the familiar clinking of leg iron chains grew louder in the hallway. He sat anxiously behind the steel mesh divider in the same interview cell where he and Carmichael had last spoken. A wave of disgust rolled through him as Kaleb Carmichael's ragged frame filled the doorway as he was led into the room by two guards. The chain links secured to his manacles rattled as he shuffled inside. His eyes fixed on Jarrod's, his gaze harsh as granite. His face was stony, expressionless. As he sat on the stainless-steel stool, the lead guard gave Jarrod a nod. He nodded back and the guards slipped from the room, closing the heavy steel door behind them. This time Jarrod would wait for Carmichael to speak first. Jarrod folded his arms tight against his chest and swivelled his chair from side to side. Jarrod held Carmichael's gaze, counting each second until he reached sixty. Carmichael's concentrated scowl gave way to a bitter grin.

Finally, he broke the silence. 'You're a hard man to read, Jarrod. What's going on in that head of yours?'

Jarrod inhaled deep through his nose, exhaled and then said, 'I'm wondering how killing innocent people makes you feel. Is there a shred of pity or humanity inside you?'

Carmichael's grin soured. He leaned forward, his elbows propped on the steel bench. 'Oh, I feel something, *Jarrod*. But it isn't pity. It's unbridled power running through my veins as I rip the life-force from their body. It's the ultimate rush, what us humans were born to do. We were bred as the planet's supreme killing machines. The only difference between you and me is that I have the courage to act on our primal instincts. I feed the black wolf inside me. He's hungry, Jarrod. So hungry! Feed the black wolf inside you and your eyes will open to the possibilities.'

'Is that what Vincent Miles taught you?'

Carmichael leaned back. 'I suppose he did.'

'But you want more. You think this book of secrets has all the answers, that it will bring you enlightenment?'

'Of course. It's the next step in my evolution.'

'Evolution into what? Are you planning on growing horns and wings so you can fly out from these walls and breathe fire down on the rest of us?'

Carmichael burst into maniacal hysterics. A twisted shriek of laughter echoed against the concrete walls of the confined space. Jarrod felt a wave of cold dread rise through him. Carmichael's laughter cut short, and his face transformed into a devilish grimace. Jarrod's heart thumped hard inside his chest. Carmichael's eyes locked onto his. It was like staring into an insect's eyes. There was nothing human in them.

Carmichael closed his eyes as though lost in prayer. 'My spirit will rise from this shell of a body and away from this pit of despair. I will join Vincent and we will live on forever in paradise.'

'But you need that book, don't you? You can't achieve this evolution without it?'

Carmichael's eyes snapped open. 'Yes, I need that book,' he whispered.

'Then let's cut the shit. You know that's why I'm here. I did what you asked. I pulled the old files. What you told me checks out. I've gone right through them. I have no doubt Vincent Miles was somehow involved, but without more information, they're still a dead end. What's the riddle? Help me find that book.'

Carmichael rubbed his chin and fidgeted with the chain fed through a steel ring welded to his handcuffs. He lingered on Jarrod's words, deep in thought. '*Look into the eye that watches the dying sun.* That's what Vincent told me. He said that's where I'd find the book after he was gone.'

'What eye? What does that mean?'

'How the hell should I know?' he snapped, irritated. 'I've turned that farmhouse upside down and found nothing. No inscriptions on the floors or walls, no engravings, no instructions. I walked around that property for days. I found nothing. It's out there though, I know it.'

He studied Jarrod's face and his eyes widened with hope. 'You're the key. Everything that's happened since Vincent died has brought you and me together. It's fate. You'll unlock the riddle. I know it in my heart.'

'You don't have a heart.'

'Maybe not in that sense of the word,' he said with a grin. 'But I have the same muscle inside my ribcage pumping blood and life to every part of my body.' He ran fingers over his scars. 'But I won't have any use for this horrid body much longer. Bring me that book so my spirit can rise. You'll then be rid of me forever and you'll solve those murders. Win-win. Find that book!'

He shot to his feet and turned his back. 'Guard!' he called out and the door swung open. He was led away in silence.

Look into the eye that watches the dying sun. Jarrod didn't know what that meant, but he knew he had to return to the root of his nightmares.

THIRTY-NINE

JARROD escaped the prison confines and negotiated the quickest route out of the suffocating city until he hit the freeway towards Lockyer. The urban sprawl thinned, and his feeling of dread lifted as the last traces of the city disappeared in his rear-view mirror. As the scenery changed to open country, he could breathe again. But he wasn't going home. Within two hours he was on the Lockyer bypass road heading towards the Miles property on the western side of town.

He veered off the sealed road, leaving behind the heat haze shimmering above the bitumen. Bitter memories resurfaced as the Miles farmhouse rose above the horizon, drawing nearer as dirt and stones crunched beneath the car tyres. The derelict structure now had a distinct lean. Its log stumps bent under its weight and had shifted off their vertical axis from the movement of earth at its foundation. Decades of harsh summers, drought and abrasive winds had stripped away its protective outer layer and white paint flaked from the weatherboards. The corrugated iron roof sheeting was bronzed with rust and curled up at its edges. It was a blight on the landscape, a stark reminder of the horrors that had occurred there.

As he turned down the gravel driveway, his instincts told him the cursed place still concealed secrets. The front windows were dark eyes peering out across the barren landscape. Late-afternoon sun stung Jarrod's eyes. A wrought-iron gate dangled from broken hinges, an open invitation for anyone brave enough to venture up the path to the veranda's warped steps.

Jarrod pulled the car up in the driveway and killed the engine. He lowered his window and listened to the long grass whispering in the breeze. He sat still, heart racing, and was struck by the eerie silence.

Fragments of glass glistened in the dirt just up ahead. His skin went cold as a flashback raced through his mind of the moment the windshield exploded and Brad's throat was torn open. He remembered the coppery smell of his blood and his last gasps for air. Closing his eyes, he shook his head to banish those bitter memories back to the dark corner of his subconsciousness. He swung the door open and willed himself from the car. Surveying the immediate vicinity, he shielded his eyes from the sun with his hand. He stepped over the broken glass and walked through the open driveway gate towards the crumbling garage.

Tattered police crime scene tape flapped in the breeze like a kite tail, snagged in the barbed wire of the side fence. He glanced into the open garage where the rotting carcass of the old Holden cowered in shame. Cobwebs clung from the side mirrors and tangled grass had sprouted from the dirt floor and engulfed the wheels. Jarrod went inside where the air was cool but thick with dust and decay. It was the same as the last few times he'd been there, cluttered with irrigation equipment, a collection of jars and tea boxes full of machinery components and junk. He knew the car and shed had been turned upside down by the forensic guys so he wasn't planning on wasting time searching in there again.

He walked back out into the daylight towards the house and climbed the rickety front stairs. As he stepped onto the veranda, the floorboards creaked. He looked out towards where his car was parked in the driveway and beyond the front yard. It was the same view Kaleb Carmichael had from his vantage point inside the house before he opened fire on him and Brad. He turned towards the front door and placed his hand on the rusting knob. The door was unlocked but as he turned the knob, he had to shove with his shoulder to loosen the stiff hinges. The door opened inwards with a loud groan. He stepped inside and moved down the hallway. The sound of his shoes on the timber floors echoed in the bare space of empty rooms. Inside, there was nothing he hadn't seen before, but he needed to look again with fresh eyes. He searched floorboards and walls for secret compartments or inscriptions. There was nothing. He felt no sense of Vincent Miles' ghost, no signs that he had ever been there. The place had been stripped bare, an empty shell. Whatever hadn't been seized or destroyed in the aftermath of the Vincent Miles case had been looted by locals. The entire house had been forensically searched but he needed to satisfy his curiosity, to know for certain nothing had been missed.

He went back outside and retrieved his torch from the car and found a step ladder lying in the dirt under the house. Lugging the ladder up the stairs, he positioned it in the middle of the lounge room. He climbed up the ladder and slid open the manhole. Dust danced in the light beam of his torch as he inspected the ceiling, only to discover a dead rat and Daddy-long-leg spiders. A discarded latex glove and boot prints in the dust on the ceiling beams were the last traces of the forensics team who had last been up there. He climbed down and brushed the cobwebs and dust from his clothes. Satisfied there was nothing more to be found, he breathed in the clean country air as he stepped outside. He swore to himself he would never set foot inside that house ever again.

He climbed down the stairs and headed to the back of the house where old tractors and farm machinery were littered around the property being devoured by rust. To the west was the hill where Kaleb Carmichael had set up his camp. The lower paddocks behind the farmhouse had been consumed by wild lantana and native scrub had reclaimed the cleared land. A mob of kangaroos, disinterested by his presence, lazed in the shade of a clump of wattle trees. The land rose to a slope towards the east, where Kaleb Carmichael had escaped on the motorcycle towards the McNelly farm. Searching the property was like looking for a needle in a field of haystacks. An emu parade search of the property had been conducted, using all available police officers and SES volunteers following the discovery of Vincent Miles' bunker. Carmichael said he'd been searching the property for days. Jarrod had no idea what he was looking for or what he expected to find that hadn't already been discovered. He looked at his watch. It was nearly 4:30pm and the sun shimmered above the tree line on the western hill. He figured he had less than two hours of daylight, so he had to make the best use of his time.

He found the thin path forged by the motorcycle tyres where Carmichael had made his escape through a dense maze of trees and wild scrub. He followed the trail along a dry gully until it reached the steep slope of the eastern hill. The tyre tracks joined a natural trail peppered with kangaroo droppings and the manure paddies of stray cattle. He pushed on, climbing the slope until he came to the crest of the hill. He bent over with his hands on his knees to catch his breath. Looking back to where he had come from, he was taken by the rugged beauty of the gully below. Orange rays of sunlight pierced the trees, casting long shadows like outstretched fingers. The earthy shades and contours of the landscape contrasted with the bottle green canopy of the trees. Despite its dark and twisted history, the land possessed a haunting charm. He imagined the scene being captured by the oil colours of an artist's palette.

He turned back towards the direction of the trail which had led Carmichael over the other side of the hill towards the McNelly homestead. His thoughts turned to Alice McNelly and her husband's heartbreak at hearing the news of her murder. Carmichael had used her as a human shield to get to him. She had served her purpose and was discarded like a piece of trash. He could have shown mercy but instead he took her life. It was a reminder of his true nature – a heartless killer.

Jarrod trudged along the ridge of the hill where a wire fence ran along its spine, separating the Miles and McNelly properties. He found a section of fencing where repairs to the chainwire had been abandoned. A leather tool belt, a pair of wire cutters and a coffee thermos were laid out on the ground beside the fence. A large tree stood about two metres from the fence inside the Miles property. The trunk had been scorched from a grassfire that had swept over the hill years earlier. Its dead branches, void of foliage, lurched outwards like the arthritic hands of an old man. Hands on hips, he gazed out over the valley towards the setting sun, wondering what the hell he was doing. It was hopeless. What did he expect to find? He looked around, having already made up his mind to head back to the car.

Just at that moment, a beam of sunlight caught the tree as the sun hovered above the western hill. There was no mistaking it. On the face of the trunk, high above the ground, a shape like a cyclops eye materialised. It gazed out towards the west. The contours of a gnarled knot were highlighted by the sun's rays, forming the distinct eye shape he hadn't noticed only moments earlier. He remembered Vincent Miles' riddle. *'Look into the eye that watches the dying sun.'*

Dead undergrowth crunched under his shoes as he stepped up to the base of the tree. In the centre of the "eye" was an opening, however it was too high for him to reach. As he leaned against the tree, he noticed a wedge about a metre from the ground that had been chopped into the trunk with an axe. It was cut deep enough to use as a foothold. He placed the toe of his shoe inside the wedge and reached up and grabbed a low hanging branch for balance. In one motion, he hoisted himself up using the wedge as a step and the branch as a handrail. With his free hand, he reached into the hollow opening of the eye until his fingertips caressed an object wrapped in a coarse cloth. His fingers found the edges and grabbed hold, pulling the object from its hiding place.

He lowered himself to the ground and gazed at the heavy object in his hands wrapped in a bone-coloured cloth. He unwrapped it to reveal a thick book the size of a bible with a leather cover the colour of dried blood. The book was bound by a thin leather strap, meeting in a cross. The strap was fastened with a bow knot at the front.

Etched by hand into the leather on the front cover was the same geometric shape Jarrod had seen before – Metatron's Cube, the symbol of Vincent Miles. He was holding the book of secrets.

FORTY

DUSK came sooner than expected. As the day faded away, the last of the sun's rays dwindled behind soft orange cloud. The tall trees on the western hill became silhouettes against the golden hue. He sat in the dirt at the base of the dead tree, captured by the spell of Vincent Miles' book of secrets. As he read the book, it took a vice-like grip of his thoughts. The distorted ramblings of a twisted mind came to life on the tattered pages. The words were scrawled in pencil, a mixture of incoherent ramblings and shocking revelations. The book told a chronological story of how Vincent, as a boy with primal urges to kill, underwent a metamorphosis of enlightenment as he entered adulthood. As Jarrod read on, he uncovered vivid descriptions of who Vincent said he had killed over the years and how. There were pathetic attempts at self-serving justifications for his actions which gave some insight into his crazed mindset. Jarrod became so engrossed, drawn in by the disturbing content, that he hadn't noticed his eyes were adjusting to the approaching darkness. Crickets chirped and birds nestled in overhead tree branches, bickering over the best perches as nightfall loomed. The temperature dropped as the shadows deepened.

Realising he needed to make his way back to the car before nightfall, he closed the book and rose to his feet, brushing dirt and twigs from his trousers. He retraced his steps along the ridge, carefully following the same path as it meandered down the slope towards the gully below. He successfully made the trek in the dying light without stumbling over the many rocks and logs in his path. He emerged from the thick scrub into the clearing at the base of the hill. The farmhouse came into view and stared back at him in gloomy silence. He became acutely aware of his solitude, alone with only the ghosts of the past to keep him company in this forsaken place. With the book tucked under his arm, he hurried towards the car as an unsettling chill swept over him. The car was his haven, a welcome refuge from the black haze of the emerging darkness. He sat in the car and locked himself in, an instinctive reaction to the unsettling fear that had taken hold. Something outside had spooked him. The warmth of his body had been drained from him as though he'd been dipped into an ice bath. His skin shuddered as the darkness outside engulfed the car like black smoke.

He sat in the gloom, his breathing loud in his ears, and stared at the farmhouse with growing anxiety. A sense of foreboding overwhelmed him, as though accusing him of stealing a precious artefact. He turned on the interior light and studied the book. As he flicked through the pages, he took in every detail of Vincent Miles' words, considering both the literal and hidden meanings of each sentence. The book seemed to start as a diary, recounting his life story from his upbringing on the farm with his church-going parents, right through to his relationship with Roxy and the birth of his child. As the story unfolded with each page, his words became darker, a deep bitterness emerging. There were gaps in the timeline and he often digressed into tangents, describing in stark detail his murderous acts and the sense of power growing inside him. The loss of Roxy and their little girl was the catalyst that sent him down an even darker path. Full of rage and hopelessness, he waged his own war on the world. He wrote that his transcendence into a higher being began when he met Clare. Through her, he discovered his true purpose in life, and they plotted a path towards eternal salvation. His words confirmed what Jarrod had known all along, that he and Clare believed they would be at peace together with the souls of their children. That's why Jamie and Olivia Kingston had to die.

The pages that followed contained chapter after chapter of prophecies of dark shadows that would engulf the world following their departure. He described fallen angels descending from the heavens to seek vengeance on humans and terrifying demons rising from the earth to feed on the carcasses. He described what he called the "path to enlightenment" for those who had the courage to follow his example to find their own salvation. These were the words that Kaleb Carmichael was so desperate to read. He believed Vincent Miles had left him a set of instructions and prophecies that would unlock the secrets to being reborn as a higher being.

To Jarrod, these words were nothing more than the ramblings of a mad man. It was difficult to decipher fact from fiction as he tried to unravel ramblings about the disappearances of Tommy Baker and Vincent Miles' parents.

Then, to his horror, he found the scrawled words that revealed the shocking truth.

FORTY-ONE

THE words *'ETERNAL SLEEP'* were etched in bolded pencil at the top of a page. What followed sent a cold shudder down Jarrod's spine. The first scribblings began with, *'I killed my parents in their sleep.'* Jarrod closed his eyes and braced for what was to follow. He took a breath, opened his eyes and continued reading.

'They had it coming – my parents. They deserved it. I couldn't bear their oppression and hypocrisy. They would never accept me for what I was and I could no longer suffer their accusing eyes. To them, I was some vile creature, tainted with an evil streak, so my father said. They were holding me back, denying my right to embrace the power within. They had to die – it was the only way. I watched them as they slept. At first, I didn't think I had the courage to go through with it but the rage surfaced and took hold of me. I slit my mother's throat with my hunting knife, and she gurgled, choking on her own blood. Her eyes stared up at me, full of hatred and fear. I smiled back at her. My father woke up but before he realised what was happening, I cracked open his skull with a crowbar. It was all over in seconds, they died in silence. I was set free as they fell into an eternal sleep.'

What he described next rocked Jarrod to the core. The words detailed how Vincent had disposed of their bodies and cleaned up their bedroom before destroying their bloody bedding and night clothes in a bonfire. He drove their Range Rover to the quarry lake and sent it hurtling off the cliff where it disappeared forever in the bottomless abyss. Jarrod avoided touching the erratic handwriting as though the lead pencil had been dipped in acid. He feared the words would burn his fingertips and send poison into his bloodstream. The toxic words were pure evil. Jarrod now knew where he would find what remained of their bodies but first, he needed some help. He had no choice but to act on a hunch, a gut feeling.

Within minutes he arrived at the front gates of the McNelly property next door. The headlights of his car revealed the chain and padlock securing the gates. As he climbed from the car, engine still running and headlights on, the front door of the cottage swung open, and the burly frame of Harry McNelly appeared as a silhouette in the porch light. There was no mistaking the sound of the cocking rifle.

'Get off my property!' he yelled. 'I'll shoot, I swear!'

'Mr McNelly, it's the police. Detective Jarrod O'Connor is my name,' Jarrod called back.

'What do you want? I have nothing more to say to you people. My wife is dead because of your incompetence.'

'I'm so sorry for what happened to your wife. I didn't come here to upset you. Can I come in? I'm hoping you can help me.'

'Help you with what?' he said, the rifle aimed at Jarrod. 'I don't owe you a thing. Why should I help you?'

'Were you friends with Margaret and Gerald Miles before they disappeared?'

'Yes, we were good friends. That was years ago. What in God's name has that got to do with what happened to my Alice?'

'Would you like to finally know what happened to them?'

'Turn your headlights off and kill the engine. I need to see you up close with your identification. Any sudden moves and I'll blow your head off.'

'You have my word,' Jarrod said. 'I just need to get my torch from the car.' He killed the engine and headlights and stood near the locked gates, shining his torch on his police badge.

Harry cautiously limped down the porch stairs, holding the rifle up with one hand, the stock wedged under his armpit. He used his other hand to steady himself against the handrail. He waddled over towards the gate, grimacing in pain with each step. Keeping his distance, he still aimed the rifle at Jarrod. In the torchlight he studied the badge and then Jarrod's face, and the badge again.

'I've seen you before,' said Harry. 'You're that hot shot detective who captured that bastard who killed Alice. I've seen your photo in all the newspapers.'

'Yes, sir. But I'm no hot shot. Far from it.'

Harry lowered his rifle and held up a bunch of keys. 'Here, catch.' He tossed them over to Jarrod who caught them. 'The big gold key, that's for the padlock. Lock the gate behind you.' He turned and headed back towards his house.

~

They sat at his kitchen table over steaming cups of freshly brewed tea.

'I also lost my wife not so long ago,' Jarrod said as he took a sip.

'Yeah, I heard.' Harry's eyes softened. 'Everyone knows everyone's business in this town. It's been in the news. They caught that man? The other driver?'

'Yep. He pleaded guilty in court. He's in prison.'

'So, you and I have a lot in common. Our wives are gone and the men responsible are still alive and well, getting three square meals a day at taxpayers' expense. Capital punishment is the only thing these animals understand. The world's gone soft. No one's accountable for their actions anymore.'

'Yep, you're right.'

'You have kids?' asked Harry.

'A boy and girl. They're great kids. My mother-in-law lives with us now and helps to take care of them. I'd be lost without her.'

'I know how that feels, to be lost, I mean.'

'Do you have anyone? Family?'

'Extended family here and there, but we're not close. Alice and I weren't able to have kids of our own,' said Harry with a sad smile. 'It's just me now. I have no one else.' He sipped his tea, and they shared the silence, lost in their own thoughts.

'So, why the visit at this time of night? How can I help you?'

'I think I know what happened to Gerald and Margaret Miles.'

Harry placed his teacup on the table and stared for a moment at the rogue tea leaves swirling on the milky surface of his cuppa. 'That mongrel son, Vincent. He killed them, didn't he?'

Jarrod held his gaze and nodded.

'I knew it. Poor Margie and Gerry suffered in silence for so long. I always knew that evil boy was behind it. That's what I told the police at the time, but they just seemed to dismiss me. Thought I was some crazy old codger.'

'I think I know what he did with the bodies…' Jarrod hesitated. 'But I need your help to know for sure.'

'My help, with what? Why don't you just call in your copper mates?'

Jarrod shook his head and stared at Harry. 'No. Not this time.'

The old man frowned.

'No one else can know,' said Jarrod. 'I want to end this discreetly, to put them at rest without the media circus. But it won't be pleasant, and I can't do it alone.'

Harry crossed his arms over his belly and rubbed the bristles on his beefy chin. 'I understand. No more bright lights, police helicopters and media camped out on the street. I can't handle any more of that. Margie and Gerry wouldn't want any fuss. Their souls deserve to be at peace. What do you need?'

'Does your tractor have headlights?'

Harry just smiled.

FORTY-TWO

THE spotlights on Harry's tractor were blinding in Jarrod's rear vision mirror. Harry followed his trail of dust down the long driveway towards the Miles farmhouse. Jarrod parked alongside the house, using his headlights to illuminate the doorway to the derelict old shed. The dense blackness inside the shed swallowed the light. The rear taillights of Vincent Miles' old Holden were cold eyes staring back at Jarrod. He climbed from the car and directed Harry towards the shed.

Harry turned the tractor around, flicked on the rear spotlight and reversed towards the shed opening. As he eased the growling machine backwards, Jarrod held up his hand and Harry jumped on the brake. The tractor shuddered to a stop and Jarrod unravelled a thick tow chain from its rear storage compartment. Harry slid from the tractor cab with a groan and shuffled his boots on the gravel towards Jarrod. He stood with his hands on his hips and watched with a raised eyebrow and a grin as Jarrod fought with the tangled chain. 'Here, son. Step aside. You didn't grow up on a farm, did you?'

'You can tell?' Jarrod gladly handed him the chain.

The chain's hook was soon expertly secured to the tractor's rear anchor point and the other end was fastened to the Holden's towbar.

Harry shrugged and headed back towards the tractor cab. 'I've spent most of my life towing farm machinery out of gullies and bog holes,' he muttered. 'You go and take off the handbrake and give me the signal.' Harry climbed back up into the tractor seat.

Jarrod stepped inside the dusty air of the shed, taking cautious steps down the side of the car through the knee-high grass consuming the rusting wheels and flat, corroded tyres. The front passenger side door was unlocked, and Jarrod heaved it open with a loud creak. The stale smell of mould and remnants of exhaust fumes still lingered inside after all those years. He leaned in and took a firm grasp of the handbrake arm. Jammed by rust, it refused to yield at first, however it finally gave way with a clunk. Jarrod moved the column gear lever into neutral and climbed back out of the foul-smelling car.

As he exited the shed, he gave Harry a wave and the tractor clunked into gear, rolled forward and the chain tightened. Black smoke billowed from the tractor's exhaust pipe, its flap bursting open as Harry gave it more juice. At first the Holden resisted but as the chain tightened and the tractor revved, the car's wheels slid in the dirt, so seized by rust they refusing to roll. The wheels finally gave way and rolled, the hardened rubber peeling off the tyre walls like layers of an onion. Harry urged the tractor forward until the car had been dragged beyond the confines of the shed and out into the cool night air.

Jarrod gave Harry the signal and yelled over the engine noise, 'Righto, that'll do!'

The tractor lurched backwards, and the chain tension eased. Harry killed the engine, and all fell quiet. Dust particles danced in the beams of Jarrod's headlights as it mingled with the musty air inside the shed. He crept to the edge of the bare patch of earth that had been hidden for years beneath the old Holden. The rectangular patch was contrasted against a border of weeds that had flourished around the car's extremities. He shone his torch on the red dirt which hadn't been disturbed in decades, unnoticed even during the forensic search of the shed. As the car hadn't been moved, there had been no apparent reason to dig into the earth beneath it. Not until now. According to Vincent Miles' book of secrets, the dry patch of soil had for years concealed unimaginable horrors.

Jarrod stood in the centre of the bare patch and prodded the dirt with the toe of his shoe. Clumps of dirt came free, but he couldn't see any obvious signs of anything buried. He shone his torch around the cluttered shed until the light beam landed on the handle of a shovel poking up through a clump of matted cobwebs in the far corner. He went over and pulled it free – a garden rake and an axe broke the silence as they fell and clattered onto the floor. The grime on the shovel's handle felt coarse in Jarrod's grip.

Harry's hefty frame formed a silhouette in the shed's entrance, surrounded by the glow of the car's headlights. He remained hesitant, unwilling to step inside. Jarrod returned to the bare patch of dirt and dug. At first the shovel mostly bounced off the hard ground until he broke free the dry, top layer. The aroma of damp earth filled his nostrils, and he sliced the dirt with more purpose. He progressively dug towards the centre of the bare patch, dotting the ground with small holes. Despite the coolness of the night air, sweat dripped from his brow and his hands ached. Harry watched on with folded arms as Jarrod dug in small bursts.

Just as he was losing hope of finding anything, the shovel came down against something hard, something hollow. He leaned against the shovel to catch his breath and returned Harry's look of anticipation. He dug again and scraped the dirt free from something hidden about a foot beneath the floor level. As Jarrod shovelled the dirt away, the surface of a wooden object emerged. He shone the torch and exposed the lid of a wooden crate buried deep into the earth. He scooped more dirt away until the edges of the timber were defined. The crate was about two feet long by one foot wide. He dug out the dirt along its edges to reveal a rusty padlock secured in the lid's latch. One swift blow with the shovel was enough to destroy the lock and it broke free. The crate was buried too deep into the earth for him to completely dig out but at least he could access the lid. He knelt and swept free the remaining dirt from the lid with his hands. Carved into the lid was the unmistakable geometric shape of Metraton's Cube.

Jarrod felt along the edge of the lid until his fingertips were able to gain some purchase. He steadied himself and pulled upwards and the lid came free and swung open on its rusted hinges. He pushed the lid all the way up, allowing it to crash backwards onto the floor in a cloud of dust. Coughing, he covered his mouth and nose in the crook of his elbow. After the dust settled, he shone the torch inside the box to reveal the round tin lids of two large pickle jars. Rags had been jammed in tight in the spaces between the jars. He pulled the rags free and tossed them onto the pile of dirt he was kneeling beside. He slid his fingers down either side of one of the jars and took a firm grip. As he eased it upwards, it felt heavy. Liquid sloshed inside the jar. He lifted it up so that the car's headlights shone through the glass to reveal the brownish, murky liquid.

A ghastly object inside the liquid appeared. The ghoulish face of a woman's severed head stared back at him through partially open eyes, wavy brown hair floating in the liquid like seagrass. The white flesh around the base of the head was jagged with congealed blood. Although bloated and distorted in death, the face of the poor woman was familiar. It was the face of Vincent Miles' mother who he'd seen in the old polaroid photo. Her face was undamaged and was locked in an eternal grimace. Her mouth was open as though gasping, her swollen tongue protruding over her white teeth. He gently placed the heavy jar on the ground and a strong smell of methylated spirits seeped from the edges of the lid. He looked up at Harry who stood frozen, his mouth gaping in horror.

Jarrod turned his attention to the other jar and lifted it free from the crate. He held it up to the light to reveal a man's severed head preserved in the same murky liquid. The flesh on the face was mangled and torn. The man's face had been bludgeoned beyond recognition. A fragment of skull bone clung to a flap of skin and floated in the liquid above a gaping hole in the back of the man's head. It had to be Gerry Miles. Jarrod placed the jar down as reverently as he could beside the jar containing his wife's head. Both faces looked up at him through the milky liquid, trapped in a single moment of horror.

'Poor Margaret and Gerry. They were good, decent people. They didn't deserve this,' said Harry in a low, gravelly voice. 'Their son was a monster. What person could do this to their own parents?' He shook his head in disbelief and blessed himself with the sign of the cross.

'You're right, Harry. Only a monster could do this.'

'What now, Jarrod? Are you going to take these jars to be paraded around like circus attractions?'

Jarrod stood and brushed the dirt from the knees of his trousers. He looked down at the grisly severed heads and in his mind flashed the images of their faces in that photograph. 'No, Harry. They deserve better. They deserve peace, once and for all.'

'What about their bodies?' Harry asked. 'How can they rest in peace when we have no idea where their bodies are?'

'I've read Vincent Miles' so called "book of secrets". That's how I knew these were buried here. He boasted about it in his writings. He chopped off their heads with an axe.' Jarrod's voice trailed off and he looked over at the axe lying in the dirt in the corner of the shed. 'He wrote that he kept the heads so that his parents would remain with him. He cremated the bodies on a bonfire somewhere out there in the bush.'

'Sick little bastard.'

'There's only one right thing to do now, Harry.'

Harry's eyes stared into his with understanding. 'I'll get the jerry can from the tractor.'

He turned and walked away, leaving Jarrod alone with the severed heads of Margaret and Gerald Miles. He knelt and placed them back into the crate and covered them with the rags. Harry returned with the fuel and handed it to him.

Jarrod unscrewed the lid and doused the jars in fuel.

'The car needs to go back in the shed. There're spirits trapped in it that need to be set free,' said Jarrod.

Harry gave a nod and soon the tractor engine thundered to life and reversed into the Holden, pushing it until it rolled back into position in the shed, coming to rest above the buried crate and jars. Jarrod unhitched the chain and Harry drove the tractor clear.

Jarrod sloshed petrol over the car, the rotting timber walls and the cluttered piles of junk. He backed out of the shed, tipping a line of petrol in the dirt to form a long fuse. He stood shoulder to shoulder with Harry a safe distance away.

Harry showed Jarrod a Zippo cigarette lighter. 'Alice gave this to me as a gift when we were newlyweds. It belonged to her dad who died way too young. It's never let me down.'

'Alice would want you to light it, Harry. It feels right that it should be you.'

Harry studied the antique lighter and then flicked open the lid with his thumb. With a flick of the flint wheel a bright orange flame sparked, the light reflected in his tired eyes. He bent down until the flame licked the end of the trail of petrol and with a whoosh the flame took on a life of its own and raced along the fuse line towards the shed. As the flame disappeared, the interior of the shed glowed and the crackling of fire broke the silence. Soon the Holden was engulfed in flames. Fire flung itself to the walls until the entire shed was consumed in red and orange flames. The pulsating heat forced them to step back. Smoke billowed and swirled, and the air smelt of burning timber infused with acrid chemicals. Flames leapt high, charring the walls and tin roof before they succumbed to the intense heat. Embers floated in the hot air like fireflies. The shed was an inferno and the walls and roof caved in on themselves in a ball of sparks and flames.

As the fire roared, devouring everything in reach, the shed and the car became a molten mass of burning debris. Everything was gone, eradicated forever. The spirits of Margaret and Gerald Miles and other ghosts of the past were finally free, disappearing into the night sky in a thick column of black smoke.

Harry turned to Jarrod and nodded his chin toward the old farmhouse that watched on with disdain. 'The shed isn't all that needs to burn.'

Jarrod nodded and grabbed the jerry can. 'Can I borrow your lighter, Harry?'

'Be my guest,' he said with a grin, handing over his cherished Zippo.

FORTY-THREE

THE following morning, Jarrod sat in his police car at the end of a dirt road beneath the looming shade of the pine forest. The morning news bulletin on the radio reported a "mystery fire that destroyed an abandoned farmhouse". He turned off the radio and smiled. On the passenger seat sat the "book of secrets". After going home the night before to see Pat and the kids, he'd sat up in bed until after midnight studying the crazed writings of Vincent Miles. He had an unsettled sleep, disturbed by the usual nightmares. Miles' sombre words clung to his thoughts like a looming cloud. He was determined to push through his feelings of dread. He had to stay the course. Miles' writings gave clues that could solve other cold homicide and missing persons cases. However, on this morning, Jarrod had one sole purpose – to give closure to the parents of Tommy Baker.

Under a heading entitled "*Fly Tommy, Fly*", Vincent Miles wrote a graphic account of what really happened on that fateful morning three decades earlier. One whole page of the book was dedicated to a hand-drawn mud map that precisely depicted the location of the cliff where Tommy had been pushed to his death. Jarrod knew the spot. It was a distinct rocky outcrop overlooking the quarry lake, the place he confronted his own demons. It was a short walk from where he was now parked. He'd driven past the Baker property on the way there. It was over four kilometres from the quarry lake. He was surprised by just how far Vincent had lured Tommy away from his home. It was a long way for an eight-year-old to ride on a tiny bicycle. He tried to imagine the sheer terror of his ordeal and the subsequent heartache of his parents who endured years of pain and unanswered questions.

He got out of the car and climbed over a log fence, following a walking track through the outer edge of the forest until it opened to a clearing bathed in warm sunshine. He walked a bit further until he was teetering on the edge of a cliff, gazing out over the turquoise quarry lake. No one could possibly survive a fall from that height. He remembered the words in Miles' book and his heart sank. According to Council reports, the level of the lake had dropped after recent years of drought. Far below, water lapped at the base of the cliff. Lines had formed on the stone walls showing the gradual decrease in water depth. A glint of sunlight caught a metal object just under the surface. Jarrod spotted the opening that led to a walking track zig-zagging its way down to the lake, once used by locals before the DANGER and NO SWIMMING signs were erected due to the toxicity of the water. He pushed his way through the overgrown vegetation and vines, cutting his own path until he finally reached the base. He scaled sandstone boulders until he was standing below the cliff edge where he had stood earlier. Rocks and logs, once submerged, reared out of the water.

Just below the waterline, a rusted object clung to the outstretched branch of a fallen dead tree. He climbed out along the trunk on his hands and knees. One slip and he'd be in the drink. The tree groaned under his weight. He climbed out further, his belly now pressed against the smooth trunk. Below him, just under the surface, a bicycle wheel was snagged by a branch. He hugged the tree with one arm and reached down with the other. His hand plunged into the icy water until it found the wheel. He grabbed hold, the texture of the tyre rubbery in his grip. He pulled but it didn't budge, and he nearly fell in for his troubles. He wrapped his legs and other arm tight around the tree to brace himself and he yanked again. The branch cracked and the wheel came free. He gripped it tight and shimmied back along the tree, pulling the bicycle free from its watery grave when he reached the boulders.

It was a child's bike, a little BMX. The frame was once yellow, now mottled with brown blotches of rust. The wheel rims and spokes were corroded green and brown. As he flipped it over, gunky water gushed out of the handlebars. He slung the bike frame over his shoulder and made the trek back up the densely wooded track until he reached the cliff above. He didn't stay to admire the view. Instead, he walked back out along the sandy track to the car where he placed the bike in the boot and drove off.

He pulled up in the driveway of the Baker farmhouse. Everyone in town knew the place, haunted by the tragic mystery from all those years ago. Mr and Mrs Baker still lived there. Their once proud gardens had withered to dust, along with their hope of ever finding their missing boy. The yard was overgrown, and the house neglected with flaking paint and rusted roof iron. A woman pegged bed sheets to the clothesline out back. A man in work clothes smoked a hand-rolled cigarette on the front porch, his skin weathered and leathery. Jarrod got out of the car and opened the boot. He lifted the bike out and carried it to the base of the stairs. The woman looked over and left her washing basket and met Jarrod on the pathway. Her eyes were bright, her face kind. Years of grief were etched into the wrinkles in her cheeks. The man rose to his feet and stood at the top of the stairs.

Jarrod held up his badge. 'Mr and Mrs Baker?'

'Yes,' said the woman.

'I'm Detective Sergeant Jarrod O'Connor from the local police.'

Mrs Baker looked at the bicycle. 'Oh my!' she gasped and covered her mouth with her hand. 'Is that what I think it is?'

Jarrod nodded.

'Tommy's bike?' said Mr Baker. 'That's our little boy's bike, isn't it?' His knees buckled under his weight. He reached for the handrail. Jarrod dropped the bike and bounded up the stairs to catch the old man before he fell. He lowered him to the top step, where he sat, his body shaking.

Mrs Baker fell to her knees, stroking the bike seat, sobbing. She looked up at Jarrod, her eyes glazed with tears. 'You brought it home to us.'

Jarrod held her gaze, a lump in his throat making it hard to swallow.

Mr Baker stared into Jarrod's eyes. 'Where's our boy?' he said, his voice pleading.

'I know what happened to him,' said Jarrod. 'The quarry lake took him. I'm so sorry. He's not coming home.'

Mrs Baker looked up at Jarrod and smiled through her tears. 'Thank you, Detective. He's free now – and so are we.'

FORTY-FOUR

AT 10:00am the next morning, the door to the prison interview room swung open and Kaleb Carmichael shuffled into the hollow cube of concrete in leg irons. As usual, his wrists were bound in handcuffs, the restraints looped through a chain wrapped around his waist. The grey walls were bleak as ever. A strange feeling of claustrophobia swept over Jarrod as he sat alone on his side of the windowless room. A green LED light flashed on the overhead security camera. He knew that returning to this place was inevitable, however it did nothing to settle the uneasiness growing inside him once again at the sight of Kaleb Carmichael. The steel mesh separating them magnified his ghastly appearance, distorting his scarred features like a circus mirror. As the door closed behind Carmichael, the layered echoes of inmates jeering at prison guards fell silent. There were no more sounds of people, just the hum of the fluorescent light bulbs and Carmichael's heavy breathing. He sat motionless, staring intently at Jarrod who wondered if Carmichael could hear his heart beating, thumping hard. Inside this confined space there was no way of knowing if it was day or night.

Carmichael fidgeted. He picked at sores on his hands with his fingernails as one knee bounced up and down. He rocked back and forth on the stainless-steel stool bolted to the floor. His bloodshot eyes were crazed with paranoia, his lips dry and cracked. He looked more unhinged than Jarrod had ever seen him. His arms were thin and the scarred flesh on his face had sunken into his cheekbones.

'You don't look well, Kaleb.'

A grin spread over his face, wide and open, showing his yellowing teeth. His eyes were unmoving – narrowed, rigid, cold. 'It warms me to know you care about my welfare, *Jarrod*.' He hissed Jarrod's name through his lips like a serpent.

'Don't flatter yourself,' said Jarrod. 'You have no idea how much satisfaction it gives me to see you wasting away in prison.'

Jarrod waited for his reaction.

There was no violent outburst, no maniacal laughter. His grin faded and the fidgeting stopped. He sat rigid. 'Do you have something for me?'

Jarrod hesitated, his arms folded. He had all the time in the world, all the time he needed to toy with Carmichael. He exhaled, long and drawn out, and reached down to his briefcase at his feet. Lifting the case onto his knees, he slid the locks so the latches snapped open in unison. Opening the lid, he removed a tattered book bound in blood red leather. He closed the briefcase and placed it back on the floor and set it down again. Carmichael's eyes widened in astonishment. Jarrod pressed the "book of secrets" against the steel mesh. Carmichael lunged forward and pressed his face against the mesh, sniffing long and hard to savour the smell of the pages.

Jarrod pulled the book away and flicked through the pages. He slammed it closed and Carmichael's eyes met his.

'The book, where did you find it?' he said, desperate.

'It was hidden inside the hollow of an old tree on the Miles property.' Jarrod couldn't help but smile from the irony. 'You would have ridden straight past it when you escaped on that motorbike. It was right under your nose the whole time. From your camp on the hill you might have even been able to see it.'

'I figured as much,' Carmichael said. 'Vincent always loved to hide in plain sight.'

Jarrod nodded. 'That he did.'

'Well come on. I need to read it. Open it up and let me see the pages.'

'No.'

'What? No? You swore you'd let me read it.'

'No, I didn't, Kaleb. I promised I would bring it to you. So here it is. To prove to you that it's real.'

'Open it!'

'No.' Jarrod kept his voice calm.

'Don't do this to me, Jarrod. I *need* to read it. My transformation will never be complete until I read his prophecies.'

'Your transformation into what?'

'A higher being, of course,' he said as though it was obvious.

Jarrod looked down at the book and then back at Carmichael.

The fires of Hell flickered in his eyes. Rage surfaced. 'Don't mess with me,' he sneered through clenched teeth. 'You have to let me read it! Please, give it to the screws so they can give it to me to read. I must have that book.'

'Would it kill you to not know what's inside it?' said Jarrod.

'Yes, it will kill me!' he spat.

'Good.' Jarrod placed the book back in his briefcase and locked the lid. He stood and turned for the door.

Carmichael pressed his face against the mesh. 'No! You can't do this,' he screamed.

'This is goodbye, Kaleb. You'll never see me or this book ever again.'

'I'll come after you!' He punched the mesh, his knuckles bleeding. 'I'll find a way. I'll transcend from this place, and I'll kill you and your family.'

Jarrod stopped with his back to him, his hand resting on the door handle. 'No, you won't, Kaleb. It's over.' Jarrod glanced over his shoulder. Carmichael met his eyes for one last time. 'You'll wither away in this place and the world won't even remember your name. You're nothing.'

As Jarrod pulled the door open, Carmichael bashed his forehead against the steel mesh, splitting open a deep gash. Blood smeared across his face, and he spat bloodied saliva on the floor. 'Bring me that book!' he shrieked like a wild animal.

Jarrod was met by a guard in the corridor, and he left the room without turning back. Kaleb Carmichael's screams echoed off the concrete walls as Jarrod followed the guard along the narrow hallway towards the elevator. He was desperate for the doors to open and to be carried up and away from that hellhole.

'I'm coming for you, O'Connor!' were the last words that lingered as the elevator doors closed.

FORTY-FIVE

OVER the coming weeks, Jarrod injected his energies into catching up on routine investigations that had been neglected over the past few months. Ross Benfield's patience had worn thin, and he was applying pressure on Jarrod to close the book on Vincent Miles and Kaleb Carmichael and focus on current cases. Local crime was on the rise and there was no end to child protection cases that needed looking into. As calls flooded in, Jarrod became lost in the usual caseload. A full-time replacement for Brad had yet to be secured. The CIB and uniform crews had been carrying the bulk of new work and it was time to focus on the present. There were local families in crisis and in need of support.

The dilemma of what to do with the "book of secrets" ate away at Jarrod. A few times he had come close to setting fire to it, destroying it along with all the bitter memories it represented. However, each time he had resolved to destroy it, to do what needed to be done, he faltered. He had a nagging feeling there were still more secrets waiting to be uncovered, somewhere in the encrypted ramblings and riddles of a madman. There were loose references to other unsolved murders, and Jarrod needed time to study the book in more detail. On the quiet, he sent a request to the Missing Persons Unit to meet with them in the city to discuss possible long-term cases that may be linked. Benfield would blow a gasket if he found out.

The "book of secrets" remained in the bottom drawer of Jarrod's desk, hidden beneath a stack of old case files. He was often drawn to it, to read back over Vincent Miles' scrawled notes to find hidden answers amid the chaos. This only served to fuel Jarrod's frustrations. The answers were buried deep in complex layers of prophecies and reflections written by a man convinced he would be born again as the one to seek retribution against God himself. Jarrod put the book away and slammed the drawer closed.

At 8:06am on a Wednesday morning his desk phone rang. 'Lockyer Youth Crime Unit, Detective O'Connor speaking,' he answered.

'Jarrod, Jeff Oldfield from the prison here. Have I caught you at a bad time?'

'Hey, Jeff. There's never a good time. How can I help you?' He immediately felt uneasy to receive Jeff's call. His stomach churned at the thought of what games Kaleb Carmichael might be playing now. He'd had no contact with him since his last visit.

'Are you sitting down, mate?' said Jeff.

'As a matter of fact, I am. This doesn't sound good. Should I be concerned?'

'Well, it depends.'

'On what?' A flutter of nerves unsettled his gut.

'Well, on whether news of Kaleb Carmichael's untimely death is of concern to you.'

'What? What happened?'

'His naked body was found this morning on the floor of the amenities block. His throat had been cut and he'd been stabbed over twenty times. It was a frenzied attack. A crude metal shank was found protruding from his chest. It was a real mess, blood everywhere. Someone got the jump on him as he was getting out of the shower.'

Jarrod was numb. 'I thought he was isolated from other prisoners?'

'He was, until recently. He put in a request to get out of isolation and to go back into general population. Maybe he realised it was a better option than going insane, or perhaps he just saw it as a way out. He knew there were other inmates lining up to have a go at him. In the end he welcomed it, dared them to have a go.'

'Any suspects?'

'Yep, about a hundred. None of the prisoners are talking. We're reviewing CCTV footage, but this was well planned. Soggy toilet paper was stuck to the camera lenses. It took less than a minute to inflict the damage. Whoever did it came and went undetected.'

'What now?'

'A major headache, that's what. An investigation, inquest, shadow minister calling for heads to roll. All the usual. These incidents are a part of life in a high security prison. The worst of humanity all locked up together. What do the shiny arse politicians expect? It's a perfect recipe for violence. We do our best to prevent a bloodbath but every now and then, ya know, these things happen.'

'Holy shit, I'm shocked. It seems surreal. Carmichael is really dead?'

'Yep, dead as they come.'

'Well, thanks for letting me know, I guess.'

'No worries. I wanted to let you know before you hear it on the news. We're keeping it hush hush, but it won't be long before the media get wind of it, then the real shit storm will start.'

'Man, what a mess. Good luck.'

'Thanks, I'll need it. Anyway, I better get back to it. Just thought you'd want to know.'

'I appreciate the heads up.'

'Oh, I do have one question for you though.'

'What's that, Jeff?'

'Is the world a better place without Kaleb Carmichael?'

'Yes, it is. Without a shadow of a doubt.'

'I thought you'd say that. Kaleb Carmichael wasn't the first crazy fucker to be let loose onto this world… and he won't be the last.'

'You got that right. Otherwise, we'd both be out of a job.'

'You take it easy now, Jarrod O'Connor. There're more monsters out there waiting for you.'

THE END

ABOUT THE AUTHOR

Jack Roney is a member of the Queensland Writers Centre, Australian Society of Authors, and Australian Crime Writers Association. He lives with his family in Brisbane, Australia. His writing is inspired by over thirty years in law enforcement where he gained experience as an investigator, tactical skills and firearms instructor, police academy instructor, strategic policy writer and media officer. He draws on his experience as a former detective to bring authenticity and realism to his writing. He was a police consultant for the ABC television series Harrow. *The Shadows Watch* is the final book in a three-book series, with the first novel in the series, *The Angels Wept,* reaching the Wattpad Awards shortlist. His speculative fiction novel, *The Ghost Train and The Scarlet Moon,* was the runner-up in the Hawkeye Publishing Manuscript Development Prize.

www.jackroney.com.au

Book reviews can make or break a book. If you liked what you read today,
please do consider posting a review on Goodreads or your favourite forum.

The Shadows Watch is available at hawkeyebooks.com.au
and all good bookstores and libraries.

BOOKS BY
JACK RONEY

**THE ANGELS WEPT
(JARROD O'CONNOR #1)**

**THE DEMONS WOKE
(JARROD O'CONNOR #2)**

**THE SHADOWS WATCH
(JARROD O'CONNOR #3)**

**THE GHOST TRAIN AND
THE SCARLET MOON**